WHERE THE
BULLETS FLY

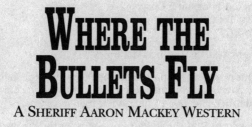

WHERE THE BULLETS FLY

A SHERIFF AARON MACKEY WESTERN

TERRENCE McCAULEY

PINNACLE BOOKS
Kensington Publishing Corp.
www.kensingtonbooks.com

PINNACLE BOOKS are published by

Kensington Publishing Corp.
119 West 40th Street
New York, NY 10018

All Kensington titles, imprints, and distributed lines are available at special quantity discounts for bulk purchases for sales promotions, premiums, fund-raising, educational, or institutional use. Special book excerpts or customized printings can also be created to fit specific needs. For details, write or phone the office of the Kensington sales manager: Kensington Publishing Corp., 119 West 40th Street, New York, NY 10018, attn: Sales Department; phone 1-800-221-2647.

ISBN-13: 978-0-7860-4342-2
ISBN-10: 0-7860-4342-3

First printing: October 2018

10 9 8 7 6 5 4 3 2 1

Printed in the United States of America

First electronic edition: October 2018

ISBN-13: 978-0-7860-4343-9
ISBN-10: 0-7860-4343-1

To Dan and Corky King—
for your friendship

Chapter 1

Dover Station, Montana, 1888

Sheriff Aaron Mackey had just finished another coughing jag when he heard the ruckus carry up Front Street from the Tin Horn Saloon. A gentle breeze carried the sounds of shouted curses and breaking glass to the jailhouse porch where Mackey sat with Deputy Billy Sunday.

Billy glanced down the street while his long black fingers built his cigarette. "Think we ought to see what that's all about?"

"No." Mackey wiped his mouth with the back of his hand and set his rocking chair to rocking once again. The Tin Horn Saloon had always been a bucket of blood, even back when it had been called Lizzie's Stopover when Mackey was a boy. "Probably some miners getting into it with some loggers or cowpunchers brawling with some cardsharp. Best let Sam's new bouncer earn his keep. Bastard's making more than either of us, anyway. If they need us, they know where to find us. Always have."

Normally, Mackey would've walked down to the Horn to make sure things didn't go too far, but that day was not a normal day. It was the first time he had been out of bed in a week. The pneumonia made him feel like hell and look even worse. A week's worth of beard stung his fingers as he rubbed his hand over them, and his hair was greasier and longer than he liked. His lungs ached something awful, and he felt like he was breathing through a wet towel.

But wheezing in the rocking chair on the front porch of his jail was better than suffering fever dreams in bed.

He didn't walk down to the Tin Horn because he didn't dare risk falling over if he tried to stand. The pneumonia had left him far weaker than he'd ever admit and was not finished with him yet, no matter how much he willed it so.

Besides, it was a beautiful afternoon and he saw no reason to ruin it over another drunken brawl down at the Horn. Hopefully, it would run its course and that would be that.

Mackey stifled a cough as he watched the town settle into the same drowsy mood it usually reached that same time each day. A few of the regular towns-people moved about their business, either shopping at the general stores or on their way someplace else. Unfamiliar men and women browsed the shop windows along Front Street the way horses nose grass. He knew they must have been waiting for the stagecoach because the train wasn't due to make a stop in town until the next day. They didn't need anything and had no intention of buying anything, either. Looking in the windows was just something to do while they were hitched to the town, waiting to move on to the next place. None of them seemed especially bothered by the sounds of the brawl coming from the Tin Horn.

Neither were the two men from the town's Veterans Committee, who were climbing atop wooden ladders to stretch a new canvas banner across Front Street. They managed to tie it off fast before the banner billowed in the wind.

Dover Station Veterans Dance – To-Morrow
Come One ~ Come All
WELCOME MR. RICE AND MR. VAN DORN

Despite being veterans themselves, neither Mackey nor Billy had attended the dance since they had returned to Dover Station five years before. Mackey had always thought of the dance as a bunch of nonsense; an excuse for old men to wear faded uniforms and tell lies about the War Between the States. Every year, he received a formal invitation addressed to Captain Aaron Mackey, United States Cavalry. Every year, he threw it away unopened.

Mayor Mason had already decreed that this year's gala would be the biggest, most impressive event in the town's history. Several bankers from New York City would be in attendance, including Mr. Frazer Rice and Mr. Van Dorn of the Rice Van Dorn Company. Mr. Rice and Mr. Van Dorn had indicated that they were seriously considering investing in the town, and Mayor Mason wanted to give them a warm welcome. The mayor said the gala wouldn't just celebrate the town's veterans, but the Town of Dover Station itself. Another crew of volunteers was over at the train station making signs of welcome for the dignitaries and hanging bunting all around the station.

It was all window dressing, as far as Mackey was concerned, like hanging lace curtains in a whorehouse. They could make the town as pretty as they'd like, but no one could hide what it really was: a cow town with decent mining and logging concerns. Mackey saw no reason to hide it, for those were the very reasons why the investors were coming to town in the first place. Men like Rice and Van Dorn weren't interested in bunting and dances and cheering crowds. They were interested in making money.

As the volunteers finished tying off their banner, Mackey watched Billy finally lick the cigarette paper and seal his smoke. Given how long Mackey had been bedridden, he decided his deputy could stand some teasing. "I've seen houses built faster than you build a smoke."

But Billy wasn't a man to be hurried. "You've got no intention of going back to bed, do you?"

"What's that got to do with how long it takes you to build a cigarette?"

"Because you get bored when you're sick and you only pick on me when you're bored." Billy tucked the cigarette in the corner of his mouth and thumbed a match alive. "You need to go back to bed."

Mackey doubted he had the strength to stand, but knew he wasn't strong enough to argue with Billy Sunday. Mackey was only thirty-five years old, but the pneumonia had left him feeling closer to eighty. Or at least what he envisioned eighty might feel like; not that he had any illusions about living that long.

"Got no time for bed," he said as he resumed rocking. "Fell behind on some things during my convalescence."

"Like what?"

He looked north toward the town cemetery behind the blacksmith's shop. Most of the men he had killed in his five years as sheriff were buried in a section the locals had taken to calling "Mackey's Garden." He usually didn't like such names because they caused a man to acquire a reputation, and reputations caused more trouble than they were worth.

But the term seemed to dampen men's zeal about breaking the law in Dover Station, so he decided to allow the name to stick. "Was planning on watering my garden."

"You're too weak to sit up straight, much less tend to any gardens. Besides, dead men don't need watering. You'll find that out personally if you don't get back to bed."

Mackey knew Billy was right, but it didn't dampen his enthusiasm to keep the argument going. "I decided the garden could wait." He ran his hands over the wooden arms of his rocking chair. "Got behind on my rocking the past week or so. Need to keep my hand in lest I lose the knack for it."

Billy blew the smoke into the wind, away from Mackey. "You're too young to be taking up a rocking chair, Aaron. Best leave the rocking to older men."

"At this rate, I may not get any older." He stifled another cough and winced. His sore lungs ached with a vengeance. "Just as soon get it in now while I can."

"You'll be doing more rotting than rocking if you don't take care of yourself. Pneumonia calls for bed rest and plenty of it. Being out here will only make it worse."

Although the sun had disappeared behind the jailhouse half an hour before, Mackey made a show of looking up at the sky. "Don't want to go in just yet. The sun feels good on my chest."

Billy didn't laugh at the bad joke. "You've had enough sun for one day. Any more, you're apt to start looking like me. Can't have two black lawmen in town. I couldn't stand the competition. I like being an oddity." Billy turned his head and blew more smoke into the wind up Front Street. "You need to go to bed."

"Jesus." Mackey closed his eyes and kept rocking. "If I wanted nagging, I'd go home to Mary."

"As if she'd have you. She might not like you very much, but you're the only husband she's got. She'll blame me if you die and make her a widow."

Mackey ignored the growing sounds of a brawl from the Tin Horn and pondered Billy's statement as he rocked. His wife hadn't said a civil word to him in years and wasn't apt to do so in the near future. If she cried after his death, it would be to mourn her own widowhood rather than her husband's passing. She had already buried one husband and knew her complexion was much too fair to look good in black. Appearances mattered a great deal to Mrs. Mary Hannon Mackey.

Mackey didn't let the growing noise from the Tin Horn distract him from his thought. "Probably get a good turnout at my funeral, though. Bet Mayor Mason, Doc Ridley, and the rest of those sons of bitches would throw themselves one hell of a planting party to celebrate my demise. Might be good for the morale of the town."

"All the more reason to spite them by going back to bed." Billy nodded at the shadow of the new banner hanging across Front Street. "Besides, your daddy's party will boost morale enough to suit me just fine.

Your death would just spoil things, and you know how much he looks forward to that shindig."

But Mackey wasn't done exploring the prospects of his own passing. The morbidity of death had lost its grip on him long ago. "He'd get over it once the bar opened up. Besides, if I kick, you'll probably get the gold star and the big chair behind the desk."

"And the big headaches that go with them." Billy took a long drag on his cigarette. "The mayor and his new friends from New York wouldn't take to having a black sheriff in town. The star you gave me suits me just fine and . . ."

Both men looked at the flurry of movement and color that appeared on the other side of Front Street.

The men up on the ladders whistled and cheered as a round, red-haired woman came barreling out of the alley between the Tin Horn and the Dover Station Dry Goods Store. She had bunched up the skirts of her faded red dress high around her hips as she ran up the boardwalk toward the jailhouse.

Mackey recognized her as one of the new sporting ladies Sam Warren had brought in on the stagecoach from Butte a month before, though he couldn't recall her name.

"Damn." Billy took a final drag on his cigarette before flicking it into the thoroughfare. "Looks like trouble."

Mackey stopped rocking. "A whore running in broad daylight usually does."

"Want to go see what's wrong?"

Mackey still wasn't sure how weak his legs were. The town was already full of rumors about his impending death. Falling into the muddy thoroughfare of Front Street would turn rumor into fact. "The girl is moving at a good pace. If she needs us, she knows where we are."

The woman skidded to a stop directly across from the jailhouse. Like most of Warren's sporting ladies, she was incredibly top-heavy and had to grab a porch beam to keep from falling into the thoroughfare. That's when Mackey realized she was in her bare feet. Another bad sign.

"Sheriff," she yelled across to him. "You need to come right quick. There's trouble in the Tin Horn, and you gotta come now."

"We already heard," Mackey shouted back, his voice cracking from the effort. "What kind of trouble."

"Some strangers wouldn't give up their guns when the new bouncer told them to, so Sam wouldn't serve them. They set to beating Sam and the bouncer, too. They're kicking holy hell out of both of them right now!"

Mackey was on his feet before he realized it. "How many?"

"Five, I think. I don't know for certain on account of me being busy upstairs when it started. I climbed out the back window to fetch you when I realized what was happening."

Five was a decent number, but not enough to worry him. "Head over to Maude's Rooming House and tell her I sent you if she gives you any trouble."

The redhead paddled on her way as Mackey went to get the rifles from the jail. He grabbed for the door-jamb as the world tilted sideways.

Billy grabbed his arm to keep him from falling. "How about you stay here and let me handle this. I'll find Sim Halstead and the two of us'll face them down together."

Mackey tried shaking off the dizziness, but no luck. After the second time, his head cleared a little. "I'm fine."

"Christ, Aaron. There's only five of them. Sim and I can . . ."

"Sim's just an auxiliary and it's not his job. It's not yours, either. It's mine, and I don't get paid to let other people do my duty."

Billy let go of his arm. "Stubborn bastard."

Mackey went in the jailhouse and took his flat brimmed hat from the hook on the back of the door. After setting it on his head, he could've sworn the ache in his chest dulled a little. It could've been wishful thinking, too.

He took down his Winchester from the rifle rack and handed Billy his Sharps. Neither man levered a round into the chamber. Since their cavalry days, they had always made a practice of keeping their weapons fully loaded and ready. Both had Colt revolvers in the holsters on their belts, too. Billy wore his on his hip, while Mackey wore his just to the left of his buckle, another tradition they'd taken with them when they left the cavalry.

Mackey weaved as another wave of dizziness hit him. He shook it off and kept walking.

Billy gritted his teeth as he slammed the jailhouse door behind him. "You are one stubborn son of a bitch, you know that?"

Mackey was too busy fighting to stay upright to argue. "Don't forget to lock the door."

Billy locked the door and followed Mackey up the boardwalk toward the Tin Horn.

Chapter 2

Mackey felt his steps grow steadier the more he walked. The sheriff and the deputy both wore Colt pistols—the sheriff with the belly holster to the left of his buckle for an easy draw and the deputy with his Colt on his hip. Both men kept their rifles at their sides as they walked. The townspeople had seen this walk before and reacted accordingly. They knew it was time to head indoors without question or protest. Doors of shops and homes slammed shut as the two lawmen walked down Front Street. The few visitors milling about the boardwalk town took a cue from the locals and made their way indoors.

The chilly spring wind blowing up Front Street helped clear the fog of sickness from Mackey's mind. He counted twelve horses hitched to the posts in front of the Tin Horn. Based on what the whore had told them, there were five men inside raising hell, but Mackey knew better than to take whores at their word. There might be more.

The exact number didn't really matter. He kept walking anyway. And so did Billy.

They stopped directly across the thoroughfare from the batwing doors of the Tin Horn just as a group of men stumbled out onto the boardwalk.

Mackey took a quick inventory:

Five men. Late teens to late thirties.

Four of them holding whiskey bottles.

The fattest of the bunch was the oldest. He was also in the middle and lugging a crate of whiskey.

All five men had guns on their hips.

All of them were drunk, too.

Mackey and Billy brought their rifles up to their shoulders at the same time.

It took a few seconds for the five drunkards to notice Mackey and Billy. It took another second for them to realize they were covered. Drunk as they were, they stopped moving when they did.

Mackey was glad his voice was strong when he called out: "You boys are under arrest for being drunk and disorderly. Set your bottles and your guns on the boardwalk and put your hands against the wall. Do it nice and easy and no one gets hurt."

The five men had formed a ragged, weaving line along the front steps and boardwalk of the Tin Horn. The two men on the far left side were still standing on the boardwalk. They were young and wide-eyed; their flap holsters buttoned. They looked eager, but unsure and scared. Mackey knew they'd pull if they had to, but they wouldn't pull first.

The fat man in the middle was holding the crate of whiskey. He'd have to drop the case to go for his gun. He'd be dead before the case hit the boardwalk, and he looked old enough to know it, too. Mackey paid him little mind.

But the two men on the far right were a different

story. They weaved just enough to be drunk, but steady on their feet. No flap holsters for them. They wore their pistols just far enough down their legs to give them a faster, easier draw. Both of them had hard eyes.

One of them was even smiling.

If trouble started, it would start with them. They'd been through this kind of thing before.

But so had Mackey and Billy.

Mackey shifted his aim to the two gun hands on the right. Billy shifted his aim left.

The last man on the right spoke up. "You're Aaron Mackey, ain't you? The hero of Adobe Flats." He smiled. "I heard of you."

Mackey sensed something was about to break and tried to stop it. "Last warning, boys. No one has to . . ."

The gunman on the far right dropped his bottle as he went for his gun. So did the man next to him.

Mackey fired, hitting the first man in the chest as his pistol cleared leather. Mackey levered another round into the Winchester and fired again, hitting the second man in the chest as he aimed. The gunman's bullet went wide and shattered a window somewhere off to Mackey's right.

Billy's Sharps rifle boomed twice; hitting the two young men on the left as they fumbled at their flapped holsters for their pistols.

As the gun smoke cleared, the fat man was the last man standing, a crate full of whiskey in his arms and four dead men at his feet.

Mackey and Billy shifted their aim to the center of that crate.

"Set that crate down nice and slow, fat man,"

Mackey said, "then throw up your hands. No reason for you to end up like your friends."

"Don't shoot me, please." The fat man tried to put fear in his voice, but it didn't work. Mackey tracked him with his rifle while the fat man took a step back up onto the boardwalk and inched over toward the porch post on the left. Billy's rifle tracked him, too. "I'm just gonna lay this here whiskey down nice and easy, just like you told me. Then you'll take me off to jail. Ain't that right?"

The fat man's knees popped as he slowly lowered the case to the boardwalk then dove for cover behind the horse trough.

Mackey and Billy fired at the same time. Both rounds caught the fat man high on the left side while he was still in the air. He was wounded but not dead yet. He still had a gun on his hip and now he had cover.

Mackey wasn't surprised to see Sim Halstead burst through the batwing doors of the Tin Horn and cut loose on the fat man with his sidearm. Mackey wasn't surprised that none of his six shots went into the trough, either. Every bullet had hit the fat man where he'd landed.

He wasn't surprised because the old army scout had always been a hell of a gun hand with a knack for turning up at the right time.

As soon as the shooting stopped, Billy called out to Sim: "Any more in there?"

Sim shook his head as he cracked open the cylinder of his Colt and replaced the spent shells with new. Everything Sim did was slow, efficient, and quiet. Even gunplay.

Mackey and Billy also fed new shells into their

rifles. An empty rifle was no good to anyone except the bad guys. "You in there the whole time?" the sheriff asked.

Again, Sim shook his head.

"Come in the back way after it started?" Billy asked.

Sim nodded as he slid the Colt back into the holster on his hip.

Some men were men of few words. For reasons of his own, Sim had chosen to be a man of no words at all. Mackey and Billy knew the reason why, but neither of them had ever discussed it. Not with each other or with Sim or with anyone else. Sim's silence was nobody's business but his own. If he wanted to explain his silence, it would be up to him to do so. But given as how he wasn't talking, an explanation wasn't expected to be forthcoming any time in the near term.

Now that the shooting had stopped, some of the townsfolk and patrons from the Tin Horn began to drift out onto the boardwalk to see what had happened. In some regards, Dover Station was different from other towns. In regard to gossip, it was about the same as most.

Sam Warren, the bartender and owner of the Tin Horn, pushed through the crowd that had gathered in front of his establishment. A pot-bellied man whose suspenders strained to keep his pants over his impressive gut, he was holding a bloody bar towel against the side of his head. A fair amount of blood was already beginning to dry on his beard.

"That's him." Warren cut loose with a stream of tobacco juice at the fat man behind the trough. "That's the bastard who hit me with my own whiskey bottle." Warren forgot about his wound long enough to check the crate of whiskey the fat man had lain on the boardwalk. "At least all the bottles are intact. Would've hated to go through all this nonsense and lose a case of good liquor in the bargain."

Billy began to check the pockets of the dead men for anything that might show who they were. "Ever see any of these boys before, Sam?"

"Never," the barman said with the piety of a parson on Sunday. "Sons of bitches rode up here from the south side of town about an hour ago. They were already drunk but peaceable enough when they walked in, so I served them. As soon as they started getting loud and sloppy, I told them to lay their guns on the bar before I'd serve them any more liquor. That's when they ripped poor Stephan, my new bouncer, out of his outlook chair and set to whaling on him." He pointed at the dead man behind the trough with his free hand. "The fat bastard broke a bottle against the side of my head when I went for my shotgun under the bar."

Mackey fed the last cartridge into the rifle. "You weren't supposed to serve them if they were packing, Sam."

Warren dabbed at his wound with his bar towel. "I know, but they were respectful enough at first and it's been a mighty slow day. I got a business to run, Aaron and . . ."

"Law says you don't serve anyone until they give up their guns. Now you're hurt, your place broken up, and I've got five dead men in the street." Mackey held his rifle at his side. "You weren't supposed to serve them if they were packing, were you, Sam?"

Warren looked like he wanted to say more, but thought better of it. Aaron Mackey wasn't known for his patience or fondness for public debate.

Billy broke the silence. "They say where they were from? Who they were?"

"All I got out of them was a beating," Warren said. "Some of my customers said they helped themselves to some whiskey while Stephan and me was out cold. Stephan's my new bouncer from the Yukon I told you about, and . . ."

"Looks like he's doing a hell of a job." Mackey nodded down at the dead men in the street. "Well worth the expense of bringing him all the way down from the Yukon."

Warren pouted and tended to his wound. "Say, how'd you find out about this anyway? They had the whole place covered. Wouldn't let anybody leave."

"That new redhead you brought on came and fetched us," Billy said as he moved to search another dead man. "Said she snuck out the back."

Sam Warren beamed with a pimp's pride. "That Molly sure is a resourceful gal, ain't she? And while she was sneaking out the back, old Sim here snuck *in* the back way." He slapped the old scout on the shoulder. "You'll be drinking on the house tonight, my friend. All the whiskey you can hold."

Sim didn't smile. He never smiled. Mackey knew he didn't drink, either. He was sure Warren knew that, too. An empty reward from an empty man.

As Billy searched the bodies, Mackey looked over the horses hitched in front of the saloon. "Anybody know which of these horses belong to these boys?"

Some of the saloon patrons on the boardwalk began pointing out which horses belonged to them. It took some sorting out, but Mackey figured the five at the end belonged to the dead men.

He looked over each horse, but the inspection

didn't take long. Each mount looked like it had ridden a long, hard trail. They were all thinner than they should've been, and their hooves were in bad shape. The blacksmith would have to give them new shoes, but they'd still fetch the sheriff's office a good price when it came time to sell them.

But Mackey was more troubled by what he didn't see.

Mackey waited until Billy stood up after he finished searching the fat man behind the water trough. "Find anything?"

"Nope. Other than the pistols, about ten dollars in silver between the five of them. That's all. No letters or anything else that says who they are or where they're from. Anything in their saddlebags?"

"No saddlebags," Mackey said, "or bedrolls either. Just saddles and rifles in their scabbards." Each rifle would need a good cleaning, but they'd bring a good price at auction, too.

Billy had always had a knack for saying what Mackey was thinking. "Awful strange, trail men like this not having gear."

Mackey never liked to make up his mind before he had all the facts. "We'll have to check all the hotels in town. See if they were staying in one of them. Then . . ." Mackey felt another wave of weakness come over him and grabbed the saddle horn of the nearest horse to steady himself.

He knew everyone saw it and tried to cover it with bluster. To Warren, he said: "Get your customers lined up inside so they can give their statements to Billy and Sim one at a time. That means you too, Sam. Billy will ask the questions and Sim will write them down." Billy didn't know how to write and Sim didn't talk. But between the two of them, they got the job done. "Make sure everyone signs their statements, too."

"Hell, Aaron," Warren said. "Half of these bastards are so drunk, they don't know what they saw and the other half can't write."

"Then they can put that in their statement and make their mark below it. I want everything they saw or didn't see on paper. Chances are these boys have friends and I want something for the official record if someone comes around asking questions." He looked at Sim Halstead. "I'd appreciate it if you'd go in and help them get started."

Sim motioned for the customers to go back inside. Most of them went with little grumbling or complaint. Everyone knew Aaron Mackey wasn't a man given to asking for anything twice; not even in the best of moods. Neither was Sim.

Mackey noticed that the boardwalk on both sides of the street were jammed with murmuring towns-people. He figured they were either speculating about what had happened or lying about what they'd seen. It was always like that after a shooting. In Dover Station. In every town everywhere in the world, Mackey supposed. He'd make sure the official report of what had happened would be in *The Dover Station Record* the following day. Until then, the rest was just a lot of hot air and nonsense.

Billy walked over to Mackey and lowered his voice. "Strange about hard-riding men like these not having saddlebags or bedrolls."

Mackey stifled a cough as the weakness lingered. "No pack animals either."

"And they don't strike me as the types to take rooms in hotels."

"No, but we've got to ask anyway. When you're done here with the witness statements, check the other hotels. Saloons, too. Warren said they were already drunk when they got here, so they either drank on the ride in or they got drunk somewhere in town. Find out where. That might tell us who these boys are and where they're from."

"And if they have friends."

Mackey finally felt strong enough to let go of the saddle horn and stand on his own. "You're getting pretty good at this deputy business."

"After five years, I should be. And while Sim and I are doing all this investigating and note taking, you'll be going back to bed."

Mackey rubbed his chest to help with the soreness of his lungs. It didn't help much, but a little. "Haven't made up my mind on that yet."

"Looks to me like your body has made up its own mind. You're either walking back to the jail or I'm gonna have to carry you back there when you fall over."

Murmurs rose from the boardwalk across the street as someone began pushing his way through the gathering crowd. "Make way," a familiar voice called out. "Make way. Let me through here!"

As soon as Mackey saw Mayor Mason and Charles Harrington, editor of *The Dover Station Record,* pushing through the townspeople, he began heading back to the jailhouse. "No need to carry me anywhere. Christ himself would've left the tomb on Saturday to avoid those two bastards."

Over his shoulder, he added, "Send someone for Doc Ridley and the undertaker so he can fetch these boys off the street. I'd say the people have gotten enough of a show for one day."

The politician and the reporter began shouting questions at Mackey's back as he walked toward the jail.

The banner announcing the next day's Veterans Dance snapped and billowed overhead in the strengthening wind.

Chapter 3

Mackey unlocked the jailhouse door and stepped inside. He didn't bother closing it behind him. He knew Mason and Harrington would only barge in anyway or pound on it until he answered it. Since his fever was beginning to return, and the throbbing headache that accompanied it, he decided to not delay the inevitable.

He had just begun to pour himself a cup of the coffee Billy had made earlier that afternoon when Mayor Brian Mason and Charles Everett Harrington of *The Dover Station Record* stormed into the jail. Neither of them took the time to close the door behind them, either.

Mayor Mason may have been shorter than the newspaperman, but he had a politician's lung power. He voiced his indignation first and loudest. "How dare you turn your back on me in front of the whole town like that? You're a public servant, Mackey, same as me."

Mackey knew Mason was spoiling for an argument, which was why he decided to stall him. He motioned toward one of the coffee mugs on the table next to the stove. "Coffee?"

The mayor reddened. "I came here for answers, damn you, not coffee. Now . . ."

"Shame." Mackey slowly filled his cup. "Billy makes a damned fine pot. Always did. His coffee saw me through many a patrol in Arizona. Texas, too, come to think of it. Can't underestimate the power of good coffee in the wilderness, Brian. Makes a man feel at home and that can make all the difference."

Mason's face grew even more florid. "Now see here . . ."

Mackey looked at the newsman. "What about you, Charlie? Can I pour you a cup?"

"A bit early in the day for me," Harrington produced a silver flask from his jacket pocket and toasted Mackey. "Maybe later."

"Suit yourself." Mackey took his time placing the coffee pot back on the stove. "But you boys are missing out on quite a treat. Like I said, Billy makes a fine pot."

He eased himself down into the swivel chair behind his desk. He knew informality frustrated Mayor Mason more than anything else.

Before coming west, Brian Mason had been a grocer from New York who had packed up his family and come west with dreams of making his fortune in California. For reasons Mackey had never bothered to understand, the Mason family's trek to the Pacific ended in Dover Station, Montana, where he now owned the second-largest dry goods store in town. The fact that Mackey's father owned the largest dry goods store in the territory still vexed Mason to no end. Mackey wondered if that was why Mason took great pride in the fact that he had been elected to the position of town mayor. The fact that he had run unopposed for his mayoralty—because no one else wanted the position—seemed to have been completely lost on him. He believed he was entitled to a certain level of respect for holding an office no one else had wanted.

Which was why Mackey intentionally took his time sipping his coffee before placing the cup on his desk. "You wanted to see me about something, Mr. Mayor?"

Mason was already reddened from being made to wait. "You're damned right I want to see you about something. I want to know about that godawful mess you left out on my street."

"It's not your street," Mackey pointed out. "That street belongs to the good people of Dover Station, the very same people we're sworn to protect and serve." He looked over at the publisher of *The Dover Station Record.* "Isn't that right, Charlie?"

Harrington took a pull on his flask. He had always made it a point to keep out of arguments between the sheriff and the mayor, though he always seemed to enjoy watching them, even provoking them on occasion.

Mason's fleshy face reddened even further. "You just killed five men, left them lying dead in the street like dogs, and you're making light of it."

"Point of order, Mr. Mayor," Mackey said. "I only killed two men. Billy killed two others and Sim finished off the fat man who dove behind the trough. Pretty spry for a man that size if you ask me." He made a show of thinking about it for a moment. "But Billy and I did wing him before Sim opened up on him." He looked at Harrington. "You're an educated man,

Charlie. Would you call that a tie or should we divvy that kill up in thirds?"

Harrington looked out the window.

Mason rocked up on his toes as he put his hands behind his back. It was a gesture intended to make him look official, but only served to make his prosperous belly look even rounder. "You obviously fail to grasp the gravity of this situation, Sheriff Mackey."

Mackey sipped his coffee. He loved when the mayor parroted big words he'd overheard or read elsewhere. "Then I'd be interested in any attempt on your part to enlighten me."

The mayor cleared his throat. "Tomorrow may very well be the biggest day in the history of Dover Station, sir. As you know, I have gone through great expense and considerable effort to bring influential investors here all the way from New York so they can see us at our finest. Mr. Frazer Rice and Mr. Silas Van Dorn of the Rice Van Dorn Company are perhaps the most influential men on Wall Street."

Mackey narrowed his eyes. "Come to think of it, I believe I've heard a few people around town mention it once or twice." Mackey grinned as he sipped his coffee. Since making Dover Station a more civilized place, tormenting Brian Mason was one of the few pleasures Sheriff Mackey enjoyed. "Don't know what Mr. Rice and Mr. Van Dorn have to do with what just happened down at the Tin Horn, though."

"They are investors, sir. They represent railroad men and financiers and captains of industry, men who are serious about making major investments in Dover Station. And, much to my chagrin, they have expressed a great interest in meeting you personally, sir. It seems the idea of shaking the hand of the Hero of Adobe Flat holds some appeal."

Mackey ignored the flattery and sipped his coffee. "Rice and Van Dorn are money men, Brian, and they won't put a penny in this place unless they think they can get ten dollars out of it. All the glad handing and sign waving in the world won't change that."

"Perhaps," Mason allowed, "but gunning down five men in the street won't help matters any, either. In broad daylight less than an hour before they're scheduled to arrive, no less!"

Mackey hadn't known they were due to arrive so soon. Or did he? He remembered hearing Mason had invited dignitaries to the Veterans Dance. He remembered they were due to arrive soon, but he'd lost track of when they were scheduled to arrive. *Was it today?* He had thought it might be tomorrow. The pneumonia had made his mind so cloudy that he might have lost track of time.

Either way, he decided it wasn't a good enough reason to concede the argument to Mason. "Investors usually like to know where they're placing their money, Brian. And I'd bet a month's wages that those men wouldn't have come all this way if they didn't already know this is still rough country. That's probably why they're coming here in the first place. Figure they can buy us up low and sell us out high later on."

Mason smiled. "I wasn't aware of your familiarity with financial matters, sir."

"I'm not," Mackey admitted. "I'm familiar with people. We've got cattlemen and loggers and miners and townspeople and every drunk, drover, and snake-oil salesman who come to town off the train all pushing each other for their piece of this place. Sometimes that pushing turns into more than that, and when it does, I'm paid to do something about it. That's exactly what we did down at the Tin Horn just now, Brian, and you know it."

"You're paid to enforce the law, not to kill people."

"That's right. So, when Mr. Rice and Mr. Van Dorn and their friends get wind of what I did today, I'd wager they'll like knowing there's some law and order in this town. Could make you look mighty important in front of all your new friends from back east. Might be why they're looking at Dover Station in the first place, as opposed to other towns out here."

Mason rocked up on the tips of his shoes again and grabbed the lapels of his coat. "Butchering men in the middle of town won't help our chances, I can assure you of that. You could have at least tried to get them to surrender or wounded them."

"Spoken like a true grocer from back east." Mackey took another sip of coffee. "And we gave them the chance to surrender and they went for their guns. But it'll all be part of the official record, if that soothes your conscience any."

Mason hadn't been expecting that. "It will?"

"Everyone who saw the shooting is giving written statements down at the Horn right now," Mackey told him. "Billy and Sim will have them in a couple of hours. I'll have the report finalized and in Mr. Harrington's paper tomorrow morning for the world to see. And, since I'm in a generous mood, I won't mention that none of this would have happened if Sam Warren had obeyed the law and disarmed those boys before he served them."

"You've always got an answer for everything, don't you, Aaron?" Mason's eyes narrowed. He didn't like losing arguments and he realized he was losing this one. "Well, even if this cost us major investment, at least you have a new crop to plant in that damnable garden of yours."

Mackey looked at Mason for a long second. "Careful, Brian."

"You need to be careful, sheriff. You've been down with pneumonia for the past month, so perhaps you haven't noticed that Mr. Rice already opened one bank over on Grant Street last week. Mr. Van Dorn and his other partners are seriously looking at developing other parcels, perhaps as a hotel. The railroad may be changing its schedule to stop here more than once a week. Hell, the telegraph is thinking of adding another line to run from here clear down to Butte. Things are changing for the better in Dover Station and changing fast. And all of that is threatened if you keep gunning men down in the street like this."

Mackey set his mug down on his desk. "When I first took this job, men like you were begging me to kill men like that. That's how the whole 'damnable garden' of mine got started in the first place. I do what I'm paid to do the best way I know how. I don't shoot drunks for pissing in the street, and I don't beat card sharps half to death for keeping aces up their sleeve. But when someone goes for their pistols, I put them down. You don't like that, get yourself someone else for the job."

"You speak of another time," Mason said. "This town's industry and commerce have matured since then and are poised for exponential growth. I'll not have you stand in the way of . . ."

When Mackey heard clapping and whistling coming

from the boardwalk, he knew his father, Brendan "Pappy" Mackey had just arrived at the jailhouse.

Mackey's father could never have been described as a tall man, but what the Irishman lacked in height he made up for in size. He had broad shoulders, a strong back, and thick forearms worthy of a black-smith rather than the shopkeeper he was. He was going on sixty, but still often did the work of three men half his age. His hair and beard had long turned steel gray, making his stern countenance appear even more so, though his eyes belied a vibrant spirit.

"A grand speech, Brian," Pappy said as he entered the jailhouse, his brogue adding just a hint of sarcasm to his words. "Too bad Election Day is so far off, or you'd be a shoe-in for another term. Maybe even governor, by Christ, if they ever get around to making this territory part of the Union."

The mayor and Pappy had been rivals since Mason had come to Dover Station and opened his own dry goods store. That had been almost twenty years ago, but the elder Mackey still treated Mason like a new-comer. "We are in the middle of discussing important town affairs that are none of your concern, Brendan."

"Nonsense." Pappy took a chair next to Harring-ton. "I'm a town founder, a town resident, and the owner of the largest store within fifty miles. I was one of the men who brokered a peace with the Blackfeet when we came to this country, so I'd say town affairs are very much my affairs." He nodded toward his son. "The fact that my boy here killed those five men just now makes it even more of my affair."

Charles Everett Harrington cleared his throat. "Technically, your son only shot two of the five men.

Billy shot two on his own, but the responsibility for the death of the last man is still a matter of some dispute."

"I stand corrected." Pappy bowed humbly. To Mason, he said, "I wouldn't fret about a couple of dead criminals scaring off these wealthy friends of yours. Those boys'll be buried and forgotten by lunchtime tomorrow. And when the dance starts, they'll be nothing more than a fart in the wind."

But Mason held his ground. "The burials won't be held until tomorrow, and I've got Mr. Rice and his friends coming in this afternoon by special train and . . ."

"Special train? That must've set you back a pretty penny."

"Not at all," Mason stammered. "Mr. Rice paid for . . ."

Pappy wagged a finger at him. "I know what this is really about. You're worried about how we're going to split the dead men's property between your shop and mine, aren't you?"

Mason's eyes narrowed again. Over the years, each store purchased the possessions of whomever Mackey had killed, then resold them to the public. The profits went to the sheriff's office, which turned a nice profit. "How dare you imply that I might allow my own personal business to conflict with my duties as mayor of this town. I . . ."

"I was thinking about how we usually split things," Pappy said. "Sixty-forty in my favor is unfair to you. And seeing as how you're under special stress given these visitors coming to town and all, I'd be amenable to cutting you a break. Maybe discussing a fifty-fifty split."

The mayor stopped sputtering.

Pappy sweetened the pot a bit. "Hell, given the occasion, I'll even give you three out of the five horses we've taken from the dead men if it'll make you feel any better."

Mackey watched Mason flinch as his brain went in two directions at the same time. The politician in him was still riled up about the possibility of the shooting scaring off investors. But Pappy's offer to increase his customary share of the dead men's possessions appealed to the shopkeeper aspect of his nature.

When the mayor's face softened, he knew Mason's shopkeeper side had won out. "A sixty-forty split in the possessions sounds even better. In my favor, of course."

"Then we have a deal." Pappy spat in his palm and held it out for the mayor to shake. Mason did the same, though reluctantly. After the two men shook on it, Pappy added, "Now get the hell out of here."

Mason quickly withdrew his hand. "I'm still the mayor and I still have town business to conduct with Aaron."

Pappy beckoned Harrington to hand over his flask, which he did. "You're only the mayor because no one else wanted the goddamned job in the first place. You're mayor because the men who built this town let you be mayor. Men like me. So when you speak to my son, you'll speak to him with respect. In public, in private, or any other time you see him. Or you'll stop being mayor and go back to being the second-largest store owner in this here town."

Mayor Mason flushed. "Now see here, Brendan . . ."

But Mackey could tell his father was in a talking mood, and there was no stopping him once he started. "You're not the only one in this town who can charm the high rollers you're bringing in here tomorrow night, Brian. Me and several of the others can put on quite a show for these folks if we're of a mind to. One more word out of you and that's exactly what I'll do. We'll bar you from the dance tomorrow night. Make you watch the whole thing from the street like a goddamned stable boy."

Pappy dismissed the mayor with a wave. "Now, off with you and not another word about it."

Mason balled his tiny fists at his sides. Like Sam, the mayor had plenty to say, but clearly thought better of it. Like Mackey, Pappy wasn't renowned for his patience of love of debate.

Instead, Mason cleared his throat and said; "Sheriff, you and I will discuss this at a later date. In the meantime, I'm headed down to the station to oversee the final preparations for our welcoming ceremony. Good day, gentlemen." He then left the jail, careful to close the jailhouse door quietly behind him.

"That's the spirit," Pappy boomed after him. "Make straight their path." He took a final pull from Harrington's flask before handing it back to him. "Jesus, that stuff tastes like turpentine."

"Perhaps, but it's still sweeter than either of you." The reporter toasted the Mackey men with his flask. "You two were a little rough on the old boy, don't you think? He *has* gone through the trouble of getting quite a number of potential investors to attend the dance tomorrow. He succeeded, too. There's something to be said for that."

"Here's what I have to say for it." Pappy hawked and spat in the spittoon by the door. "To hell with him. That weasel is only doing this because he sees something in it for him, just like with them horses." He laughed. "Probably thinks I gave in too easy on that score. Well, I checked them over before I came over here. Never saw a sorrier example of horseflesh since the one my son married."

Mackey looked at his father over the rim of his mug. "Enough."

But his father ignored him. "Every single one of them mounts is fit for the glue pot and little else. I just gave Mason sixty percent of nothing. Poor things seem to still be alive out of sheer habit and little else."

"Kind of like someone else I know." Mackey got up and refilled his cup at the stove. "I was handling Mason just fine before you walked in, old man."

"Old man?" Pappy flexed his arm so the muscle bulged against the sleeve of his shirt. "How's that for an old man? Besides, if anyone was ever born to be given a hard time, it's Brian Mason."

"He'll sulk for the rest of the week." Mackey sat behind the desk again. He was still lightheaded and hoped the others couldn't tell. "He'll take it out on me in a thousand different ways, not you. You think you did me a favor, but all you did was make things worse. Like always."

Pappy laughed and slapped his own leg. "You're just grumpy because you're feeling so poorly." He eyed his son closely. "Say, how are you feeling anyway? You look like hell."

As if on command, another wracking cough overcame him.

"You sound wonderful." Pappy got up and walked around his son to pour his own cup of coffee. "Serves you right for staying in a damned drafty jail instead of with me at my place."

"I'm better off here." Mackey spat phlegm into the spittoon by his desk. "You run your goddamned mouth so much, I'd never get any rest."

Pappy spiked his coffee with a healthy pour from Harrington's flask. "Maybe, but you should be home in your own bed where you belong, if you ask me. And you would be, too, if you hadn't gone and married that miserable wife of yours."

Even when he was in the best of health, Mackey knew winning an argument with his father was next to impossible. Given his present condition, he didn't even try. "Mary's a complicated woman with a strong will. She . . ."

Mackey realized Harrington was still sitting there, taking in every word, as reporters were apt to do. Harrington might drink all day and most of the night, but he never forgot anything he heard. And whatever he heard was often repeated either in conversation or printed in his newspaper.

Mackey pointed at the newsman. "If I hear or read one word of this anywhere else, Charlie, I swear to Christ, I'll . . ."

Harrington threw up his hands in surrender. "My only concern is the chronicling of the town's daily affairs. The domestic bliss or lack thereof of Sheriff Aaron Mackey falls far beyond the scope of official town business."

Pappy grinned. "If you're so damned honorable, Charlie, what the hell are you doing running a paper way out here in the wilderness?"

Harrington regarded his silver flask for a moment. "A valid question I've asked myself a great many times." He took a healthy pull and screwed the cap back on. "And while I might not have any interest in your familial difficulties, the matter of the five men lying dead out on Front Street is of great interest to the town and to my readership. I plan on using it as my lead story in tomorrow's edition. Might even manage to get a whole week out of it if I play the angles right. What can you tell me about the newly departed strangers?"

Mackey had nothing to tell him, so he stalled. "Everything you need to know will be in my official report."

"And when will that be ready?"

"The sooner you two bastards leave, the sooner I can get working on it and get it to you."

Pappy spat his spiked coffee back into his cup. "Heathen. Calling your own father a bastard. Your own flesh and blood."

"You've call me a bastard at least once a day for most of my life. A stupid bastard at that."

"I'm your father," Pappy said. "I'm entitled."

But Harrington wouldn't be distracted by the banter between father and son. "Nice try at distraction, you two, but I still have an open question on the floor. Can you tell me anything in advance of the official report? Who were these men? Where were they from?"

Since Harrington would know the truth soon enough, Mackey saw no reason to stall. "There's not much to tell. None of the men had anything on them. No letters, no pictures. Nothing in their pockets, either, except about ten dollars between the five of them."

Pappy lowered his cup. "Nothing?"

"No bedrolls. No saddlebags. No pack animals,

either. At least none we've been able to find yet. None of them had a goddamned thing but the clothes on their backs, the guns on their hips, and the boots on their feet."

"Damned strange, isn't it?" Harrington asked. "For men all the way out here to have nothing by the way of trail gear?"

Mackey felt his lungs begin to clog again, and he stirred them to clear them. "Those mounts show signs they've been on the trail recently, maybe even as late as today. They should've had provisions, but we didn't find as much as a slice of bacon among them."

"Maybe they were staying somewhere in town?" Harrington offered.

Mackey was seized by another deep coughing spasm, so Pappy answered for him. "If they did, they would've had a hotel room key or a receipt on them for the room. And if not, some hotel keeper would've claimed them by now. No saddlebags or bedrolls or pack mule means they were most likely camped somewhere else. Somewhere they felt comfortable leaving their things behind."

Harrington still didn't look troubled. "I know I'm still naïve to quite a few things about life out here, but I still fail to see the cause for concern. Perhaps they simply left their things at an isolated camp site and rode into town."

"Men like these wouldn't do that," Pappy said as Mackey struggled to get his breath. "They rode in on tired mounts. They were armed and ready to fight when Aaron and Billy braced them outside the Tin Horn. Men like that wouldn't be apt to just leave their gear behind unguarded and ride into town."

Mackey stopped coughing and wiped his mouth

with the back of his hand. The effort weakened him even further. He felt like he was breathing through wet cheesecloth. "They're probably camped some place close by. At least one of them stayed behind to mind their gear, but I've got a feeling there's a lot more than just one of them."

"And when their dead friends don't come back," Pappy added, "whoever's watching their stuff is liable to come looking for them."

Harrington looked as though he had finally grasped the complexity of the situation. "Could be just one man. A reasonable man at that."

Pappy said, "If those men were reasonable, they'd be in Aaron's jail cells right now, sleeping off their hangovers."

Mackey drank his coffee. The warmth of it felt good in his raw throat. "Let's not jump to any conclusions. We won't know anything until they get here, if anyone shows up at all."

But Harrington never had any shortage of questions. "But what happens if they have friends who ride in here looking for trouble?"

Mackey set his coffee mug on the desk. "That'll depend on them."

Pappy cleared his throat. "Sounds like you, Mr. Harrington, have plenty of material to get started on that story of yours. Better get back to your shop and get a jump on that morning edition. Them articles don't write themselves, now do they?"

"I get it." Harrington tucked the flask into his coat pocket as he slowly stood up. "The men of the Mackey clan wish to discuss certain matters that are not for my ears."

Pappy smiled. "Your powers of perception are

rivaled only by my own, Charlie darling. Drop by the Tin Horn later for a snort or two. On me. I'm sure Sheriff Mackey will be by your shop with the official report once it's been written."

Mackey stifled a cough.

The newspaperman bowed, then closed the door behind him as quietly as Mayor Mason had, but with much more of his dignity intact.

Once they were alone, Pappy said, "I found out something I didn't want to tell you in front of that nosey lush."

Mackey wasn't surprised. His father was the biggest gossip in the territory and usually heard everything first. The only thing he liked better than a good fight was good dirt. "What is it?"

"I heard those boys you killed were drinking down at Katie's Place for the better part of the morning. Before they raised hell over at the Tin Horn, that is."

"Katie's Place?" Mackey repeated, though he'd heard it clear enough the first time. "You sure?"

"I'm sure that's what I heard. As for whether or not it's true, that'll be up to you and Billy to find out."

But that didn't make much sense to Mackey. "Why would they be down at Katie's? Her place is too spiffy to cater to that kind of trash."

"Don't ask me." Pappy drained the last of his coffee and stood. "I'm just an old gossip who hears things. Take it with as many grains of sand as you are of a mind to."

"I'll head down and ask her." Mackey stood up, but was hit by another wave of dizziness. He felt his father's thick hand grab his arm to steady him. Mackey didn't like being touched, and he had been grabbed twice within the past hour.

Pappy eased him back over to his chair. "You should be in bed, boy, not running around town. You'll need to be in good form for the dance tomorrow night."

Mackey pulled his arm free. "I've never gone to that goddamned costume party of yours, and I'm not going to start now."

If his father was hurt, he hid it well. "Even so, let Billy dig around about these boys today. He's more than capable and . . ."

"Billy's every bit as capable as I am. Maybe even more capable." It came out harsher than he'd intended. He'd always been touchy when it came to talk of Billy's abilities. "But he's not paid to be the sheriff. I am. Finding out who those men were and where they were staying is my job, not his. Or yours, either. I've been sick long enough. Time to get back to work."

Pappy moved away from his son. "You're a disagreeable, stubborn son of a bitch."

"Runs in the family." Mackey took his straight-brimmed hat from the desk and set it on his head. "I'll head over and talk to Katie myself. Find out what those men were doing there, if they were there at all."

Pappy opened the jailhouse door and let his son walk out first. "How about I walk with you for a bit?"

"And disappoint all your old army buddies waiting at your store? I'll be they can't wait to hear all about the shootings. Like the mayor said: the people of Dover Station deserve better than that."

Pappy pulled the jailhouse door shut behind him. "I didn't beat you enough when you were a boy."

Mackey pulled out the key and locked the door. "You never laid a hand on me. Not even once."

"And I'm paying for it now. 'Spare the rod' and

all that. And if you had any sense, you'd take up with Katie instead of that wizened beast you're chained to now."

Mackey didn't bother arguing with his father. He walked away from him instead, down Front Street toward Katie's Place.

But Pappy still wasn't done. "Christ, the woman moved all the way out here just to be with you. That ought to count for something."

Mackey lowered the brim of his hat against the strengthening wind and not break his pace. There was no use in arguing with his father.

Especially when he was right.

Chapter 4

The few people who were still on the boardwalk made it a point not to meet Mackey's eye as he walked along Front Street. It was widely known that the sheriff was a man to be avoided in general and after a shooting in particular.

That was just fine with Mackey. Their avoidance allowed him to see Cy Wallach, the town undertaker, and an assistant loading the bodies of the dead men in front of the Tin Horn onto a flatbed wagon. The old German would most likely take the cadavers over to his workshop to prepare them for burial the following day in that part of the cemetery the locals had taken to calling Mackey's Garden. Every year since he'd been elected sheriff, a couple of rows were added to the garden. Come tomorrow, there'd be five more holes dug. A good number, but by no means a record for a single planting. Not by Mackey's standards.

Wallach had recently taken to calling himself a "mortician," an artist with cotton wadding and chemicals and powder that made the dead seem more alive. He always cleaned up the men Mackey killed as practice for the higher-paying clients in town who eventually requested his services on behalf of their newly departed loved ones. Mackey didn't see the point in Wallach's experiments because Wallach was the only mortician in town. People had no choice but to use him, no matter how much rouge he slapped on a corpse.

But Mackey had never seen the value in cleaning up a body or praying over it, either. He'd seen enough death in the cavalry to know there was nothing lifelike about death. If it was up to him, he'd just drop them in a hole and shovel the dirt back on them the same day they died. No reason to draw out the inevitable rot that always followed life.

But life was never that simple, so he shouldn't expect death to be simple, either. Morticians had to eat. Coffin makers and preachers, too.

As Mackey navigated the buckboards that had been laid across the muddy thoroughfare to reach the next boardwalk on his way toward Katie's Place, he spotted Doc Ridley trudging toward him through the dense mud of Front Street. Given his weakened condition, Mackey did his best to outpace the pious town doctor and the sermon he knew would follow his greeting.

Although Doc Ridley had once been Captain William Ridley of Virginia in the War Between the States, he now saw himself as a Christian soldier sitting at the Lord's own right hand. He'd never made a secret of disagreeing with what he viewed as Mackey's harsh, sometimes brutal enforcement of the town's laws. Now that Mackey had just shot five men, he knew he was in for a healthy dose of fire and brimstone from the good doctor.

But Mackey was only interested in getting to Katie's

Place to find out if those dead men had been drinking there before the Tin Horn.

Doc Ridley called to him when he got within earshot. "You must be awfully proud of your handiwork here, Aaron. Feel like justice has been done?"

Mackey stepped up on the boardwalk ahead of Ridley. "It's already been a long day, Doc. How about you skip the sermon and sign those death certificates? I'll need them as part of the official report."

"I don't need you to remind me of my duty, sir. You'll get your damned certificates in due course." Ridley climbed up to the boardwalk after him; trying to keep pace with the taller, younger man. "For although I may disagree with your butchery, the Lord tells us to give unto Caesar that which is Caesar's and give unto to Him that which is His."

"Well, seeing as how old Caesar's gotten his due from you, how about you shut your mouth and head back home?"

"You can avoid me all you want, but your conscience won't let you rest."

Mackey smiled. "Hell, I left my conscience among the Apache down in the Arizona Territory, Doc. You know that."

"Do you mean to tell me, before God, that you had no choice but to kill those men this afternoon? That you couldn't have merely wounded them and taken them to jail so that they may have had a chance to repent and change their lives?"

"You're the second man today who's trying to tell me how to do my job." Mackey stopped short so the doctor would bump into him. "I expected that from a civilian like Mason, but not from a man who has shed his share of blood. Billy and I gave them more of a chance than the men you killed at Bull Run or Vicksburg or anywhere else you fought."

As Mackey began walking again, the doctor scrambled to follow. "That was war, damn you. This is civilization."

"And civilizations have laws, Doc. Laws that need to be enforced. The town pays me and Billy to enforce those laws. Any time you or Mayor Mason want to run us out of office, go right ahead. Our stars come off just as easily as we pin them on."

"It's not as simple as all that, and you know it." Ridley struggled to sidestep the townspeople on the boardwalk as they cleared out of Mackey's way. "Why, Mr. Rice and Mr. Van Dorn are coming to this town within the hour. Dover Station is changing in big ways. It's on the verge of growing and becoming a better place to live. A more God-fearing town. Even you must be able to see that."

"So you and Mason keep telling me. But after what happened here today, looks like we've still got a ways to go before anyone mistakes Dover Station for the new and eternal Jerusalem."

"Blasphemer," Ridley spat. "You're such a barbarian that I often forget you're an educated man. You should use the skills and experience West Point gave you for His purposes instead of those of the Devil."

"You want a glimpse of the Devil, Doc? Get Billy and me fired and see what happens in this town. Let the drunks and the drovers and the cowpunchers and the miners go back to cutting loose without us to keep them in line. Let the flakes and the gamblers who come in off the train have a free hand if you want. They'll be strolling up Front Street with whores and squaws in broad daylight before you can blink. Why,

I'll bet old Beelzebub himself will be knocking on your front door inside of a week, and . . ."

Another coughing spasm seized his lungs, causing Mackey to double over.

Doc Ridley guided him out of the growing foot traffic along the boardwalk and eased him against the side of the town's apothecary. Before the coughing let up, the doctor dug his stethoscope out of his bag, put the cold steel against Mackey's shirt and listened.

Mackey tried to push it away, but Ridley kept the stethoscope in place, frowning at what he heard. "Your lungs still have fluid, Aaron." He felt Mackey's forehead with the back of his hand. "Fever's picking up again, too, and you feel clammy. I've already told you that you'll need constant bed rest for the foreseeable future if you hope to improve your condition. It might take another week. A month. Might never completely go away. Pneumonia runs its course in its own time, but the best thing for you right now is bed rest."

"Hardly have a bed to go home to, Doc. Mary's not exactly given to tending to the sick."

"She was practically a child when you married her," Ridley said. "You were a man of the world. It was up to you to make her love the man you are, not the one she had dreamed you would be."

Since there were no women in sight, Mackey stirred his lungs clear, hawked, than spat into the mud of Front Street. It made him feel a little better. "You're a hard man to peg, Doc. A minute ago, you were damning me to Hell. Now you're trying to save my life."

Doc Ridley put his stethoscope back in his bag. "I hate the sin, not the sinner, Aaron. I'm fighting for your life the same way I would have fought for the lives of the men you've just killed if I had gotten there in time."

"Then you would've been pegged with lead from both sides, Doc. That ended the only way they wanted it to end. I know it and so do you. You can bang that Bible of yours all day long and you won't change it."

"Maybe, maybe not. But I believe life means hope for redemption, Aaron. I only wish you could find it in your heart to do the same."

"Not likely." Mackey shook off his dizziness and drew a full breath of air into his lungs. He didn't feel good, but good enough to resume his walk to Katie's Place. "But thanks just the same."

This time, Doc Ridley didn't follow. "There's still goodness in you, Aaron. I saw it in you before you went to West Point, but I haven't seen it in you since you've been back. I know it's still in you."

Mackey stirred his lungs again and spat phlegm into the street. "That makes one of us."

Chapter 5

Mackey was surprised to find Mrs. Katherine Campbell reading a book in a rocking chair on the boardwalk in front of the hotel that bore her name. He felt his breath catch and his pace slow. He wanted to blame it on the pneumonia, but it wasn't. It was always this way whenever he saw her. Even a glimpse of her reminded him of what they once had meant to each other. Of what they could have been together if circumstances had been just a little different, though he knew if they had been different, their paths never would have crossed at all. Even the briefest thought of her was enough to remind him of what it was like to feel something. It had been that way even before the pneumonia and long before his marriage to Mary.

He was surprised to see her on the boardwalk because he knew she had never been one for sitting outside her own hotel, especially with dusk coming on. She despised mosquitoes and bats and other flying things that tended to come around in the early evening. Mackey figured she had decided to sit outside for a reason. He hoped that reason could have had something to do with assuming he would be paying her a visit about the dead men. She might even be concerned about his well-being following the incident. He was just glad to see her.

Mrs. Katherine Campbell was as handsome a woman as Mackey had ever seen, not that he had seen many before leaving—or upon returning—to Dover Station. She was tall for a woman, though not as tall as him. She was thin, but not as scrawny as Mary or hefty as some of Sam Warren's whores. Her hair was light brown and suited her fair complexion. Her high cheekbones and bright blue eyes gave her a friendly countenance. Peaceful, Mackey thought, though not innocent. She came from a good bloodline, too good for a Montana town, yet here she was. And he was the reason why.

It had been ten years since he had first been introduced to her at the Cavalry Officer's dance she and her husband had hosted in their Boston home. He had decided that evening that it would be the last dance he would ever attend, for he knew he could never hope to meet another woman like Mrs. Katherine Campbell.

She had smiled at him all those years ago when they first met at her home, when she was a major's wife and he was the newly appointed Captain Aaron Mackey, the Hero of Adobe Flats. She smiled at him now on the boardwalk of her hotel, a building unlike her family's townhome back east. But the smile was the same now as it had been that evening. The same smile whenever they found themselves alone. The smile she kept just for him. He felt himself smile back.

"I'm glad you're here." She closed her book and

tucked it between her and the arm of the rocking chair. "I was worried."

"I figured. I . . ."

The spell was broken when Old Wilkes trudged out of the hotel and began to sweep at the dirt and dust of the boardwalk. He was careful to sweep in the opposite direction of the wind and away from Mrs. Campbell's rocking chair, of course.

"Evenin', Aaron," the old Union sergeant said. "How's your pa?"

Wilkes had asked Mackey the same thing every time they met for as long as he could remember, and Mackey had always given the same response. "As good as he's liable to get. Thanks for asking."

"Good enough is better than most when you're talking about your father. Served with him under Sherman, you know?"

Mackey had grown up listening to Pappy's war stories, and Wilkes had been a central character in most of them. "I think you may have mentioned that before."

Wilkes returned to his sweeping. "Great man, your Pappy."

Mindful that Wilkes was there, Mackey tipped the brim of his hat to Katherine and kept it formal. "Evening, Mrs. Campbell. I didn't expect to see you sitting outside this time of day."

He saw her smile dim now that he had come closer, and she could see him better. She could see how gaunt he was and how much the pneumonia had taken out of him. "Wilkes, go back inside and check the tables, will you? I don't trust those scoundrels at the blackjack table."

Mackey watched Old Wilkes set his broom aside

and go into the saloon. He knew a lecture was coming and tried to delay it for as long as possible. "I can remember a lot of other people who've owned this place, but I can't remember a time when Old Wilkes didn't work here."

"Don't try to distract me." She nodded at the chair across from her. "You'd better sit down before you fall down, Aaron. You look awfully tired."

He would've liked nothing more than to sit beside her, but such familiarity between the married sheriff and the rich widow would've only given more grits for the town rumor mill. Mackey split the difference and leaned against the porch post instead. Now that Wilkes was out of earshot, he could at least drop the verbal formalities. "I'll be fine, Kate. I always am."

"And you're always working, too. That's why I know you're here in an official capacity."

"You do?" He suddenly felt playful. "Guess you've added fortune telling to your long list of charms."

"One doesn't need to be a mystic to hear what people are saying, Aaron. I've heard that foolish rumor that the men you killed were drinking here before they went over to the Tin Horn. I knew either you or Billy would be coming over to ask about it yourself before long." A bit of her smile returned. "I'm very glad it was you."

He could've looked at that smile all day, but she was right. He was here on business. "Were they here, Kate?"

"They stopped here," she admitted, "but Wilkes thought they looked too rough for our kind of crowd, so he refused to serve them. He wouldn't allow them to gamble at the tables, either. But, seeing as how their money's as good as anyone's, he *did* sell each of them a bottle of whiskey and sent them on their way. Last he saw of them, they were headed down to Madden's corral to drink in private."

If he'd been talking to someone else, he would've asked more questions. Most people didn't like to give up the truth easily, but Katherine wasn't most people. She'd never lied to him before, not even when she'd told him he was the love of her life all those years ago.

Like most rumors, there was a kernel of truth to it, but not enough to lay blame on Katherine or Wilkes and he was glad of it. "They say where they were from or where they were headed?"

"We didn't have the occasion to get that familiar, Aaron. They left after they paid for their whiskey. Next thing we heard, they were causing trouble up at the Tin Horn, and I knew they weren't long for this world. Not when you got wind of their hell-raising."

Maybe it was the sickness or his raw nerves from sparring with Mason and Doc Ridley most of the afternoon, but Mackey didn't know whether to take it as a compliment or an insult. "Billy and I gave those dumb bastards every chance to surrender, but they chose different. We . . ."

A deep chill coursed through him as he sagged against the porch post, and sweat broke out all over his body. She went to help him but he motioned for her to stay where she was. The town gossips had already seen them talking, an event that would set their tongues wagging for days and cause even more trouble for him with Mary. The shootings had already given them enough material. He saw no need to add to it.

She didn't get up, but leaned closer toward him.

"Please sit, or we'll go inside where we can talk alone. You look about dead on your feet, my love."

Mackey wiped at his sweat with the back of his hand. "You and me walking inside together? Head upstairs to your room, maybe? Set this town's tongues wagging for years if we did that."

"You can always use the staircase around back." She was quiet for a second longer than she needed to be. "You've used it before."

He felt himself blush. He didn't know if it was from the fever or the memory of those times. "That was different. Things weren't like this."

"You mean the shootings?" she asked. "Why? You've put down men like them before."

"I know, but there's something different about this." He blinked away his growing dizziness and looked up Front Street. "Something different about those men. Men like that usually travel hard and usually travel in packs."

"The dead are dead, Aaron. Leave them to God and take care of yourself. You look ready to fall down if you don't get some rest, my love. Please go around back and go up to my bed. I'll stay down here so no one talks, I promise. I know Mary won't let you come home while you're sick, and you'll never get better sleeping in that drafty old jail all by yourself with no one to take care of you."

"I'm not alone. Got Billy with me."

She sat back in the chair and allowed the wrap around her shoulders to fall open. She was fully clothed underneath, but her dress showed the vaguest outlines of her body; enough for him to remember what she looked like. "You're saying Billy's better company than me?"

Mackey took his time looking away from her. "No, no he isn't. But I've got to handle this shooting until it's settled, and I can't do that from bed. Yours or anyone else's."

She sat back in her rocker and looked up Front Street as well. "That's funny. I can recall us settling quite a bit together in my bed."

He felt himself get flush again. This time, it wasn't the pneumonia. "Yeah. That's my recollection, too."

She hid a smile as she put a hint of Bostonian aristocrat in her voice. "Why Sheriff Mackey, is that a blush I see on your pallor?"

"Just the fever." For the sake of his own dignity, he changed the subject. "You going to Pappy's dance tomorrow night? I hear the mayor's putting on quite a show for some New York types. Organized himself a welcoming committee down at the station as we speak."

She laughed in that way that always warmed him. "So I've heard. I'm sorry I'll have to miss both events. I'd like to see Mayor Mason's attempts at impressing Frazer."

Mackey caught that. "You know Mr. Rice?"

"Our paths crossed in various social settings back east." She looked at Mackey and smiled. "You're jealous. My, first you blush and now you're jealous. So much emotion in one day. I could be mistaken for believing you're actually a human being."

"Knock it off, Katie."

He was glad she did. "Mr. Rice is not one for social graces and he won't be impressed by a bunch of eager townspeople at the station or a room full of old soldiers in faded uniforms, either. Ledgers make him swoon, not waltzes. I'd love to watch Mason make a fool of himself trying to impress him, but alas, duty calls."

"What duty?"

"One of the girls out at Hill House is close to term. The pious Doctor Ridley won't help a fallen woman give birth, so I'll have the honors of bringing the child into this world. The old hypocrite has no problem tending to Warren's whores at the Tin Horn but won't help an unfortunate girl on the outskirts of town."

Hill House was a brothel on the outskirts of town where the respectable men of Dover Station enjoyed the company of women far from the prying eyes of their wives in town.

"Warren pays Doc for his services. The Hill House girls either don't or can't. I'm not defending it, just explaining it."

"Doesn't make it right." She took a breath as she regained her composure. "Will you be going or continuing your silent protest for another year?"

"No protest, Katie. Just not going."

"What a shame. You cut quite a figure in a uniform, Captain Mackey."

He felt himself blush again. "That was a long time ago, Mrs. Campbell. Went to one gala in my dress uniform. Don't see how this one could top it, so I figured it best to quit while I'm ahead."

Mackey couldn't be sure, but he thought she looked pleased to hear that. He knew that after her husband died, she had decided to leave Boston and her widowhood behind to join Aaron in her new life. She had used her contacts to find out he had been discharged from the cavalry and returned home to Dover Station.

She decided to follow him there without invitation or warning.

But by the time she had arrived in town unannounced, Aaron had already been unhappily married for almost a year. Another woman might have asked him to leave her, but not Katherine. All she had asked was that he didn't ask her to leave. He didn't. The near distance between them made life easier for them both to bear.

"Which one did most of the shooting?" she asked. "You or Billy? I know you boys keep score of such things."

"We each got two a piece, but only managed to wing the fat man before he dove behind a trough. Fat bastard was a spry one. Sim came out of the Tin Horn and finished him off for us."

"Sim's a good man."

"Yes he is," Mackey said.

Her expression changed. "He'll probably help bury you after that bitch you're married to lets you die in that drafty old jail."

Mackey had been waiting for her to run down his wife, and she didn't disappoint. He didn't defend her, either. "Mary's a peculiar woman. More peculiar than I knew at first." He kept looking up Front Street. He didn't dare allow himself to look at her. "Guess I didn't realize a lot of things back then. Wish I had."

Katherine kept looking up Front Street, too. "It's not too late, Aaron. You're no more married than I am. We're both wedded to corpses. Only difference is that yours is still aboveground."

She surprised him by grabbing his hand and held it against the side of her face. He was glad the crowd on the boardwalks had thinned out a bit. Her face was soft and smooth and cool. Mary's skin had always been dry and rough.

"God, you're burning up," she said. "And you'll only get worse unless you let someone take care of you."

He didn't want to, but he slowly eased his hand away. He hoped none of the gossipmongers saw her do that. "No reason for you to get sick, too. Besides, I'll be fine in a day or so."

"It's already been a month, and you're worse now than you were before. Mary can't take care of you because she resents you for not being the man she'd dreamed you to be. That's the difference between us, Aaron. She fell in love with a myth in a uniform. I fell in love with the man wearing it."

Mackey hated it when she said things like that. Not because it wasn't true, but because it made him want to forget about his wife and his duty and his responsibility to the town that had been his home for his entire life.

She went back to looking up Front Street. "I love you, Aaron Mackey. I love you enough to wait for you no matter how long it takes because I know we are meant to be together one way or the other."

She had said things like that before, and he had always found a way to avoid answering her. But on that day, he was too tired to avoid an answer. The pneumonia and events of the afternoon had left him too weak to care about the consequences of agreeing with her. Maybe he'd been tied to his duties too long. It seemed the longer he was sheriff, the more the townspeople hated him. The more people like Frazer Rice came into town, the more they would grow to resent him. The wealthy New Yorker represented riches and the future they clung to. Mackey only reminded them of their past they wanted to forget.

He could take their resentment, but had reached a point in his life where he wondered why he should have to. And why he should not agree with Katherine's ideas.

But all thoughts of love and the present escaped him when he saw Billy Sunday riding at a slow trot down Front Street. He was trailing Aaron's horse on a lead rope, a black mare he had named Adair after the Arizona town where he had found her. Anyone who knew horses could see she had the powerful, exotic look of the Arabian breed about her.

Adair strained against the lead rope as soon as she saw Mackey. Billy let the rope go and she trotted over to the boardwalk, knocking Mackey back a bit as she nuzzled into him. It had been more than a week since he had seen her and this visit did both of them good.

Katherine said, "At least you show affection for one female in this town." Before he could answer, she greeted Billy. "Good to see you, Billy."

The deputy smiled. He knew their history, but observed formalities by touching the brim of his hat by way of a proper greeting. "Afternoon, Mrs. Campbell. Thanks for keeping an eye on the sheriff for me. As you know, he's a most stubborn son of a bitch and refuses bed rest."

"A fact of which I am well aware, deputy," she said, "but as you know, the sheriff isn't a man to let something as trivial as pneumonia keep him from performing his sacred public duties."

For the horse's sake, Aaron kept his voice calm. "And as both of you know, I'm standing right here, goddamn it." Adair moved her head to his other shoulder. "You're supposed to be up at the Horn taking statements from the witnesses."

"Finished a little while ago," Billy said. "Pappy found me and said you were in no condition for walking. Figured I'd better bring Adair around for you to ride back to the jail, seeing as how weak you were. Carrying your sorry ass back to the jailhouse in front of the whole town would be an affront to your public persona of being indestructible."

Katherine giggled.

Mackey didn't. "You weren't this insubordinate in Arizona."

"You were a captain then. Listened to reason, too. Besides, riding Adair will do her as much good as you. Old girl's been cooped up in the livery all week. Horse like that needs some exercise."

"She's not old," Mackey stroked her as the mare nuzzled into him again. "Plenty of good miles ahead of her. In me, too."

"That's good to hear because you're going to need them and right soon."

Mackey stopped stroking the horse. "What's wrong?"

"I got word that Jeb Taylor's on his way into town. Supposedly has ten hands with him. Maybe more."

Mackey rested his head against Adair's neck. With the shootings that afternoon and the mayor on his back, the last thing he needed was the hotheaded owner of the town's largest ranch making one of his grandstanding scenes in the middle of Front Street. "Why doesn't that crazy bastard just stay up on his ranch and leave people the hell alone?"

"Because he heard about the men we killed today. Just so happens that Jeb found himself a few ranch hands short at this morning's count. Seems to think some of those men we killed at the Horn just might be from his ranch."

"Lucky me." From the boardwalk, Mackey slid his boot into the stirrup and pulled himself up into the saddle. He was glad for the added height of the board-walk, because he didn't think he would have mounted so cleanly otherwise. He fought a wave of dizziness as he asked, "Those boys working at Taylor's ranch would explain the lack of gear and saddlebags, wouldn't it?"

Katherine tried to help. "But if they worked for Taylor, wouldn't someone at the Tin Horn have recognized them? Taylor's men are always in there."

"Probably," Billy admitted. "But there's no way of convincing Taylor of that before he gets here. And he'll be getting here around the same time as the train carrying the mayor's dignitaries is due."

"Best if we try to catch him on the trail before he reaches town. I'm in no mood to let him shoot off his goddamned mouth in front of the whole town."

Mackey felt Katherine looking at him. He saw the concern in her eyes, so he touched the brim of his hat. "Afternoon, Mrs. Campbell, and thank you for the information."

She gave him a polite smile. Back to formalities, even in front of Billy. "Afternoon, Sheriff Mackey. Hope you'll be able to stop by for another visit, and soon." She looked at Billy. "Take care of him, deputy. He's not much, but he's all the sheriff we've got."

Mackey brought Adair around and rode away.

Billy smiled as he tipped his hat, too, before joining Mackey on Front Street.

Chapter 6

Mackey allowed Adair to move along at her own pace up Front Street toward the jailhouse. He saw no reason to hurry and believed the jail at the edge of town might be the best place to meet Taylor and his men. If the official surroundings didn't cool the rancher's temper, then cramped conditions might. Taylor never went anywhere alone and could only get four or five of his men in the small building at a time.

Mackey had another reason for heading back to the jail—he needed to sit down. The idea of being in his rocking chair was an inviting one. The effort of climbing up into the saddle had weakened him more than he wanted to admit, but now that he was riding, he had begun to feel better, despite the fatigue. Climbing down would probably take even more out of him, but he would worry about that when the time came. For now, he had a good horse beneath him and a destination in mind. Such clarity was good for his soul.

Billy brought up his horse next to Mackey. "What do you plan on doing when Mr. Taylor hits town."

"Meet him head-on like I always do. At the jail if there's time, but anywhere will do. He'll want to mouth off in a public setting, so that's where I'll meet him."

"Just you against him and his men?"

"Yeah. And you somewhere close by. You covering me with that Sharps gives me all the edge I'll need against Taylor."

"Sometimes, I think you take me for granted."

"No, I don't."

Billy didn't argue.

They had only gotten about a quarter of the way up Front Street when Jeb Taylor and ten of his men rounded the corner into town. The owner of the largest ranch in the territory signaled his men to fan out along Front Street, so they rode five on either side of him with the rancher out front. The entire party stretched the width of the thoroughfare, presenting an impressive display of force. Mackey knew that was the point.

It looked like his rocking chair would have to wait.

Mackey didn't need to tell Billy what to do next. They had lived through enough encounters like this to know how to handle them. Billy edged his mount over to the nearest hitching post and tied her off. Mackey knew he'd slip his Sharps from the saddle scabbard and slowly make his way along the boardwalk up Front Street, covering him from a doorway or an alley while Mackey met Taylor head on. A Sharps was a powerful weapon in the hands of someone who knew how to use it. Billy had a fine eye and a steady hand. He didn't need to be too close to cover him properly.

Mackey adjusted his belly holster so the handle of

his Colt was closer to the saddle horn. Easier to grip without much effort.

He edged Adair forward and stopped in the middle of Front Street. He didn't have to rein her in to bring her to a halt. The mare liked a good fight as much as her rider did. She stood stock still as the eleven men and their mounts rumbled toward them.

Like Billy and Mackey, she had been through this kind of thing before.

With a great flourish of mud and commotion, Jeb Taylor threw up a gloved hand and brought his men to a halt a few yards shy of Mackey and Adair.

Mackey knew the rancher may be a braggart and a bastard, but he never took him lightly. The rancher had carved a thriving cattle and horse ranch out of the Montana wilderness at a time when there had been nothing in that part of the territory but Blackfoot Indians, disease, harsh winters, and broiling summers. He had given more than blood and sweat to building his JT brand. He had given a wife and a son.

The same grit and perseverance that had cost him his family had served to make him one of the wealthiest men in the Montana Territory. His struggles hadn't made him humble. Mackey knew Taylor was every bit as tough and mean as the land he had tamed.

Mackey grazed his Colt's handle with his thumb. It was close if he needed it. He could feel the bulk of his Winchester in the saddle scabbard under his left leg. Billy must have put it there. He could get to it quick enough after emptying his pistol, if it came to that.

He hoped it wouldn't.

He hoped this was just Taylor saber rattling in front of his men and the town he believed he owned. He'd ridden into town for answers about his missing men, not blood.

Blood could always come later, if it had to come at all.

Mackey sat easy, hands crossed on his saddle horn as the line of men and horses slowed in front of him. Just a man on his horse in the middle of Front Street. With the handle of his Colt only an inch or so away.

Against eleven armed men.

"Afternoon, Jeb. What brings you boys into town? Hope it's not for the big dance. If it is, I'm afraid you're a day early."

Taylor was a big, dark-eyed man well over six feet tall and over two hundred pounds. He had a thick brown mustache that bore no hint of gray, though it should have. He looked Mackey up and down with a glare that would've given most men pause. Mackey simply looked back.

"Didn't expect to see you up and around quite so soon, sheriff. Heard you were laid up with an illness."

"You heard right. I was."

"Looks like you still are. You look like hell."

Subdued laughter rippled through the Taylor men.

Mackey laughed, too. "Guess I've got a knack for rallying myself when I need to, Jeb." He looked over Taylor's men. Mostly familiar faces. A few strangers. All of them armed. "What brings you boys into town on such a beautiful day?"

The rancher wasn't smiling anymore. "Heard you gunned down five men today. Just so happens that I lost a few men off my ranch this morning. I'm wondering if your dead men might be mine."

"They're not yours. Billy and I shot five drunks who pulled on us as they came out of the Horn. No one ever saw them before and none of the witnesses said they were yours."

"So you say."

"I do, but you're welcome to look for yourself if you want. They're over at the undertaker's right now. Bet Cy Wallach is already practicing some of his new mortician techniques on them. If they're yours, you'll probably get them back in better condition than they left."

A few of Taylor's men laughed. He moved his head a fraction of an inch to his left. The laughter stopped.

"I planned on going to Wallach's anyway," the rancher said. "I don't need your permission."

"Sure you do, especially armed like you are. But I'm willing to let that go for now until you have a chance to look at the bodies. I figure you should be able to do that and be on your way in about half an hour."

Taylor sat a little taller in the saddle. "You don't seem to care if those dead men are mine or not."

"That's because I don't. Whoever they were, they broke the law by raising hell and wearing guns into town and refusing to submit to arrest. They died because they drew on Billy and me when we tried to arrest them for it. The shooting was as legal as it gets."

Taylor looked at the men on his right, then on his left. "All the men I brought with me are armed. You gonna try to arrest them, too?"

Mackey made a show of looking over Taylor's men. "Only if they try something stupid. Or if you do."

The rancher sat taller in the saddle. "They won't do anything stupid, Mackey. They're all trained men. You know I don't hire greenhorns."

Mackey looked at the men. "No you don't. But their mounts are green, aren't they?"

Jeb Tyler had been accused of a lot of things since coming to Dover Station, but being a fool had never been one of them. He knew what Mackey meant.

For the benefit of the men, Mackey said, "They're all fine mounts. Fast and strong and well fed, unlike the mounts the dead men dragged into town with them. They've also most likely never heard a gunshot before. Now, Adair here was damned near weaned on gun smoke. Hardly anything spooks her anymore. But, those grazing horses you boys are riding? Hell, they'll buck if a bee comes too close." He looked at Tyler. "You've been in battle, Jeb. You know good men aren't much good when they're getting thrown by their horses."

Tyler knew it, but he didn't seem to like it. "Damn you, Aaron. I . . ."

Mackey decided to give the rancher a way out of it. "Given your aggrieved state over the possible death of your men, I'm willing to overlook the infraction, so long as they stay mounted and they all leave with you after you've had a look at the dead bodies for yourself."

Mackey looked up at the clock tower over the bank. It was already four-thirty. It felt a hell of a lot later than that. "The firearm ordinance gets enforced at five o'clock. Any of your men still in town wearing a gun when the clock strikes five will get arrested and fined. That includes you, Jeb."

Taylor gripped the reins of his horse tighter. "I'd like to see you try."

Taylor's horse sensed the tension and snuffed and shifted. Some of the other mounts did, too.

Adair didn't move.

Neither did Mackey. "No, Jeb. No you wouldn't."

Taylor looked the sheriff over while he weighed his options. Mackey saw Taylor taking in his gaunt appearance and sickly pallor. He might seem like he was alone, but he knew Billy was probably covering the area from somewhere he couldn't see.

After he'd seemed to think about it enough, Taylor asked, "You have an official report of what happened?"

"If they're your men, I'll show it to you now," Mackey said. "If not, you can read about it tomorrow."

"I want to read it now."

"I don't care. And I don't repeat myself."

"I'm not sure I like that."

"You don't have to like it." He glanced up at the clock. "Twenty-five minutes, Jeb. Best put each second to good use."

The rancher brought his horse close to Mackey. Adair didn't move. "I don't respond well to threats, boy."

Mackey leaned closer to him. "Neither do I."

Mackey refused to move out of their way and Adair wouldn't move without prompting. Jeb Taylor and his men had to ride around them. None of them touched Mackey or Adair as they rode by.

Sometimes, he thought his horse loved this work as much as he did.

At five minutes to five, Mackey was back in his rocking chair on the boardwalk in front of the jailhouse. Billy was leaning against the porch post building another cigarette. They had both leaned their rifles against the wall. Close enough to reach, but not close enough to be threatening.

They heard Taylor and his men riding up Lincoln Street, which ran behind the jailhouse. Streaks of bright yellows and pinks were beginning to appear in the sky as the day drew closer to sunset. A sharp breeze had just begun to blow up Front Street as Taylor's men rounded the corner.

Mackey could tell that afternoon had all the makings of becoming a damned nice evening. Too nice to ruin with gunplay if Taylor forced it. But if Taylor forced it, gunplay was fine with Mackey.

The sheriff and the deputy watched as all of the rancher's men took the road leading back to the JT Ranch. The only rider who came back into town was Jeb Taylor himself.

Mackey stopped rocking. His hand was flat on his stomach, close to the Colt's handle by his buckle. Billy stopped building his cigarette, but kept leaning against the porch post. He held the half-built smoke in his left hand while his right moved flat against the holster on his leg.

Taylor reined his mount to a stop in front of the jailhouse. "You were right, Mackey. None of them were mine."

Billy went back to building his cigarette.

Mackey's hand stayed where it was. "Glad you saw it for yourself, Jeb. Helped put your mind at rest."

But Taylor didn't seem satisfied by that. "You could've saved us both a lot of time and trouble if you'd just told me that in the first place."

"I did, but you decided to try showing me up in front of your men instead of listening to reason.

That's the last time. Next time you run your mouth at me in front of anyone, I'll kill you, Jeb. I won't care who you have with you or how many. I'll put a bullet in your belly. Whatever happens to me after that won't matter, but you've talked down to me for the last time."

Mackey followed Taylor's eyes. He could tell he was thinking about going for his gun. He saw the rancher look at the rifles leaning against the wall, then at the pistols on each man's belt. He'd be lucky to get one of them if he pulled, but not both of them. Not men like Aaron Mackey and Billy Sunday.

The rancher grabbed the reins with both hands instead. "You've got to be one of the most miserable, disagreeable sons of bitches I have ever met."

Mackey looked up Front Street as he resumed his rocking. "Get home safe, Mr. Taylor."

Taylor swung his horse around and headed up the road toward his ranch and his men. The bell in the clock tower rang five times just as Taylor cleared Front Street.

Billy kept building his cigarette. "Bastard sure cut it close, didn't he?"

Mackey went back to rocking. "Jeb Taylor is not an easy man."

Billy licked the paper and rolled his smoke. "Kind of like someone else I know."

Mackey set his head back against the cool wood of the rocking chair and closed his eyes. Billy never let anything rest. Just like Pappy.

He decided to change the subject. "You file the statements you and Sim took down at the Horn earlier?"

"On your desk awaiting your perusal."

Now that Taylor and his men were gone, Mackey wanted to settle in and enjoy the sunset from the jail-house porch. The town had drifted back into its usual rhythm after that afternoon's shoot-out. He was sure it'd pick up again once the train carrying the mayor's dignitaries arrived at the station, but it wouldn't last. Dover Station responded to new things at first, but quickly absorbed them as it moved about its daily routine. "At least the conversation at tomorrow night's gala won't be boring," Mackey said. "Between the shooting and Jeb Taylor's ride and those wealthy New Yorkers being in town, the rumor mill's well stocked with grist."

Billy thumbed a match alive and lit his cigarette. "As long as all they do is talk, we've got nothing to worry about."

Mackey wanted to keep rocking in his chair, but there was another bit of business he needed to settle. He'd done his best to put it off for as long as he could, but he couldn't put it off any longer. He waited until a wagon rolled past before he spoke of it. "I know you and I usually dig the graves of the men we kill together, but . . ."

"Our grave digging is a custom, Aaron. Not a law. You can barely dig into a bowl of porridge right now; much less dig earth for a grave. I've already got a crew lined up to do the digging. Petty cash ought to cover the expense."

"I appreciate that," Mackey allowed. "Asking people to do my job for me isn't my way."

"Paying men to dig a grave don't count as a favor. It counts as a job. No shame in it on either side of the agreement."

But although the matter was already settled, Mackey

figured it still required explanation. "I've always thought that killing ought to cost a man something. Burying the men we kill always seems like a fair trade for us getting to live. Without the effort of the result, the killing might get too easy. I never want that to happen."

Billy kept building his new cigarette, carefully laying the tobacco onto the paper. "Just because killing's never been hard for you and me, don't mean it's ever been easy. It's not likely to get easy for us, either. We're simply not the type."

Maybe it was the fever. Maybe it was other things preying on Mackey's mind. "What type are we?"

"Whatever we need to be right now. That's the best anyone can hope for."

The two men watched the softening colors of the coming sunset deepen as the day began the slow change into night. The wind up Front Street had calmed down to a breeze, carrying with it the smell of flowers blooming on the surrounding hillsides. The scent made a pleasant scene even more so.

"You know how to get around me, don't you?" Mackey asked.

"I'd never do that, Aaron. But I know how you think. After all this time, I'd be a damned fool not to. You're not a complicated man."

"Just a stubborn son of a bitch."

Billy flicked his dying cigarette into the middle of Front Street. "Stubborn just about covers it."

Since that matter seemed to be settled, too, Mackey pushed himself out of the rocker. Weakness and dizziness settled over him again, but he managed to steady himself on the porch post without help. He felt weak, but not as weak as before. "Think it's time I go sleep in my own bed for a change."

Both men looked up when they heard the train whistle echo through the valley, followed by a loud chorus of cheers from the railroad station.

Mackey shut his eyes. *Just when I was about to go to bed.* "Sounds like the mayor's guests have arrived."

"You're not going down there, are you?" Billy asked. "You can't hardly stand as it is, much less walk over to the station."

But Mackey felt a second wind coming on as his weakness subsided. Maybe it was the arrival of new people to town that did it. Maybe he just wanted the pleasure of seeing Mason make a damned fool of himself in front of the bankers he'd brought all the way from New York City.

Or maybe he was just looking for a reason to delay going home and seeing his wife.

Mackey wasn't sure why he stepped off the board-walk and headed toward the station, but he did. "Might as well see what all the fuss is about. Take the Sharps with you. A show of force will impress our guests."

Billy didn't look pleased, but went with him anyway.

Chapter 7

Billy and Mackey got there just as the train bringing the dignitaries to Dover pulled into the station. The engines stopped with a great hiss, and the engineer let out a long blast from the whistle, bringing the crowd that Mayor Mason had assembled to a fever pitch.

A sudden wind from the north blew the thick smoke from the engine's great smoke stack away from the platform and all of the Doverians who had gathered there. Mackey knew the mayor would see it as divine providence, a sign that the Almighty Himself had blessed the arrival of these saviors from back east.

Mackey had been sick for the past few days, so he hadn't seen the station since Mason's volunteers had begun to work on it. He hardly recognized the place. Normally a plain building with minimal signage and decoration, the station bore a fresh coat of new brown paint. The busted handrails and stairs had been fixed, and the brickwork of the chimney had been re-pointed. Every straight edge on the station was covered in red, white, and blue bunting. Lace curtains had been hung

in the freshly cleaned windows, and the loading area
had been cleared of all freight.

Several of the fifty or so people Mason had either
convinced or cajoled into attending thrust signs in the
air, reading **WELCOME TO DOVER STATION** and
GOD BLESS MR. RICE and **GOD BLESS MR. VAN
DORN**. Men threw hats aloft while women clutched
baskets filled with home-baked pies and other treats
for the visitors. Mackey was surprised to see the tinny
piano from Hill House had been brought all the way
down the hill on the back of a flatbed wagon, most
likely because it was more presentable than its battered
counterpart at the Tin Horn. Doc Ridley stood before
a brass band, which Mackey could see had been cob-
bled together from the various musicians from every
whorehouse and hotel in the territory, as it began
playing "The Battle Hymn of the Republic." A mixture
of muted curses and boos rose from the old confeder-
ates in the crowd, and the band drifted into a rendition of "Dixie," which served to quell all objections.

All of this bother, Mackey thought, and neither
Rice nor Van Dorn had even stepped off the train yet.

Mackey looked for his father in the crowd and
wasn't surprised to see he wasn't there. Public meetings weren't his style. He'd meet with the potential
investors while they were in town, but in his own time
and in his own way, at the gala tomorrow night in full
uniform with the Medal of Honor pinned to his tunic.
He'd make more of an impression that way.

But Mackey did see Mary in the crowd, exactly
where he had expected her to be, at the bottom of the
rail-car steps, waiting for Mr. Rice and Mr. Van Dorn
to appear. If either of the men failed to hear her

brogue or see her blue eyes, her blond hair would be impossible to miss among the plump gray women with baskets in hand. She always liked to stand out from the crowd. It was why she had married the Hero of Adobe Flats in the first place.

The crowd grew louder when two men appeared at the end of the coach car and walked down the stairs.

Mackey had kept up with the news from back east by reading newspapers and periodicals that were often months old by the time he got them. He had seen photos and illustrations of Mr. Rice and Mr. Van Dorn before, which was why he knew the first man off the train was Silas Van Dorn.

The young investor had come from a wealthy New York family that could trace its lineage back to the days when New York had been New Amsterdam and a thriving Dutch colony. But the young Mr. Van Dorn had already earned his own solid reputation—and fortune—in the complicated world of finance. He was tall and gangly to the point of looking feeble. The adoration of the crowd appeared lost on him as he dabbed at his head and face with a linen handkerchief, clutching the banister as he descended one step at a time.

"Guess traveling doesn't agree with him," Billy said. "That man looks worse than you do, if that's possible."

Mackey ignored the comment and watched the second man step off the train. Mr. Frazer Rice was as tall as Van Dorn, but older by about twenty years and much healthier looking. His silver muttonchops gave him a sophisticated air, while his years made him appear more at ease with himself. More certain. He doffed his hat to the cheering crowd, a simple act that generated even more enthusiasm from the townsfolk.

Mackey watched Mayor Mason step in front of Mary just as she offered up a basket of goods to Mr. Rice and Mr. Van Dorn. He blocked Mary's view of Rice as he pumped the hands of the wealthy men and ushered them up to the raised wooden platform he had built for the occasion. Mackey smiled. Mary had just learned one of the oldest lessons of Dover Station: the most dangerous place in town wasn't in front of Mackey's gun. It was between Mayor Mason and an important man.

The band drifted back into "The Battle Hymn of the Republic." Mason practically pulled the investors through the bustling crowd and up the stairs to the wooden platform. Mr. Rice seemed to have begged off as someone helped him to the waiting carriage.

Rice nodded solemnly to the cheering crowd as Mason beckoned Doc Ridley to leave his post with the band and join them on the stage. But Mackey knew the people weren't applauding any of the men on the platform. They were applauding the money they had brought with them, or, more precisely, the letters of credit they had from practically every major bank in the world. They weren't cheering for the future of Dover Station or even the New Yorkers' vision of what the tiny Montana town could be. They were cheering their own good fortune and how Rice and Rice's money could buy it.

These strong, independent people had sacrificed enough forging a town out of the wilderness. Now they were looking to cash in on their hard work by sticking their hands in Mr. Rice's pockets. But Mackey knew no one took anything from someone like Mr. Rice that he didn't give freely. And men like Mr. Rice often took more than they gave. He would give them his money, but not before he had their gold, their lumber, their beef, and their farms. And he'd make it look like he was doing them a favor by taking it away from them.

Mackey knew every single one of the people cheering for the newcomers. Most of them had watched him grow up, though in that moment, Aaron Mackey didn't recognize any of them.

Mayor Mason was at the foot of the stairs to greet his guests and quickly ushered both men over to the wooden platform he had constructed.

As Doc Ridley scrambled up to the platform, Mason caught sight of Mackey and Billy standing at a good distance from the crowd.

He used his impressive lung power to call out to the sheriff. "Ah, there's our sheriff, Mr. Rice. Aaron Mackey, the Hero of Adobe Flats. Aaron, come join us and . . ."

But Mackey acted as if he hadn't heard the mayor and turned to leave the ceremony. He was beginning to feel poorly again, only he wasn't sure if it was from the pneumonia or the proceedings. And he was in no mood to be around strangers.

Billy started to follow him, but Mackey said, "You stay here and keep an eye on things. With Mary here, I'm going to grab a few hours of sleep in my own bed for a change."

"You don't look too steady on your feet," Billy observed. "I'd like to walk with you."

Mackey grinned as he patted his old friend's arm.

"I've got my Winchester with me. What could go wrong?"

As he headed home, he could still hear Mason calling out to him from the platform, but he saw no reason to stop.

Chapter 8

Mackey woke in another cold sweat.

His fever had brought him back in time; back to that sunrise on the arid hillside of Adobe Flats all those years ago. He could smell the dry desert air and the gun smoke from the skirmish that had made him famous and earned him a promotion to captain. The sounds of Apache war cries and dying men still echoed from his dream.

It took him a few moments to remember he was in his own bed and in his own house. Memories of the shootings at the Tin Horn and seeing Katie in the rocking chair and his run-in with Jeb Taylor on Front Street slowly reminded him it had only been a dream. He wondered if all of that had been a dream, as well. But the tightness in his right hand and the soreness in his shoulder from the recoil of the Winchester reminded him the killings had been all too real.

He didn't know how long he'd been asleep. He remembered it had been going on dusk when he'd first come upstairs and crawled into bed. It was now completely dark on Front Street, save for the lanterns some stores lit each night.

His pillow and bedclothes were soaked in his sweat. He felt like he had just stepped out of a warm bath on a cold night. But as cold as he was, he didn't have the chills he'd felt every time he'd woken up for the past month. In fact, he felt better than he could remember. He wondered if the fever that had been plaguing him had finally broken.

In the darkness, he felt at the mattress beside him in the hope that Mary might be there.

She wasn't and he understood why.

Mary had lost most of her family to the fever sickness on the trek out to Montana from back east. She'd been touchy about germs and sickness ever since.

He remembered the first time he saw her. It was the day he had returned to Dover Station after being drummed out of the cavalry. He'd brought Billy back home with him, expecting Pappy to be waiting to meet the train.

Instead, Pappy had arranged for a crowd to greet him as he stepped off the train. There was bunting and cheering and even a band from Ridge Haven, the next town over. Mayor Mason and the town elders made a great show of lining up to shake his hand and give speeches that welcomed home the Pride and Joy of Dover Station. The hero of the Battle of Adobe Flats.

He remembered suffering through the ceremony, almost cringing at every mention of Adobe Flats. He hated how they praised him for the battle, yet ignored that he'd been sent home in quiet disgrace. He thought the grounds for his dismissal were far more heroic than anything he'd done on Adobe Flats that morning.

But no one saw any point in allowing the truth to get in the way of a great party. Old women who had remembered him from boyhood lined up to kiss his cheek and asked God to bless him. Young women looked at him longingly while their jealous husbands, who had tended crops or worked mining claims instead of soldiering, refused to look his way. Young boys crowded around him and told him they wanted to be just like him when they grew up.

But neither the adulation of his town nor the scorn of his army could compare with the memory he had of Mary from that day. Her hair had been fairer then, and her eyes held a reverent love of a returning hero.

He later understood why. She had arrived in town two years before his return, recently married to a mean old drunk she had wed out of need, not love. After her husband drank himself to death, she heard the townspeople tell stories about Dover Station's Favorite Son: Captain Aaron Mackey, graduate of West Point and the Hero of Adobe Flats.

He knew Mary had been in love with him before she had ever met him. Before she even knew what he looked like. He should have put her off. He should have pushed her away. But upon his return home, Captain Mackey had been a man who had needed to be loved by someone, even if the reasons for Mary's love were based on tall tales and lies.

A few days after Mackey returned, Pappy saw to it that his son ran unopposed for sheriff. Mackey's first act was to appoint Billy his deputy. When his future was set, Mary and Aaron were married within two months of his return.

But Mary soon realized her husband was neither the hero of whom she had long dreamed nor the myth she had chosen to believe. He was just a man who had done the job he had been trained to do, the job he had loved, but would never be allowed to do again. He was no longer a captain in his beloved United States Cavalry. He was just the sheriff of a small town of miners and farmers and ranchers in the middle of the Montana wilderness.

He had little prospect or inclination to be anything else. Mackey knew this troubled his wife above all else.

He recalled what Katherine had said earlier that day: Mary had fallen in love with a myth in uniform. He knew this was true. She could not abide the flawed man who wore it. Despite her lowly upbringing on the streets of Dublin, she had never fancied herself to be the wife of a lawman in a small wilderness town. She had pushed him to use his fame as the Hero of Adobe Flats to get a job as a banker, a railroad man, or a territorial official. She wanted him to do something with prestige so she, in turn, could live the life of which she had always dreamed. But Mackey had been elected sheriff of a town that had fallen into recklessness. He and Billy were too busy with the present to give much thought to the future.

The weight of all these memories forced him to sit on the edge of her side of the bed. He laid a hand on what should have been her pillow, but had rarely been used. He knew the reason for that, too. Mary had gotten pregnant on their wedding night, but lost that baby and the one after that. Neither of them had been at fault, but Mary held him responsible just the same. For the death of their babies as much as for the death of her dreams. For not being the man she had hoped he would be. For not being the man she needed him to be.

The disappointing reality of her condition changed her. Mary's soft Irish beauty soon became as faded as the memory of his supposed exploits against the red savages at Adobe Flats. Her eyes became swollen from tears and lack of sleep. Her blond hair had taken the color of dry straw as her fair skin became blotchy. She walked with a slight stoop. She looked and acted like an old woman, but she wasn't even thirty yet.

Things had slowly grown worse with every passing week in the five years since. She railed at him over everything. Even the most minor infraction sparked her rage. Mackey stayed in the marriage because he wanted to make up for whatever disappointment he had caused her. But her resentment only grew worse. Katherine's arrival in town had done nothing to change that except make it even harder for him to do his duty. But for all his faults, being a quitter wasn't one of them. He still had to try to make Mary happy.

Mackey struggled out of bed, struck a match, and lit the lamp on his bedside table. He washed himself off at the washbasin and toweled himself dry. He ran his hand across the thickening stubble along his face and thought about shaving. But when he saw how much his hand shook, he thought better of it.

He put on clean clothes, unpinned the copper star from his old shirt and pinned it on his new one. He was surprised by how loose his shirt and pants had become in only the last couple of days. The fever had burned through more weight than he'd realized. As loose as they were, the clean clothes made him feel better than he had in weeks. He was even a little hungry. He pulled on his boots and walked downstairs.

He had just reached the bottom step when Mary began shouting at him from the kitchen.

"Well, there he is." Her brogue was sharper and more cutting than Sim Halstead's Bowie knife. "If it isn't the grand man himself come home to pollute my house with his filth and disease. Here I am, workin' my fingers to the bone night and day to keep this miserable hovel clean and in you come dirtyin' the place up again. I don't know just who in the hell you think you are, mister, but I'll not be allowin' you to spread your vermin to me. You can save that for your drunks and your jailbirds and your fancy whore down the street. And don't think for a moment that I believe you're as sick as all that, either. Just a way of gettin' sympathy, if you ask me."

Mackey tugged at the loose fabric of his shirt. "Then how do you explain this? I must've lost ten pounds in the past week."

But Mary had never been one to allow evidence to get in the way of a good rant. "You sure seemed spry enough to kill five men today. But then you come home wheezin' like a bunch of old bagpipes. It's all a great big charade; just an excuse for you to sit down at the jail with Billy, getting' drunk and chasing after that Boston whore who came chasin' out here after you. And don't think I don't know about that one because I do. Why it was only just an hour ago where Belle Ridley herself told me . . ."

Mackey stopped listening. There was no point in arguing with her, especially when she invoked the name of Doc Ridley's wife. Mary believed Belle Ridley was as infallible as the Pope and just as pious. He knew arguing with her was pointless. She wouldn't listen; not when she was like this and she was like this all the time. She would just get quiet while he explained himself, only to take up the argument exactly where she'd left off as soon as he stopped talking.

Lately, insulting Katherine had been Mary's weapon of choice. He hadn't asked Katherine to come to Dover Station after her husband died, but Mary would never believe him.

He had killed scores of men as a cavalry officer. As a sheriff, he'd faced down scores more. He had commanded men in battle, cornered renegade Apache on the warpath and faced down lawless men intent on killing him. But an Irish girl who was a hundred pounds soaking wet laid into him every time she had the mind to, and he let her. He was a fighting man who never had the will to fight his own wife. He didn't know why he took it, but for some reason, he did.

This was why he simply pulled on his flat-brim hat and took his gun belt off the newel post as the hate and venom spilled out of her. He had to buckle the gun belt several notches below normal and move the holster farther back from the buckle, closer to his left hip. The handle of the Colt still curved closer to the buckle; giving him an easy draw if he needed it.

Mary's litany of insults rose even louder when she saw him take his Winchester down from the rifle rack beside the front door.

"And just where the hell do you think you're off to at this time of the evenin'?" she yelled.

"Patrol." It was his standard excuse whenever she got like this, because when she was this bad, he preferred to be anywhere but home. He had no idea what time it was, but he hoped he still might be able to get something to eat over at Katie's Place or that new café that had opened down the street last week. Or was it last month? He'd been sick for so long, he'd lost all sense of time. He didn't care where he wound up, as long as it wasn't here with her.

When he opened the door, he saw a man leaning against the beam of the boardwalk.

Chapter 9

Mackey drew his Colt and aimed it at the stranger's belly.

The stranger let out a long whistle as he raised his hands. "Gun metal clearing leather. Ain't a more dignified or deadlier sound known to man."

Mackey saw the man was lanky as hell, a few inches taller and a few pounds thinner than he. He had dark eyes beneath the brim of a beat-up bowler, from which a mess of scraggily brown hair hung down to his shoulders. His long beard was thinned out in patches, like he pulled on it too much.

The holster on his hip and the one on his belt were empty. But Mackey knew unarmed men weren't necessarily harmless, especially a man who carried two guns. "What the hell are you doing on my porch, boy?"

The stranger kept his hands raised. "I meant no offense, sheriff. I wanted to see you, but didn't want to be so forward as to knock on your door and disturb your evening. My name is Alexander Darabont, but my friends call me Lex."

The name meant nothing to him. He kept his gun

on the stranger as he glanced at a group of four strangers on the boardwalk across Front Street watching the house, every one of them as grizzly as Darabont. Dusty clothes and long, greasy hair and lean, hungry looks. It was tough to be certain in the dim light of the boardwalk torches, but they seemed to be unarmed.

One of the four stood out. He had high cheekbones and a darker complexion than the others. His hair was longer, blacker, and straighter. Mackey had seen his share of half-breeds and knew he was looking at one now. Half Mexican, half Apache and probably as dangerous as he looked.

"I see you've noticed my friends," Darabont said. "The exotic looking one who seems to have caught your eye is Concho. His mother was Mexican and his father is believed to have been . . ."

"Apache," Mackey said.

Darabont's smile grew. "I see Concho's reputation precedes him."

"No. I just know the type." He looked back at Darabont. "What I don't know is why you're here. I asked you once. I won't ask again."

"Forgive me. All this time on the trail seems to have dulled my manners. I probably should have knocked, but I didn't want to trouble your lovely wife." He looked past Mackey at the inside of the house, and offered a crooked, yellow smile. "She sounds like a lovely woman. I've always loved the gentle music of an Irish brogue."

Mackey pulled the door shut with his left hand while keeping Darabont covered with his right. "State your business."

"My associates and I have come to town looking for some friends of ours who have gone missing."

Mackey looked across the street at the four men. None of them had moved. "That so?"

"When our friends failed to return to our camp by nightfall this evening, we naturally grew concerned for their welfare. We looked for signs of them on the trail between our camp and this here lovely town of yours. Failing to find any sign of them, we thought it best to continue our search within town limits. We expected to find them drunk in an alley or spending time with the ladies in that whorehouse up on the hill." Darabont's eyes didn't look so friendly any more. "We didn't expect to find them murdered. By you."

"They're dead, not murdered," Mackey said. "There's a difference."

"Yet the result is the same."

Mackey had no intention of debating him. "You sure they're your friends?"

"Of course. The whole town is abuzz with your thrilling exploits this afternoon. How you and your deputy bravely cut down five rabid dogs threatening the citizenry of Dover Station. Some of the townspeople were so proud, they directed us to the undertaker so we could see them for ourselves. The undertaker, Mr. Wallach, was kind enough to show us their bodies. At ten cents per corpse, of course."

Mackey was glad his back was to his house. No one could get behind him. Darabont was in front of him, and his four men were across the street. If anything was going to break, it would break now. He'd make sure Darabont died first. He'd worry about the four men across the street after that.

"I didn't know about Wallach charging to view the bodies," Mackey said. "I'll put an end to that tonight."

Darabont's eyebrows rose. "You object to the fee, but not their deaths?"

"Your friends had a chance to surrender, but went for their guns instead. You'd have done the same thing in my spot and don't tell me otherwise."

"You think we are violent men, sheriff?"

"You boys don't look like a band of roving preachers."

Darabont gestured to his empty holsters. "Yet, as you can see, we are unarmed. We only seek information about what happened to our friends, not gunplay or vengeance."

Mackey didn't trust Darabont or the men he had stationed across the street. But since they were friends of the men he'd killed, they were entitled to some answers. "Your friends got drunk and started trouble in the Tin Horn. They terrorized the customers and beat the hell out of the owner and his bouncer. When we ordered them to surrender their weapons, they tried to pull on us."

"Tried?"

"Tried but failed. The shooting was legal, Darabont. Straight down the line, all the way legal. I've even got sworn statements from over twenty witnesses who were in the Tin Horn and on the street at the time of the shooting. It's all written up in an official report down at the jailhouse if you want to read it."

"No need," Darabont said. "I'm sure the report will read exactly as you say, but then again, I've never held much stock in written reports. I prefer the oral tradition, to hear things from the people who've actually done them. I owe my dead friends that much, because, like the saying goes, 'there is special providence in the fall of a sparrow.'"

Mackey recognized the quote from Shakespeare and responded in kind. "'When beggars die, there are no comets seen.'"

Darabont's pleasant demeanor became something else. "And just what the hell is that supposed to mean?"

"It means me and my men legally gunned down five drunks who refused to disarm when ordered to do so. It means it was one of the most cut-and-dry shootings I've ever been involved in and I've been involved in my share." Mackey kept the Colt level as he took a step closer. "And it means my patience for your grandstanding is wearing thin."

"You consider a polite request for information on the death of my friends 'grandstanding,' sheriff?"

"I consider your air of refinement to be grandstanding," Mackey said. "And the implied threat of you and your men lurking around my house unsettles me. Bad things happen when I'm unsettled. You already lost five men today. Best cut your losses and ride on."

Darabont's smile returned. "I could be forgiven for taking that as a threat."

"Take it any way you want, so long as you take it with you on your way out of town."

But Darabont was in no hurry. He leaned against the porch post and rubbed at his beard in the same places where it was thinnest. "I'd wager that you don't know much about the whiskey making process, do you?"

"Can't say as I do." Mackey subtly moved his thumb to the hammer of his Colt. He didn't cock it, but he kept it there. He kept the gun aimed at Darabont's belly, too. "Couldn't care less, either."

"When bourbon is placed in the barrels for the aging process," Darabont explained, "a certain amount of it always evaporates, no matter how well the barrel is sealed. Distillers call that 'the angel's share.' They just bottle what's left and sell it. But the strongest, most potent liquor is still in the pores of the wooden barrel. And if you can get it out, one sip will send you on your way and then some. That stuff in the barrel is called 'the Devil's cut.'"

Mackey smiled. "Let me guess. You and your bunch over there think of yourselves in pretty much the same way."

Darabont laughed and slapped his leg. "Well, sheriff, that just about sums it up. We're just about the best and the worst all at the same time." He nodded back toward the others across the street. "And there's plenty more of us out there. A whole lot more."

Darabont's friends heard him and cheered him on.

Mackey kept his Colt level. "Never been much for whiskey. Never been much for talking, either. So why don't we settle this right here and now." He thumbed back the hammer of the Colt. "Tonight."

Darabont kept his hands raised and eased off the porch post. "You sure you want to do that, sheriff? Especially after your run-in with Mayor Mason this afternoon? What would those fancy guests of his think when they heard you'd just killed five more in the same day, especially when five of those men are unarmed, as my friends and I are most certainly unarmed now? That'd put your score at ten men before the clock strikes midnight. All those wealthy New York types might get scared off by all that violence. Surely, they'd be shocked to see such behavior from the hero of Adobe Flats."

Mackey didn't have to ask where Darabont had heard about his run-in with Mayor Mason. If the townspeople talked about the shooting, they had probably talked about that, too, and a lot more.

Darabont held his hands even farther away from him as he began to slowly back away toward his friends. "Now, I don't want to take up any more of your precious time and I don't want to get arrested for loitering, so my friends and I will be on our way. I want you in good spirits for the next time we meet."

Mackey matched him step for step; the Colt leading the way. "Next time we meet, you won't be enjoying anything."

"So many have said." Darabont grinned. "Yet here I am."

"Don't forget to collect your friends on your way out of town. The dead ones."

"We won't forget." Darabont stepped down the two steps to the street without even looking. A sure-footed man. "We don't forget anything, sheriff. Ever."

Mackey got to the edge of the boardwalk just as Darabont reached the four men across the street. "Then you won't forget to stay out of Dover Station."

Mackey expected some kind of comeback from Darabont, especially now that he had rejoined his friends. But all he did was touch the brim of his bowler as he led his men across the dense mud of Front Street and back toward the livery.

Mackey watched them the whole way. He managed to hold his coughing jag until he got back inside.

Chapter 10

Mackey had already been sitting alone at the Dover Station railroad station for some time before the sun began to rise. The cold air of the morning should have hurt his lungs, but he was glad it hadn't. For the first time since he could remember, nothing hurt him at all. He felt quiet and peaceful, even on the hard wooden bench outside the deserted station building.

The bench he sat on wasn't nearly as comfortable as his rocking chair on the porch of the jailhouse, but he hadn't come to the station for comfort. He had come for solitude.

There were other quiet places in town where he could've gone, of course, especially so early in the morning, but Mackey believed there was nothing as quiet and peaceful as a train station at an off time. The creatures of the night were already headed home and the creatures of the morning were still asleep. The sky had only begun to brighten, but he could sense a quiet renewal already in the air. And if Mackey needed anything following his run-in with Darabont, it was quiet.

He didn't want to go to the jailhouse and risk waking up Billy with his rocking and sporadic coughing fits. His deputy was a light sleeper; always had been, even back in their cavalry days. A church mouse pissing on cotton would be enough to wake him. Billy needed his sleep. Mackey didn't. The pneumonia had made him sleep long enough, maybe too long.

The events of the day before had shown him that.

His run-ins with town elders and with Mary. His disgust at the welcome ceremony at the station. Tangling with Darabont on his front porch, too. He'd handled it all, but it had taken more out of him than it should have, even considering the pneumonia. All day long, people had been telling him that Dover Station wasn't the same any more. Mackey was beginning to wonder if he wasn't the same any more, either.

As the sun began to rise, he could see the remnants of the previous day's celebration. The flatbed carrying Hill House's piano was long gone, as were all traces of the ramshackle band that had come with it. Some freight had been placed at the loading area again, but not as much as usual. The red, white, and blue bunting still hung on the railings and the windowsills, billowing and forgotten in the indifferent morning breeze. The decoration that had looked so festive the day before now looked forlorn and ridiculous, like a ball gown at breakfast or a Christmas tree in the middle of January.

Mackey supposed Mason would keep the decorations in place until Mr. Rice and Mr. Van Dorn boarded their train back to New York with the dreams of the townspeople in their wallets.

He wondered what would happen during the course of their visit. He wondered about Darabont and his men, too. He didn't like how the stranger knew how far to push him without going too far. He had made his point carefully and clearly and refused to lose his temper when Mackey had baited him.

Mackey had come up against men like Darabont before. Smart, unpredictable, and prideful men; too prideful to let an affront to their honor pass without adequate satisfaction. And Mackey was pretty sure that losing five men to a small-town sheriff would rank as an affront to Darabont's honor.

Mackey was sure Darabont would do something to avenge the men—and the honor—he had lost. The question was what. And when.

Mackey's hand went for the handle of the Colt when he heard something thumping on the station's boardwalk. He relaxed a little when he saw a man with a walking stick round the corner of the station building.

The man walked with a slight limp but was not stooped. Despite the chilly morning, he was hatless and wore a black coat lined with fur at the collar and sleeves. The tweed suit beneath his open coat fit his thickening form too well to have come out of the Sears Roebuck catalogue.

Mackey noticed the brass handle and tip of his walking stick must have cost him a pretty penny. But, then again, the man could afford it, for Mackey recognized this man from the celebration of the previous day. He was Frazer Rice of New York City.

Mackey took his hand away from the Colt on his belly. "Morning, Mr. Rice."

"Morning," the man called out as he hobbled closer. "I take it you're Sheriff Mackey."

"You take it correctly, sir."

"Thought so," Rice grunted. "I've heard of you."

Mackey didn't know how to take that, so he took it as it was. "Same here, though the newspaper likenesses don't do you justice."

"Damned things never do. Just as well. Never liked my picture being taken anyway. Fame never does the infamous any good."

Mackey was glad they had at least that much in common. "I hope you'll accept my belated welcome to Dover Station."

"And I hope I'm not disturbing you by wandering over here like this," Mr. Rice said. "Needed to stretch my legs a bit after being crammed in the same train car as those ninnies the entire ride out here. If my cigar smoke didn't bother them, my silence did. And when I needed their silence, they chattered on like old hens, mostly complaining about the conditions of my train car. Silas Van Dorn was the worst of them." Mackey watched him bend forward at the waist, then slowly ease himself back upright. "You'd think railroad men would be made of tougher stuff than that, but I guess that's the difference between railroad men and investors. I'm a railroad man myself."

"I knew that, too."

"From the gossip or the papers?"

The sheriff smiled. "Heard about it plenty from both sources. Given how the mayor talks about you, I half expected you to be carried into town by a company of angels."

"Yeah, I gathered that." Rice squinted into the mist of the near distance. "Everyone's always looking for a Messiah even though they didn't treat the last one very well. And when they find out all I am is a man with a railroad and some money to spend, they tend to think less kindly of me."

Mackey remembered how people's opinions about him had changed since he'd come out of the army, especially Mary's. "Yeah. I know something about that, too."

"I noticed you walked away yesterday when the mayor called you to the stage," Rice said. "I'd like to know why."

"Why?"

"Just curious is all," Rice admitted. "Men usually like adulation, especially men like you and the good mayor."

"I'm nothing like the mayor."

Rice nodded. "Didn't think you were, but I'm glad to hear it for certain. Hope you didn't come to the stage on account of the shootings. I heard all about that, no matter how Mason tried to cushion it for me. Got to say I'm impressed. I like my money to be secure. Your conduct yesterday puts me more at ease about investing in a wilderness."

"Might want to let the mayor know your sentiments," Mackey said. "He's afraid you'll think we're barbarians."

"Heard you went to West Point," Rice said.

"Yes I did." Mackey saw no reason to say more. This was Rice's discussion. Let him take it where he wanted to.

"Me too, though it was well before your time. Never graduated, though. Slipped on ice and shattered my knee while getting on my horse." He thumped his cane on the boardwalk. "Not much room in the cavalry for a cripple with a bad knee. I was only there a year before it happened, but I'd like to think some of the training stuck. Acquired a taste for history while I was there, an interest which has stuck with me my whole life. Barbarians get a bad rank as far as most history books are concerned. But it takes barbarians to win wars and build things. Things like Dover Station. There's profit to be made in law and order. My kind of profit."

"Glad we're of the same mind, Mr. Rice."

He watched the investor place his hands on his hips as he looked along the track bed. The railroad engineers had placed the tracks so they skirted the hills that surrounded the town, creating a gradual, meandering curve. The diversion had made for a wider distance between two points, but bending track was cheaper than dynamiting through the hills that surrounded the town, so the railroad had taken on a meandering path.

Rice's chest expanded as he drew the chilly Montana air deep into his lungs. "You smell that, sheriff?"

Mackey didn't smell anything except Dover Station. "Not sure what you mean, sir."

"Sure you do. You just don't know it. Same smell in every train station and depot the world over. Some say it's just train grease and steel with a little anxious sweat from the waiting room thrown in, but I know better. That, sir, is the smell of progress. Of opportunity." His eyes narrowed as he seemed to look at nothing in particular. "Of money." He nodded in agreement with his own point. "That's my kind of smell."

Mackey didn't know what to say, so as was his custom, decided it was best to say nothing.

Rice went on. "I hired a perfumer once to try to duplicate that smell. Brought the son of a bitch all the way from Italy to do it, too. Guinea bastard tried like hell to match it, but failed at every attempt." Rice shrugged. "Guess some things aren't meant to be duplicated."

Mackey thought of it another way. "My guess is you have too much money."

Rice laughed. "No such thing as too much money, sheriff, and the only people who believe such nonsense are the people who never had much in the first place."

Judging by the words, Mackey might have taken offense. But the way Rice had said it told him no offense had been meant. And if there was one thing Mackey had learned, it was that a man's tone made all the difference. "Kind of hard for people to get any money, especially when people like you have it all."

"True," Rice admitted, "but that won't be the story in this town. Not if Silas and I have anything to say about it, and I have plenty of say in that matter. I hope you don't have any designs on leaving anytime soon, sheriff, because I've got big plans for Dover Station. Bigger than anyone has dared to dream. Lumber, cattle, horses and farmland all within spitting distance of my station. In two years, I plan on making this town a full-fledged depot that will bring wood and cattle and crops to every point on the compass."

"Don't forget about the miners," Mackey said. "They're awfully proud of what they do and get testy when they're forgotten."

"Mining men are speculators," Rice told him. "Gamblers. Plenty of men are ready to waste their lives and fortunes digging holes in the ground. Let them. I'm not a gambler, son. I've always been interested in the things I can see shit and grow. Things like cattle and crops."

"And railroads."

Rice smiled to himself. "I like your thinking, sheriff."

Mackey looked out on the brightening dawn. Faint pink ribbons had just begun to appear in the eastern sky, just as they had on similar mornings back when he had been a cadet at West Point and a lieutenant in the Arizona territory and a newly appointed captain as the Hero of Adobe Flats back in Boston all those years ago, back when the future was something to be dreamed of and hoped for. Back when the future had meant something to him.

But those days were long gone and the hopes and dreams of those mornings past gone with them. He hadn't thought much about the future since returning to Dover Station. And he didn't like how Frazer Rice reminded him of how long ago that had been.

Maybe it was his lack of sleep or the worries about Darabont on his mind, but he decided to make his point. "You're a blunt man, aren't you, Mr. Rice?"

"Don't have much tolerance for a man who'll use twenty words when five will do. Men like your Mayor Mason."

"Good, because I've lost count of all the men who came here with a flourish and wagonload full of promises that they'd make everyone rich. All we ever got out of it was hot air and hard feelings. I don't mind talk, so long as that's all it is."

"I spent most of last night hearing the stories about the broken promises and the broken hearts, sheriff. I'm normally more of a doer than a talker."

"That's good because I'd hate to see you build up everyone's hopes by making a lot of grand announcements, only to up and disappear like a fart in the wind. I've lived here most of my life when I wasn't in the army. I can remember back to after the war when my old man and his friends built this town out of nothing more than a skinner outpost in the middle of nowhere. The people who live here do their best for as long as they can until they can't do it anymore. They take loss hard here, and there are some disappointments people just can't come back from. It's my job to protect them. Not just from drunks and men with guns, but people who'd harm them in other ways. So if you're just here to speculate and decide if this is a good investment, keep it to yourself. Because if you build up their hopes and knock them down later, I'm going to have to sweep a lot of drunks off the streets. A lot of bodies of men who kill themselves over the disappointment, too. I won't be happy if that happens." He looked at Rice. "And you won't be happy, either."

Rice blew into his hands as he looked out again at the vast land that raced away from the station toward the mountains. The hillsides around the town were becoming clearer in the strengthening sunlight. "That's quite a speech for a quiet man. Guess what they say about still waters running deep is true."

"Wouldn't know about that," Mackey said. "Just looking out for my town."

Rice smiled as he blew on his hands some more. "You're a hard man, Sheriff Mackey."

Mackey stifled a cough. "Stubborn, too."

Chapter 11

Later that morning, long after the sun had risen much higher over the ridgeline, Mackey and Billy watched a stranger ride toward the jailhouse from the south.

Mackey had long since resumed his place in the rocking chair on the jailhouse porch by then. Billy was on the bench, enjoying his morning coffee and cigarette. Mackey found something peaceful about the way Billy did things, even everyday things like brewing coffee and building a cigarette. Everything was done with an easy purpose and motion day in and day out. Nothing about Billy ever felt sudden, but as if he had planned it out long ago. Billy moved with the slow confidence of a man who didn't care who might be watching or if anyone was.

Billy nodded toward the approaching stranger from the south. "Rider coming."

Mackey stifled another cough. The effort hurt a little less than it had the day before. "I see that."

He hoped Billy hadn't heard him cough but knew

better. Billy said, "You were over at the station this morning, weren't you?"

Mackey kept rocking. He saw no reason to deny it. "Needed to be alone for a while. I go there sometimes when I need to think."

"I know. How long you been up?"

Mackey winced at the rebuke he knew would follow. "Since I woke you to tell you about Darabont last night."

"Hell, Aaron. On a cold morning like this? Thought you was going back home to bed where you belong."

"I tried that," Mackey admitted, "but when I got there, Mary was sore about Darabont coming by the house. Said I'd brought danger to her front door, then started laying into me again about being a sheriff."

Mackey knew Billy could have said a lot. He may have even wanted to. That's why he was glad his deputy just sipped his coffee instead. "That woman sure does have a flair for the dramatic. Should've been on the stage."

Mackey saw no point in denying that, either.

The two of them sat quietly; watching the stranger approach the town. Mackey didn't think he was one of Darabont's men. Darabont probably never went anywhere alone. He preferred a pack. This man rode alone and made no effort to conceal his approach.

Mackey kept rocking as he watched the man approach. "Mr. Rice happened by while I was over at the station. Says he's got big plans for this town. Says the place smells like promise and opportunity."

Billy drank his coffee. "All I smell is stale beer from the Tin Horn when the wind blows right."

Mackey kept rocking. "I think he's a serious man."

Billy set his cup down. "All rich men are serious about money. And scared when it comes to pulling it out of their pocket." He finished his cigarette and flicked the dead butt into the muddy thoroughfare of Front Street. "You know Darabont went by Cy Wallach's and took his dead friends away."

Mackey nodded as he suppressed another coughing spell. His lungs ached, but not as much as before. "He said he was going to do that when he left my place last night."

"But you don't think that's the end of it, do you?"

"I'd be lying if I said Darabont didn't have me worried some."

"Worried is one thing," Billy said. "Afraid is something else."

"Yes it is. If we were still in uniform, I would've killed that son of a bitch last night out of pure efficiency."

"But we're not in uniform anymore," Billy reminded him. "We haven't been for some time. There's a difference between what soldiers can do on patrol and what sheriffs can do in the confines of a town setting. Killing Darabont would've forced Mayor Mason to do something foolish. Darabont knew that. I'm glad you didn't give him the chance, but I don't like Darabont knowing how far to push you."

"Neither do I." Mackey rested his coffee mug on the arm of his rocker. "Got a feeling I'm going to resent letting that bastard live."

"We'll handle it if we have to."

Mackey nodded. "Always have in the past."

"Always will, too." Billy stirred his lungs and spat into the street. He nodded toward the distant rider. "Wonder what the hell he wants."

Mackey watched the growing dust cloud trailing behind the rider. "I suppose we'll find out soon enough."

As the rider reached Front Street, Mackey could see he was a large man on a big sorrel. Neither man nor mount was built for speed but for power instead. A pack mule weighed down with supplies was on a lead line trotting right behind him.

The stranger's long blond hair flowed out from beneath a black, wide-brimmed hat. The hat itself had a silver band with turquoise stones in it. His moustache and beard were as blond as the rest of him and just as well groomed. His duster was black, which made it easier to see the gold star pinned to his chest.

Mackey had never seen the big man before, but judging by the size and shape of the star, knew he was a deputy United States Marshal. What Mackey didn't know was why a federal marshal would be in Dover Station without sending a telegram announcing his arrival.

"Quite the dandy," Mackey said to his deputy.

Billy looked the man over. "Seems awfully impressed with himself. Probably lick himself all over if he could manage it."

Mackey sipped the last of his coffee and rocked slowly as he watched the rider turn onto Front Street.

Mackey hadn't noticed Pappy had come out of his general store across the street until his father let out a long, loud whistle at the approaching rider. "Well, well, well. Will you look at the lovely vision that's come to call upon us this morning?"

The marshal eyed Pappy as he swung down from

the saddle and hitched his horse to the post in front of the jail. "Been called a lot of things, old timer, but a vision ain't never been one of them."

Pappy spoke out of the corner of his mouth as he struck a match and fired up his pipe. "There's a first time for everything, young man, because I believe I just did."

Mackey set his mug on the porch floor and stood to greet the visitor who'd stepped up onto the jail-house boardwalk. Mackey's legs were stronger than he'd expected them to be. The man was a few inches taller than Mackey, putting him at well over six feet tall. He was wider and heavier, too, which must've put him at over two hundred pounds. All the long, blond hair made the man look even bigger than he already was.

"You the sheriff around here?" the big man asked.

Mackey said he was and introduced himself as such. He nodded at Billy, who was already standing. "This is Billy Sunday, my deputy."

The big man pulled off a yellow gauntlet. "I'm Walter Underhill, Deputy U.S. Marshal out of Texas."

The two men shook hands. He didn't offer his hand to Billy and Billy didn't look for it.

"Montana's a little out of your jurisdiction, ain't it, marshal?" Billy asked.

"Not really." He tapped the star pinned to his chest. "That's a federal badge, boy."

Billy didn't miss a beat. "Attached to a federal judge in a federal district over a thousand miles away from here, boy."

Mackey moved between the two men. The marshal might be out of his jurisdiction but he was still a federal and a federal could be a big pain in the ass. He already had enough trouble with Darabont lurking around. He didn't need to add to it. "That's just Billy's way of saying he's curious about what brings you up this far north, Underhill. Quite frankly, so am I."

Underhill began pulling off his other gauntlet. "Been chasing a couple of men I understand are from these parts. Go by the name of the Boudreaux brothers. Know of them?"

"Known of them most of my life," Mackey said, "but they've never given me any trouble. Not enough to draw federal attention, anyway. What are you after them for?"

"If it's all the same to you, I'd prefer to talk about that inside in private. What I've got to say ain't for everyone to hear." He thumbed back toward Pappy. "And that old bastard back there is a town gossip if I ever saw one."

"Got good hearing, too." Pappy puffed his pipe as he looked up at Underhill's back. "He's telling the truth, Aaron. About being a Texan, I mean. Saw a lot of them in the war. I couldn't be sure when he first rode in, but I can see it clear as day now that I've laid eyes on the back of him."

Underhill turned just enough to answer him. "I'm not surprised. The only way a Yankee could ever kill a Texan was to shoot him in the back."

Smoke billowed out of Pappy's pipe. "Had no choice, seeing as how they always headed the other way once the shooting started. Yep, all braggin' and no sand. A Texan's just about the lowest form of white man alive in my book."

Underhill slapped his gauntlets against his leg as he turned to face Pappy full on. "Old men like you ought to learn to curb their tongue."

"Tried it once," Pappy winked. "Never quite found the knack for it. How about you try to teach me?"

Mackey opened the door of the jailhouse. "If you two ladies are done carping at each other, maybe we can talk about the Boudreauxs now?"

Underhill reluctantly broke eye contact with Pappy before he strode into the office. He ducked his head as he went inside, even though he didn't need to. Mackey and Billy looked at each other before they filed in after him.

Chapter 12

"Don't know why you cut me off," Underhill said as he sat down. The old wooden chair creaked beneath his bulk. "If you ask me, that old bastard is in dire need of a beating."

Mackey went to the stove and poured coffee into three cups. "That may be true, but I'd give that particular old man a wide berth if I were you."

Mackey noticed Underhill's hand tremble as he quickly took the cup of coffee. He tried covering it up by settling back into the chair and stretching his broad shoulders even wider. "I think I could take one mouthy old man. Doubt you'd miss him. World's full of them."

Mackey handed a mug to Billy before taking a seat behind his desk. "Maybe, but I'm kind of partial to that one. He's my father."

Underhill lowered his mug to Mackey's desk. "That so?"

Mackey shrugged. "My cross to bear. So, how about

you tell me why you've come all the way up from Texas looking for the Boudreaux boys."

Underhill reached into his pocket and handed him a wanted poster. "It's all right there and legal. They're accused of raping a pair of women just outside of Fort Worth, then shot their husbands after."

Mackey took a look at the poster. It was a wanted poster from the Fort Worth Sheriff's Office offering a thousand dollar reward for the Boudreaux brothers. It said they were wanted for rape, assault, and general mayhem.

Mackey read the poster again, then looked back at Billy. Billy couldn't read, but didn't need to in order to recognize their likenesses drawn on the paper. "Don't look nothing like the Boudreauxs who live here, Underhill."

"Still, it's them I'm after." Underhill drank his coffee. "You going to help or not?"

Mackey asked, "Let me see the warrant."

"Don't have one."

Billy spoke before Mackey did. "You mean to tell me a federal marshal rode all the way up here from Texas without an actual warrant in his pocket?"

Underhill pointed at the poster. "My warrant's right there in black and white." He tapped the star on his chest. "And here, stamped in gold."

Mackey handed the wanted poster back to Underhill. "Paper and gold don't make it legal. We all know that."

Underhill grew very still. "You calling me a liar, Mackey?"

"No. I'm saying things don't add up like they should. Every marshal we've ever had up here had a warrant with them or had one wired in advance. You just ride in here and expect me to hand over two men I've known my whole life to a total stranger on charges that are hard to believe."

Underhill looked at Billy, then at Mackey. "So that's how it is. They're your friends and you're sticking up for them. Locals sticking up for locals."

"No. I'm saying these boys might get a little loud and a little drunk sometimes, but neither of them ever forced a lady to do anything."

"Here, maybe," Underhill said, "but boys on the trail have a tendency to act up in ways they wouldn't while at home."

"If you told me they killed men in a bar fight, I'd be apt to agree with you. But I have a tough time believing they raped anyone. They're two mighty fine-looking boys, marshal, way better than their pictures on your wanted poster show. Dark hair, good skin, even got most of their teeth. Charming as hell, too. They even speak fluent French. They've never had cause to rape a woman because they get more than their fair share of attention from the ladies wherever they go."

Billy added, "Hell, half the whores in town don't even charge them full price on account of them being prettier than they are."

"Don't know about whores," Underhill said. "Don't care how pretty these boys are supposed to be, either. All I know is that they're charged with raping two women and killing their husbands and it's my job to bring them back to stand trial."

"Without a warrant," Mackey said.

Underhill's eyes narrowed. "I'll get the judge to wire a warrant to you if it'll make you feel any better."

"We'll get to that in a minute," Mackey said. "Tell me about these husbands you're so hell-bent on avenging. "Where'd the killings take place?"

When Underhill's eyes flickered, Mackey realized the marshal didn't know as much as he should have. "What difference does it make? They're dead just the same."

"Makes all the difference in the world," Mackey said. "If these two men walked in while the boys were having a go at their wives, they could've shot at them and lost."

"Which means the boys were defending themselves," Billy added.

"And if they got killed elsewhere," Mackey went on, "like on the trail, then these men might've stalked the Boudreauxs after they left town and gotten killed for their trouble. They're skilled hunters and they're not apt to letting someone try to ambush them."

Underhill looked at Mackey, then at Billy. Mackey noticed the bags under the marshal's bloodshot eyes. When put together with the shaking hand, he figured Underhill was either hung-over or a drunk. It didn't tell him much, but it told him something.

"I see what this is." Underhill began to stand up. "Sounds to me like you two are covering up for your friends."

"Sounds to me like you don't know what the hell you're talking about," Mackey said.

The big man got up and walked toward the door. "These two won't be the first men I've brought in alone and they won't be my last. Just tell me where I can find them and I'll be on my way."

"I'll be going with you." Mackey stood up and adjusted the Colt a bit closer to his left hip. "You go out to their place on your own, I'll be bringing you back here across your saddle."

Underhill stood up to his full height again. "I already told you these two ain't the first hardcases I've brought in."

"They're crack shots, Underhill. They learned how to shoot squirrels before they could walk. Either of them could put a bullet through your eye before you even knew they were there."

Mackey took his Winchester down from the rifle rack and opened the door. "They're likely to be a bit more welcoming if they see a friendly face." To Billy, he said: "Keep an eye on the store while I'm gone. See if any of our friends come back for a visit."

Billy took down the Sharps and headed out to the porch. "I'll set a fine table for them if they do."

The Boudreaux place was a good three-mile ride out of town; up the gradual hill that led out of town and through the edge of the timberland where the loggers plied their trade. Underhill's sorrel was more interested in Adair, but Adair kept her mind on the trail. Birds sang deep in the forest as a cool breeze rustled the leaves that had begun sprouting. It was the kind of day best enjoyed by a slow ride through the tall grass. Not worrying about men like Darabont. And not hunting down old friends with a stranger, either.

Judging from Underhill's silence as they rode,

Mackey figured the marshal was chewing over more than just the idea of tangling with the Boudreauxs. He looked like he had a lot of questions about a lot of things, but Mackey decided to let him take his time asking them. He wasn't a big fan of answering questions from strangers anyway. They rarely appreciated the answers he gave.

About a mile out of town, Underhill began unburdening his mind. "Tell me something, Mackey. What made you take on a nigger as a deputy?"

Mackey drew Adair to a halt.

Underhill brought his sorrel to a stop a few steps after. "What the hell is wrong with you?"

"I don't like that word, Underhill. I don't use it, and I don't allow people to use it around me."

"Hell, Mackey, it's what he is, ain't it?"

"Billy Sunday is my deputy. He's also my friend. If you use that word around him, he's likely to kill you. And I'm just as likely to look the other way when he does and so would most people in town."

Underhill clearly didn't like the rebuke, but he took it. "Just not common to see a . . . one of them as a lawman is all. No offense meant."

Mackey figured that was as close to an apology as he was likely to get. He let Adair begin to walk again. Underhill followed.

"His name is Billy Sunday," Mackey said again. "And I'd appreciate it if you'd start referring to him by his name instead of as my deputy."

Underhill's jaw clenched. "I heard what you said to *Billy* before we left. Sounds like you're expecting some kind of trouble."

Mackey wasn't given to sharing his concerns, especially to strangers. But it was a long ride up to the

Boudreaux house. It would be an even longer ride back to town if the brothers didn't come peacefully. He might as well be sociable while he could.

"Yesterday, we had to kill five drunks who wouldn't disarm when we told them to. Some of their friends came by to collect the bodies last night. Came by my house after. Their leader threatened at avenging his friends, though in a very roundabout way."

"And you let him ride out? Just like that?"

"Making subtle threats isn't against the law. Carrying them out is." He left it at that. There was no point in explaining his other concerns, especially how Mayor Mason would react to more dead men.

"How many men did this bastard bring with him?" Underhill asked.

"Four plus himself. Ring leader was a creepy little bastard with a fancy way of talking, but dead eyes."

This time, Underhill stopped short. "Kind of a short fella with long, greasy hair. Scar under the right side of his jaw? Called himself Darabont?"

Mackey reined in Adair. He'd noticed the scar in passing, but hadn't paid much attention to it. "You know him?"

"I know the man who gave him that scar on his neck. Tried hanging him for rustling cattle down in Texas. Hanging party got attacked by thirty of his friends just when they were about to slap the horse out from under him. Bastards killed everyone in the party, then hung *them* from every tree on the road into town."

Mackey set Adair in motion and the two men started riding again. "Jesus."

"Happened about a year ago," Underhill went on.

"Heard they rode north, but no one went after them, and I haven't heard much about them since. Story's gotten bigger as time's gone on, though. Most folks say there were a hundred of them and they desecrated the bodies before they hung them, but that's all nonsense. Thirty men stringing up a lynching party's bad enough as far as I'm concerned."

Mackey caught a thread of something. "Seeing as how your judge friend sent you all the way up here for the Boudreaux boys, I'm surprised he didn't send out some marshals after Darabont."

"He sent out three marshals right after. All friends of mine, too. Never heard from them again, either."

Mackey didn't know how much of that was true, but he knew his own impression of Darabont. Despite his fancy talk, he didn't seem like a pushover. "You be willing to lend a hand if they start trouble while you're here?"

Underhill laughed and sat a little taller in the saddle. "Whatever your old man's opinion of me might be, don't worry. I'm damned handy to have around when the lead starts flying."

Mackey kept riding. He hoped Underhill was as good as he said he was, though in his experience, it was often the other way around.

Another half a mile passed before Underhill said, "You never told me how you chose Billy as your deputy. I'd like to know."

"We served together in the cavalry and he's been with me ever since. Finest man I've ever had the honor to know."

"Cavalry?" Underhill repeated. "Hold up! You're *that* Aaron Mackey, aren't you? Hero of Adobe Flats?"

Mackey kept riding. "My men were the heroes, marshal. All I did was lead them."

"Heard they made you a captain after that," Underhill said. "What the hell are you doing with a tin star in the middle of nowhere?"

"Had to be somewhere," Mackey said. "Dover Station's as good a place as any. My old man and his army buddies came up here after the War Between the States. Wasn't much here back then. Just wilderness and a hell of a lot of Indians. But then they started finding gold and silver in the mountains. Copper, too. Loggers came after, followed by the farmers and the ranchers. Lived here from the time I was about six all the way until I went off to the Point."

"West Point?" Underhill asked. "How'd you swing that? I thought you could only get into West Point if you were the son of an officer. And your old man don't strike me as officer material."

Mackey smiled. "He wasn't, but . . ."

Adair stopped short just as the crack of a rifle shot echoed through the timber. Mackey heard the bullet whiz by and land in the tall grass on the other side of the trail not five feet away.

Underhill already had his Colt in his hand while Mackey stood high in his stirrups and yelled out: "Who was that? Who's the dumb son of a bitch who just shot at me?"

"Aaron?" a voice Mackey recognized as Jack Boudreaux called back. "That you?"

"Goddamned right it's me. Get your dumb ass out here where I can see you. Right now!"

Jack Boudreaux and his brother, Henry, stepped out of the tall grass onto the trail. Both men were land-work lean and medium height. Despite their dirty work clothes and faces, it was clear they were fine looking boys. Dark haired and strong features that belied their French stock. Heads hung low in shame. Henry rifles at their sides.

Mackey was not in a welcoming mood. "The hell you think you're doing shooting at me like that?"

"Sorry, Aaron." Henry looked down at the ground. "Didn't recognize you. You don't look like your normal self is all."

"Yeah," Jack added. "You look like hell. How was we supposed to know you'd . . ."

"You two bastards are going to look even worse in a while. You know who I got here with me?"

Both brothers looked up at Underhill. And both brothers shook their heads at the same time before looking back at the ground.

"His name is Walter Underhill, Deputy United States Marshal out of Texas. And I've got a feeling you boys know why he's here."

Both brothers shook their heads again, so Underhill told them: "You boys remember those two women you forced yourselves on down in Fort Worth? And the husbands you killed?"

Jack quit looking at the ground. "We didn't rape no women."

Henry quit looking at the ground, too. "And we didn't kill no husbands, either. Killed a couple of bastards who bushwhacked our camp when we was headin' home though. It was self-defense, plain and simple, Aaron. Honest."

"And if they was those ladies' husbands," Jack

added, "they didn't announce themselves. And those ladies never mentioned they were married."

Mackey had known the Boudreauxs a good portion of their lives. They were given to raising a bit of hell now and then, but he'd never known them to be violent or cruel. But a trail was no place for a trial, especially with a federal marshal in tow. "You'll still have to ride in with us while we get this straightened out. Now get your things and let's go."

"You gotta believe us, Aaron," Jack said. "Them cowardly bastards opened up on us while we was sleepin'. Ain't our fault they missed."

"I swear to God," Henry added, "we thought they was out to rob us. We didn't know it had anything to do with them ladies we poked."

"Them ladies who happily poked back," Jack said. "We didn't force them to do anything they didn't want to do. And they wanted to do plenty. They was in better shape when we left them than when we found them. Hell, they even cooked us breakfast the next morning."

Mackey was inclined to believe them, but knew Underhill still had a job to do. And he wouldn't be apt to listen to reason until they'd brought the Boudreauxs back into town. "I'm not going to tell you boys again. Get your horses saddled and let's get back into town. The quicker we settle this, the quicker you'll be back here."

Neither man protested again. They just started walking up the trail to their home about a mile away. Underhill and Mackey ambled along quietly a good distance behind them.

Underhill broke the silence first. "What the hell is all that about getting this settled? Nothing's settled until the judge says it is. Those boys are coming back to Texas with me."

"We've got a lot to settle," Mackey said. "You, me and those boys. But we'll settle it once we get back to town."

Underhill looked like he wanted to say something more but held his tongue. Under his breath, he said, "Those boys are coming back with me."

Mackey let it go. He'd already said they'd settle the matter back in Dover Station. And he wasn't given to repeating himself.

Chapter 13

It was just before noon when Mackey and Underhill rode into town with the Boudreauxs in tow. The town was well under way towards getting things ready for the Veterans' Gala that night.

Women in their best Sunday dresses were already heading for The Dance Hall with plates of food and baked goods. Many of the veterans had already put on their uniforms hours before the dance was scheduled to begin. He saw men in faded Union blue and Confederate gray tunics, trading old stories and comparing the wounds they'd received during the late War Between the States.

"Looks like someone's having a party," Underhill said as they rode past Katie's Place at the south end of town.

"Not much gets by you, does it, Underhill?"

The Boudreaux boys laughed.

The marshal looked at him. "How about you stick your sarcasm up your ass and tell me what the hell is going on?"

Mackey decided he'd probably ribbed him enough for one day. "All the old vets in town get together once a year to throw a big party. My old man heads up the Union side. Doc Ridley heads up the rebel side. They march into the ballroom, salute each other, then set to dancing and drinking." He motioned at the Boudreauxs riding ahead of them. "Our prisoners are part of the band. Best damned fiddle players in the territory. Ain't that right, boys?"

"If you let us out in time to play," Jack grumbled.

"I will," Mackey said. "Don't worry."

Underhill didn't like that idea. "Hold on just one damned minute. These men are my prisoners, and I'm not . . ."

"They're my prisoners until you produce a warrant from a federal judge proving otherwise. Besides, they're being held in my jail and they'll be held under my rules. No one's talking about letting them run free, Underhill. You can keep an eye on them while they're playing and bring them back to their cells when they're done. It'll be the easiest duty you ever drew because the last thing on their minds will be escape. Every woman in town will keep their eyes on them the entire time."

"Thanks, Aaron," Henry Boudreaux said. "We've been looking forward to this all winter."

Underhill said, "You'll be there too, won't you, Mackey?"

"Never have, never will," Mackey said. "But I'll be around if I'm needed."

"Why not? You were in the army, same as the rest of these fellas?"

Mackey felt himself getting annoyed. "I've got my reasons."

As they rode past Katie's Place, he felt a pull toward her hotel. He felt pulled toward her. He knew Darabont wasn't done with Dover Station yet. He wasn't done with Mackey or Billy either. The only question was when and how he would take his revenge. He knew it wouldn't be long. He had to quietly warn her and Wilkes to be on their guard without sparking a panic throughout the town. All of the old vets would be itching for a fight to prove they still had their virility. He didn't want them shooting at every shadow that moved until it was absolutely necessary.

"Underhill, how about you run these boys over to the jail. If you get lost, they'll show you where it is. I'll be along in a bit."

The marshal did not look happy. "Where the hell are you going?"

But Mackey wasn't one to give an accounting of his time to strangers, even if those strangers were federal lawmen. "Tell Billy to put the brothers in the same cell. We'll need the extra room for drunks from the gala tonight."

Mackey rode Adair over to Katie's Place, but stayed mounted. He had things to do and couldn't risk getting pulled in by Katie's charms. He found Old Wilkes on the porch instead, sweeping dust out onto the thoroughfare. The old Union man was already in uniform. The buttons on his faded tunic strained against his belly. "Evenin', captain! How's your pa?"

"Doing just fine," Mackey said. "And it's sheriff,

Wilkes, not captain. Hasn't been captain for a long time."

"On any other day, you'd be right. But with the gala coming on and all, today you're Captain Mackey."

Mackey didn't like it, but decided to let it go. "Katie about by any chance?"

Wilkes shook his head. "She went off up to Hill House to tend to one of the whores who's with child. Poor girl seems to be having a rough time now that the baby is so close to getting born. Katie said it might take most of the night before she's done. Looks like she'll miss the gala, which is damnable shame if you ask me. She always does herself up nice for the dance."

Mackey looked up the hill just outside of town to where Hill House stood alone at the top of the ridge that surrounded Dover Station. Although the place was only half a mile out of town, Mackey didn't like Katie being out there alone with Darabont and his men on the loose. With the gala going on that night, he couldn't neglect his duties in town, but he'd be sure to take a ride out to Hill House this afternoon once he got the Boudreauxs settled in the jail.

Wilkes broke his concentration. "You goin' to the ball tonight, Aaron."

Mackey closed his eyes. The old man had asked him the same question every damned year for the past five years. "You ever see me at the ball?"

"Nope, but your pa and me and some of the others keep hoping you'll change your mind. Be kind of nice having you there, with your medals and all. Ain't seen them since the day you got back to town. Only officer this town ever produced. Probably the only one it ever will. We're mighty proud of that, son, even if you're not. What you did that day on Adobe Flats is a hell of a thing. Be kinda nice to have you there this year in particular, given all those fancy men the mayor's brought out here from back east and all."

Mackey didn't want to think about Adobe Flat or the gala or his damned medals. He was more concerned about the present. About Katie. "Who will be minding the place while you're at the dance?"

"Got a couple of men keeping watch here and . . ."

"I mean with Katie up at Hill House."

Wilkes set his broom aside and thought about it. "They got that old Swede up there who minds the place and does repairs for them. Andersson, I think his name is. He don't speak much English, but he's always handled any trouble with the customers. Why the concern, Aaron?"

"Remember those five men we shot yesterday?"

"Sure do. Did us proud, you did, keepin' us safe and all."

He knew Wilkes was one of Pappy's best sources of gossip, so he chose his words carefully. "Well those men have friends who've made some threats against the town. With the dance going on and with Katie up on the hill, I'd . . ."

"Say no more, captain." Wilkes may have preferred to play the doddering idiot who swept up the place, but Mackey knew the former cavalry sergeant was no fool. "I'll make sure I'm up there this evening to keep an eye on Miss Kate."

Mackey was glad to hear it. "I don't want you missing the dance, Wilkes. I know how much it means to you."

"There'll be other dances, Aaron, but there's only one Miss Kate. I'll keep an eye on her. Hell, maybe I'll spur her along to bring that young one into the world and come back to town with me before your pappy drinks all that punch."

Mackey felt himself smiling. No, Wilkes was no fool. "Thanks, Wilkes. I'll be up to check on things when I can."

"You'll find me at my post when you do." Mackey almost flinched when the old man snapped a salute at him. It was the first salute Mackey had received in years.

He humored him by returning it. "You're a good man, sergeant. Carry on. I'll swing by after the dance gets started."

"Be good to see you when you do, sir." Wilkes resumed his sweeping. "Don't forget to give your pa my regards. Good man, your pa. Served with him under Sherman, you know?"

"I know, sergeant. I know."

Mackey gave Adair her head and let her lope at her own pace toward the jailhouse.

After making sure Billy and Underhill got the Boudreauxs squared away at the jailhouse, Mackey felt a pang of hunger—his first in weeks—and decided to head home for an early supper. He knew it would be a late night for him. Veterans Gala dances always lasted most of the night, with the town jail filled to capacity. If he was going to eat at all, he decided it was best to eat early.

He knew Mary had been cooking all day for the dance and usually made extra. She would most likely already be at the hall helping the ladies set up, allowing him to eat in peace in his own house for once.

He usually put Adair in the livery when he didn't

expect to need her again, but today, he decided to ride her the short distance up the street to his house.

He knew why, though he didn't like to admit it. Not even to himself.

The sight of all the men in their uniforms for the Veterans Gala had been an annual happening since he had been a boy. He'd grown up dreaming of the day he'd be able to attend in full uniform. Most of the men on the Union side had been sergeants and lower. Doc Ridley had been a captain in the Confederacy and, by rank, had always been the most senior old officer in attendance. Pappy was glad the day his son had finally matched the old rebel in rank.

But when Mackey had been drummed out of the cavalry, he swore he'd never wear the uniform again. The town may have given him a hero's welcome, but the burn of dismissal still stung.

He'd been dismissed because he'd kept a lieutenant from beating a captured Apache to death. Mackey had hit the young officer too hard, scrambling the man's brains in the process. The assault was justified, but the lieutenant was the son of a prominent southern senator. The army had refused the senator's demands that Mackey be court-martialed, as they had no intention of disgracing the man they'd built up as the Hero of Adobe Flat. They quietly dismissed him from the service instead.

He'd never attended the gala since he'd come back and been elected sheriff, choosing instead to stay in the jail or on patrol while most of the town drank and danced and ate. He'd grown to hate the gala and what it represented. A bunch of old men indulging in old glories. He had no time for that.

But as he rode past the men in old uniforms—

some blue and some gray—and the ladies in their finery, Mackey allowed himself to remember what it had been like on nights such as this one, back on the forts he'd served. Men in uniform, united in a common purpose and common danger. God had had little to do with it. Love of country even less. They served for the man next to them. They served to keep each other alive.

He admitted that he missed that. He missed being in command and having the authority to deal with threats in his own way. Threats like the men he'd killed at the Tin Horn. Threats like Darabont. He began to wonder if the dance was less of an indulgence and more of a celebration of survival and life. A celebration that pushed away the horrors of a time gone by. A celebration of clarity. The same kind of clarity he had longed for as he watched the sunrise at the station earlier that morning.

He also wondered if his bout of pneumonia had made him sentimental. He knew what Katherine had said about Mary had been true. Maybe Mary had fallen in love with a uniform and not the man in it. Maybe Mary was right to resent him for rejecting who and what he had once been. Until his dismissal, his years in the cavalry had been a simpler, happier time before mayors and investors and drunkards and men like Darabont were on the loose.

Perhaps his resentment about his dismissal was softening just a bit. Fighting Mary for so long hadn't gotten him anywhere. Seeing things from her point of view might.

The waves and salutes he drew from the happy old men in their old uniforms as he rode home made him reconsider his position. And for the first time in five years, he thought about putting on the uniform again. If only for one night.

He hitched Adair to the post in front of his house and began to walk inside.

Mary was already hurrying toward the door, a big steaming pot of stew in her hand. She wore his favorite dress—the green one he'd bought for her as a peace offering for a long-forgotten argument the year before—and her hair was washed and straight. She smelled of rose water and perfume, like Katherine had the day before, only not as nice. No one ever smelled as nice as Katherine.

He was about to pay Mary a compliment when she said, "There he is. The grand man coming home whenever he damned well pleases. I left a bowl of stew for you on the stove, knowing you'd think yourself too good to escort your wife to the biggest event of the year. And why should you? You've got more medals than the rest of 'em in there put together and here I am, your wife, sloppin' out stew instead of havin' the pleasure of dancin' with my husband as is my right."

She shifted the pot into her left hand as she buffaloed past him and grabbed the doorknob with her right. "Selfish bastard. That's what you are. Damned selfish."

And with a slam of the door, she was gone. She'd managed to fight and win the argument without Mackey even saying a word.

He hung his hat on the peg next to the rifle rack, placed his Winchester in the rifle rack, and headed upstairs. He walked into the bedroom he had once shared with Mary before she relegated him to the smaller room down the hall over a year before.

He opened the large chest at the foot of his bed

and gently removed the blankets and quilts Mary had piled there now that the nights had grown a little warmer. The chest had been the only bit of furniture that had survived her family's journey west.

He found his old uniform beneath some blankets. His sword and scabbard were on top and he lifted them from the trunk. It was the same sword with which he had led the charge at Adobe Flats all those years ago.

He gently laid the sword and scabbard at the foot of the bed and took out his tunic. He stood and held it against his chest as he looked at his reflection in Mary's long mirror.

He was surprised by the tall, gaunt figure looking back at him. The sunken eyes and gray specked stubble on his fallow cheeks. The years had not been kind to him, he knew, but why would they? He hadn't been kind to himself. He had been hiding for a long time.

And Aaron Mackey—the real Aaron Mackey—didn't hide from any man or any thing.

Not Darabont or his men. Not even the past.

He rubbed his hands across the stubble on his chin. Nothing a good bath and a shave couldn't fix.

Chapter 14

Two hours later, after a good scrubbing of both cloth and body, Captain Aaron Mackey stepped out onto the boardwalk of his house and pulled the door behind him.

His boots gleamed and his sword shone in his scabbard, jingling a familiar sound as he walked. His heavy army Colt was in the holster on his belt set high on his left side, butt facing out. He had always worn it that way on patrol, making it easier to draw the pistol while mounted. It wasn't a formal dress uniform, but the uniform of an active soldier. It was his, and it would do for the occasion.

The black hat had required a bit of brushing, but the brim was as straight as it had ever been. It felt good to be wearing it again.

Adair looked up from the scrub grass she'd been munching beside the hitching post. She hadn't seen him in uniform in five years, either, and raised her snout to catch his scent. She nuzzled her face against him when he untied her from the post.

"I know, old girl," he said as he stroked her neck. "Been a long time."

For the first time in five years, Mackey swung up into the saddle in full uniform. He brought Adair around to the south and rode down Front Street to the dance hall.

Many of the old timers and civilians hurrying to the gala stopped on the boardwalk as Mackey rode by. Many of them had seen him grown up and none of them had seen him in uniform since the day he'd stepped off the train. He felt himself blush as they smiled up at him. The old soldiers too surprised by the sight to even salute. Some of the young boys and girls did, and he returned the favor.

For the first time in a long time, and longer than his bout with pneumonia, Aaron Mackey felt good.

He saw Billy Sunday leaning against a porch post on the boardwalk just up the street from the dance hall. He had never worn his uniform since leaving the army, either, choosing to leave it behind when he mustered out of the cavalry and became a scout.

The deputy touched the brim of his hat. "Evening, captain."

Out of habit, Mackey offered a casual salute, then realized how ridiculous he looked. "Knock it off. Any sign of Darabont or his men?"

"Not unless they've disguised themselves as fat old men in uniforms on their way to a dance."

"Not likely. I meant around the town."

"Sim Halstead and I did a patrol while you were resting. He took one end of town and I took the other. We met in the middle and found no signs of anyone lurking around." He held up his hand. "And before you ask me, I went up to Hill House to make sure Old Wilkes and Andersson were on the lookout for Dara- bont's boys, too. They're both armed with about a hundred rounds a piece and they'll fire off a couple of shots if they see anything strange. I'll also start patrolling after the dance starts, so you . . ."

"We'll be patrolling together within the hour," Mackey said. "I'm just going inside for a little while to . . ."

"None of my business why you're doing it, Aaron. I'm just glad you're doing it. The present is hard enough without the past making it harder."

There were too many people milling around them on the boardwalk for them to have this kind of con- versation. He heard the strains of violin music and gladly changed the subject. "The Boudreauxs inside already?"

"Yep. Underhill didn't like it, but he's in there, too, keeping an eye on them. Fetched himself a new outfit from his rig just for the occasion. With all that yellow hair of his, he looks prettier than half of the ladies. He already glad-handed Mayor Mason and his investors from back east. Mr. Rice saw my star and asked me if you'd be coming by. He asked me to pass along his regards."

Mackey would make a point to talk to Mr. Rice once he was inside. There was something about the railroad man he liked, even if he was wealthy. Maybe it was because he seemed like the one man who'd come to town with intent instead of just words. "I'll be out of there in an hour at the most. If I'm longer than that, come get me. One of us should ride up to Hill

House to make sure the girls up there are okay come nightfall."

"Consider it done, captain."

Mackey ignored him as he rode down the street and tied Adair's reins to the hitching post in front of the dance hall. Granderson, one of Pappy's old comrades, snapped to attention at the doorway and offered a smart salute. "Welcome back, captain. And if I might say, you look beautiful."

Mackey returned the salute, then pulled off his gauntlet to shake the old man's hand. "No need for formality, Mike. Pappy inside?"

"Of course. The bar opened ten minutes ago."

Then that's where Pappy would be. Mackey walked into the dance hall and found men in uniforms from both the north and the south already mingling with each other. The dancing part of the evening hadn't started yet, but he was glad he had missed the formal ceremony of Gray meeting Blue in the center of the hall. He had always found the ceremony grating, even as a little boy.

The band was already in full swing with the two Boudreaux boys working their fiddles to the delight of the crowd. Underhill was watching close by. He spotted Mackey from across the room and gave him a slight bow. Mackey returned the gesture.

He spotted Mayor Mason on the left side of the hall talking to Mr. Rice, Mr. Van Dorn, and a few of the business owners from town. Van Dorn looked like he had recovered from the long train ride, but only just. Even in evening attire, he looked like a stiff wind might blow him over at any minute.

The sheriff found Sergeant Brendan Mackey at his

familiar station behind the bar. It had always his custom to serve the first round of punch to the guests before joining the party himself. He warned them all that it had a bit of a kick to it, but Mackey knew it had more than a bit of a kick. His old man had always had a heavy hand when it came to whiskey.

Pappy's old blue uniform still fit him, since he hadn't changed much—save for the gray hair—since the day he had left Sherman's command and come west. The medal congress had given him for his bravery under Sherman at the Battle of Smith Creek in Georgia looked as good as it had upon the morning he had received it.

Pappy blindly attempted to hand his son a glass of punch as he came up the line. "Be careful that you mind the punch. It . . ."

He dropped the glass back into the bowl when he realized his son was standing before him in full uniform. He looked his son up and down from head to toe. "Christ almighty, boy. You showed up. I never dreamed you'd . . ."

Then he remembered himself, snapped to attention and offered a salute. All the other men in uniform serving the chow did the same. "Evening, Captain . . . Mackey."

Mackey had always known his father had wanted him to come to the gala, but he'd never known how much until that moment. He returned the salute and said, "Evening, sergeant. At ease."

The old man pawed at his eyes with the back of his hand. "I've always wanted to be able to salute my boy."

"Knock it off and hand me some punch."

Pappy did, but couldn't take his eyes off his boy as he moved toward the chow line to find Mary.

He found his wife coming out from the back lugging a large basket of bread. She stopped short at the sight of her husband and slowly lowered the basket on the table before she dropped it.

For the first time in as long as he could remember, she smiled at him. Not because he was her husband, he knew, but because he was in uniform. The uniform. He was once again the man she had fallen in love with, not the man he really was. Just like Katherine had said.

"Aaron," was all she could say. "You look . . ."

The band began playing the first formal waltz of the evening. Mackey extended his hand to his wife. "Want to dance?"

She took his hand and placed her hand on his shoulder as they began to glide around the dance floor with some of the other couples. She wasn't as good a dancer as Katherine had been. Not by a long shot. But she was no longer the haggard, angry woman she'd been only a couple of hours before when she left their home.

Now, she looked up at him with a glowing adoration that he hadn't seen since after they'd been married. She normally looked thin and pale and close to fifty even though she wasn't even thirty yet. But as he held her as they danced, a youthfulness came over her that Mackey found quite remarkable.

As they danced, she ran her hand across the breadth of Mackey's tunic and the gold captain's bars on his shoulders. She forgot about the dance and threw both arms around his neck and held him tighter than he'd thought possible. She buried her face in his chest as she sobbed. "Where did you go, Aaron? Where did you go?"

He stopped trying to dance with her and put his arms around her waist. He was surprised he could feel the bones of her back through the dress. She hadn't let him hold her like this in over a year and she'd lost a lot of weight since then.

He put his cheek against her head and held her close as she gently cried into his uniform. She wasn't the angry, bitter woman she'd been before, but the young girl he'd fallen in love with when he'd returned home.

He stroked her hair and whispered that he loved her and for the first time in a long time, Aaron Mackey knew true peace.

And that's when he smelled it.

At first, he thought someone had left a roast on the fire too long in the kitchen.

But as the smell grew stronger, he knew it was a richer, thicker smell than burnt food.

He quickly picked his head up to smell the air better. He noticed Pappy had stopped doling out punch. He'd smelled it, too.

Underhill was on his feet and the Boudreaux brothers had stopped playing, though the rest of the band played on.

The smell wasn't coming from the kitchen. It was coming in the front door.

Mary protested as Mackey pulled away from her and began to walk to the door of the dance hall. When he got out to the boardwalk, there was no mistaking the nature of the smell.

A building was on fire.

Billy Sunday was already running down the opposite side of Front Street toward the jail. "Hill House is on fire and going up fast!"

One name flashed before his eyes.

Katherine.

She was up there helping one of the whores give birth.

Mackey ran back into the ballroom and yelled over the music, "We've got a fire up at Hill House. I need all available men to get up there as soon as possible."

Pappy bolted past him toward his store yelling, "I've got a flatbed and plenty of buckets at my store. Come help me load them."

Every man and most of the women broke into the street scrambling for horses and wagons. Mackey climbed into the saddle and swung Adair away from the fray and up the street toward the fire. He thought he heard Mary calling his name over the chaos but couldn't be certain. He didn't have to look behind him to his right to know Billy was already riding right behind him.

Mackey and Billy rode at the front of the pack up Front Street, then broke right at Lincoln Avenue, riding out of town past Katie's Place up toward Hill House. The building was a mile out of town and most of it uphill. Mackey knew Pappy's wagon would have a hell of a time making it up the hill quickly, but he'd get there.

Mackey could see the dim glow of the fire against the night sky just above the crest of the hill.

He didn't have to spur Adair on to run any faster.

The horse was already running flat out. Billy and his mount struggled to keep up.

As soon as he crested the hill, Mackey found Sim Halstead already there, his mount already tied to a small tree off the path. Sim threw up his hands and motioned for them to slow down, but he didn't have to. An invisible wall of heat prevented Mackey and Adair from going any closer to the house.

Katherine.

Mackey dismounted and had to fight to keep Adair steady as the entire building of Hill House succumbed to the inferno. Orange flames leapt through the broken roof and from every window of the two-story house. The sounds of wooden boards snapping under the intense heat echoed through the hillside. The walls of the house began to sag inward before the roof finally collapsed with a sickening crack, bringing the four walls of the house inward. The gray smoke drifted toward them, burning his eyes.

But despite the heat and the smoke, Mackey wouldn't look away. He owed Katherine that much.

Neither did Billy. "Jesus Christ."

Mackey kept watching.

As the wind shifted and began to blow the smoke and the heat toward the north. Mackey could hear the clamor of wagons and other riders coming up the hill from town. Sim Halstead tapped Mackey on the shoulder and pointed down toward a body at the foot of the stone path leading to the house.

Even in the shimmering light of the blaze, he knew it was the body of a man on his back with his arms and legs spread wide like a starfish. Mackey had seen enough corpses to know no one ever died like that.

Someone had placed him that way. Displayed him that way. And as his eyes grew accustomed to the flickering light, he saw that the man's hands and feet had been tied to pegs in the ground.

Mackey handed Adair's reins to Billy as he went to check the man for signs of life. He had to hold his hand out in front of his face to shield himself from the growing heat of the building. He crouched low to the ground and found it slightly more bearable there.

The man on the ground was Old Wilkes, still in his sergeant's uniform. His outstretched arms and legs had been tied to small stakes pounded into the ground. His body was crushed and broken and looked like it had been trampled to death by a herd of horses.

He knew this manner of death. Apaches usually killed this way.

Old Wilkes's mouth hung slack and both of his eyes were covered with a silver dollar coin. A paper note had been pinned to his blue tunic. Mackey yanked the paper from the pin and moved back to the edge where the heat of the blaze was a bit less intense.

Mackey showed the note to Sim. "Did you read this?" The silent man nodded.

By the light of the flame, Mackey read the handwritten note to Billy without reading it first himself:

Sheriff Mackey—
   As I don't believe in free advice, please accept the dollars I have left on Mr. Wilkes' eyes as payment for the wise words you offered me in front of your home yesterday. I've also helped relieve your town's moral burden by taking some of the whores of Hill House with me. They should bring a hefty price.

I know you felt cheated when we took the bodies of our murdered friends with us last evening. That's why I left a few people in the house to burn. I'm sure they'll make lovely additions to your garden.

I set pen aside, assured in the knowledge that you'll try to stop me. In fact, I'm rather looking forward to it.

> With Warm Regards,
> Darabont.

P.S.—The pregnant whore foaled. It was a girl.

Billy kept looking at the burning house. "Damn."

Mackey folded the note and slipped it into his saddlebag.

Sim kept a look out for the other riders coming up the hill behind them.

Mackey watched the flames engulf the remains of the house. He didn't know if Darabont had taken Katherine or if she was still inside. He didn't know if the girl and the baby were still inside either. That was the damnable horror of it.

That was what Darabont had wanted.

Underhill and some of the townspeople came up the hill just ahead of a dozen other men on horseback. Pappy was whipping a team of horses pulling his wagonload of sloshing buckets from his store up the hill.

The heat from the burning building kept the men and horses at a tight ring around the top of the hill. Pappy brought his team up beside Mackey and threw the brake on the wheel.

"It's burning too hot," Pappy said. "We'll never get near it."

Mackey handed Darabont's note up to his father. "I think that's the general idea."

Pappy read the note, then looked up at the fire. "My God."

Mackey stared at the burning building and took a step closer, ignoring the heat and the smoke of the shifting wind.

Katherine.

Chapter 15

As the sun began to rise the following morning, Mackey's blue tunic was filthy, as were the tunics of all the other former soldiers and the clothes of the regular citizens who had worked through the night to clear the smoldering rubble of Hill House.

The remains of the house had burned for more than three hours throughout the night before it cooled down enough for the men to get close enough to dump Pappy's buckets of water on the flames. A pump out back hadn't been damaged in the fire and a line of men passed full and empty buckets to and from the pump. Several torches had been set up to make sure the men had enough light by which to work.

Mackey spotted Mr. Rice at the front of the line working the pump, passing buckets along as soon as they were filled. Mr. Van Dorn was right behind him. It was a sight that Mackey knew should have surprised him, but didn't.

As the flames had gradually begun to die down and the rubble had begun to cool, Mackey, Billy, and some of the others tied ropes around the biggest pieces of rubble and had the horses pull them away. There was no need to be gentle. No one expected to find any survivors in the remains of the inferno. Darabont would have never left anyone alive.

It was already close to seven in the morning by the time the largest parts of the rubble had been cleared. A thick cover of haze and smoke had settled over the hilltop, blurring everything around them, including the sunrise. The women, led by Mary, had brought up coffee and food from the dance hall. They had also thought to bring up blankets to cover the charred remains of the people they had found inside.

Frontier women were nothing if not practical.

So far, the burned remains of seven people lay beneath blankets in the back of Pappy's wagon. Four women Mackey believed to be prostitutes. Two men, one he believed to be the Swede. And a blanket with a much smaller bundle beneath it. The infant Darabont had written of in the letter he had pinned to Wilkes's chest.

The veterans of Dover Station had already brought Old Wilkes's remains back to town.

Eight bodies in all. So far, none of them had been Katherine.

So far.

After a night of grizzly labor, most of the townsmen were exhausted. Many sat in various places around the rubble, drinking their coffee in quiet solemnity as the coming dawn brightened the sky around them.

But Mackey had no time for coffee. He hadn't found Katherine yet, so he ignored his own fatigue and kept working. So did Billy. And so did Sim and Underhill.

No one had any idea of how many other bodies might still be in the debris, or if they did, none of the townsmen had the decency to admit to it.

The dead people beneath the blankets in the back of his father's wagon were the charred remains of those he had sworn to protect, but didn't. Much like Nero, he had been dancing while his people burned. He had indulged in fantasy and nostalgia and guilt of a by-gone age while his own citizens were being slaughtered by Darabont's men. But at least his father had seen his son in uniform and his wife had one last night with the man of her dreams. Unfortunately, that man wasn't Aaron Mackey. Not anymore.

He knew he should have thanked God that Katherine hadn't been one of the women he had pulled out of the rubble. But Mackey wasn't in the mood to thank God. If she wasn't in the rubble, then Darabont had taken her with him, and he cursed himself for wondering if being dead might not be a better fate than being Darabont's prisoner.

As Mackey and Billy pulled another piece of debris from the pile, they saw Doc Ridley and Mayor Mason approaching him slowly. They'd been on the hill the entire time, as well, helping with the effort as best they could. Mason's shirt was black and filthy as was Ridley's gray Confederate tunic.

When Doc Ridley spoke, his voice was deep with emotion and smoke. "If it's any comfort, all of the victims appear to have been dead by the time the fire started. I can . . ." He paused to clear his throat. "I believe they were all shot before they burned."

Billy's movements faltered for the first time all night. "And the little one?"

"Given its size and condition," Doc Ridley explained, "I believe it was stillborn, thank God. I never thought I'd ever say a thing like that, but in this case, it's the most Christian thought I can have at the moment."

Mackey pushed aside a large piece of charred timber. "Nothing Christian about what happened here last night, Doc."

This time, it was Mayor Mason who cleared his throat. "I heard there was some kind of letter pinned to Wilkes's shirt, Aaron. I'd . . . I'd like to read it."

Mackey grabbed another piece of debris and threw it to the side.

Doc Ridley glared at Mackey. "Don't waste your breath asking him for anything, Brian. He won't show it to you because he knows what it says. It says the monster who did this was getting back at the good sheriff for killing his friends the other day."

"The men who set the fire are responsible for this," Mason said. "Not Aaron. It's been a raw night for everyone involved." He cast a look over at Mr. Rice, who was still manning his station by the pump. Of all four investors, he was the only one who had ridden with the rest of the townspeople when the fire broke out.

Doc Ridley stormed away as Mayor Mason nervously wiped his blackened hands on his blackened shirt. "I . . . I'm sorry about that, Aaron. You and I have had our differences, of course, but . . . Ridley's wrong. I . . . I'm sorry. Please let me see the letter whenever you're of a mind to."

Mason moved away to join the doctor.

But Mackey didn't move. He just kept looking at the pile.

"Sorry I didn't keep them away," Billy said. "Doc Ridley's a good man, but he's wrong."

Mackey threw a final piece of debris off the pile and stood up. "No, he's not."

Underhill handed Mackey a canteen full of water. The sheriff took it, but didn't drink from it.

"I think we've found everyone there is to find, Aaron," Underhill said.

Mackey knew he was holding a canteen, but drinking from it was the furthest thing from his mind. He looked at the debris area and saw most of the large piles had been pulled apart by the various work crews on the site. He could see charred ground and the smoldering remains of the foundation of Hill House. He thought Underhill was right. They'd probably found everyone there was to find.

Mackey handed the canteen to Billy without touching it. Billy took a healthy swig. "I've got to agree with Underhill, Aaron. I think we found everyone. It's cold comfort, I know, but . . ."

"Yeah." Mackey looked at the seven blankets in the back of his father's flatbed wagon. "If there was anyone else, Darabont took them with him."

Billy handed the canteen back up to Mackey. "What do you want to do next?"

Again, Mackey took the canteen, but didn't drink. The sight of the seven blankets haunted him; the smallest most of all.

"I'm going to kill him, Billy. I'm going to kill him and everyone whoever rode with him." He took a deep pull from the canteen, gargled it to clear his throat, then spat the rest of it into the pile. "I'm going to kill them all."

Sim snapped Mackey out of it by reaching up and

quickly tapping him on the shoulder. Sim never spoke. He never touched anyone either.

Mackey looked at where Sim was pointing. The other men of the fire brigade gasped as they saw it, too.

The gray smoke of Hill House had begun to clear enough to reveal the upper portion of the hillside.

And the bodies of three of the men they had shot the other day, crucified on wooden planks.

Townspeople gasped as the sight slowly came into view.

The fat man had been placed on the middle crucifix, with two others flanking him, exactly like biblical paintings portrayed Jesus and the two thieves on Golgotha. The two youngest gunmen had been propped up at the foot of the fat man's cross. Their bodies buffeted by the morning wind.

"Jesus Christ," someone said.

And once again, Billy spoke for Mackey. "Jesus got nothing to do with this."

Chapter 16

Most of the men who had worked the rubble eventually made their way to the Tin Horn once Mackey told them to go home. Many began drinking away the images of what they had seen that night. They were still in their clothes from the gala, but there was nothing festive about them. Each man looked dark and grimy. Their minds needed cleansing before their bodies or clothes.

Those men who had been working on the pile told the few who hadn't been on the hill about what they had seen and done. They spoke about the destruction of the whorehouse and removing the charred remains of the whores they had pulled out of the ruin. Of the baby, too. The Tin Horn's sporting girls gasped at the tales. Most of them went up to their rooms without customers. A few drank at the bar without soliciting business. And Sam Warren, in a move contrary to his entrepreneurial nature, allowed them to do just that. He even made sure every one of the workers drank their fill for free.

Doc Ridley was already a good part of the way through a bottle on his own, but insisted on paying his way. Sam Warren didn't argue with him.

Any chatter died away when they realized Sheriff Mackey had just walked in to the saloon flanked by Billy, Sim, and Marshall Underhill. Pappy trailed in behind them at some distance.

The sheriff took his time looking over the crowd, making eye contact with every man he could. His own face and tunic was smeared blacker than anyone else's in the Tin Horn, making his face appear even thinner and sharper than the pneumonia already had.

But when he spoke, his voice rang out strong and clear. "I know all of us have had a rotten night. A lot of you worked hard up there without rest or complaint, and for that I'm grateful. I wish our job was done, but it isn't. Far from it. After we bury those people tomorrow morning, Marshal Underhill and I will be riding out after the men responsible for all of this. Darabont and his men will have a couple of days head start on us by then, but we'll be traveling light and with a smaller group, so I expect we'll catch up to him pretty quick. Sim Halstead has signed on as our tracker. His reputation speaks for itself. I'm announcing that anyone else who wants to come along will be welcome. A two-week's supply ought to cover it. The town will pay all your expenses."

Mayor Mason, the least filthy of the men who had been on the hilltop all night, practically leapt to his feet. "No just hold on a minute, Aaron. The town can't . . ."

"The town's not paying for anything," a single, weary voice rang out from the back of the room. "I am."

Everyone turned to see two men at a table. Their skin and clothes were blackened by as much soot and grime as most of the others in the Tin Horn. Their evening jackets and starched collars were gone, their silk top hats forgotten and their dress shirts were blacker than they were white. One of the men's walking sticks leaned against the wall at his side, though even its brass handle had lost its luster.

The thinner of the two men was Silas Van Dorn. He was staring down into a glass of whiskey he hadn't touched.

The man who had spoken was Frazer Rice and he poured himself another glass of whiskey. "Provisions, bullets, mounts, men, anything you need, Sheriff Mackey. Buy up ever damned bit of ammunition and food you can carry. You buy it. I'll pay for it. Whatever you need while you're out there, you wire me and you'll have it."

"The wire's been cut," someone said.

"Then we'll make it our first priority to get it back in order," Rice said. "Tomorrow, right after we bury those people."

A low murmur went through the saloon as Mayor Mason said, "But Mr. Rice, that's liable to be a steep price."

"Price of justice is always steep," Rice said. "I'd ride out with the sheriff myself, by God, if I didn't have this damned knee holding me back. But just because I can't go personally doesn't mean my money can't do some good in my absence. Spend what you need, Sheriff Mackey. The firm of Rice and Van Dorn will back you all the way."

Silas Van Dorn nodded in distracted agreement.

Another murmur rose from the crowd before someone said, "All that money to avenge some dead whores?"

Rice took a slug of whiskey from the glass. "Whores? Maybe. They're worth avenging as much as the men who died protecting them. And that infant, too, who never did anything wrong to anyone except being born at the worst possible moment. And to bring Mrs. Katherine Campbell home where she belongs." He poured himself another shot. "Now, if the man who just said that has the balls to walk over here to my table and repeat it, I'll be happy to cave in his skull with my cane."

The crowd murmured, but no one stood up.

Mackey doubted anyone would, so he said, "You've heard Mr. Rice's generous offer. Now, I've known most of you people my whole life, so I know a lot of you agree with whatever that idiot mouthed off about dead whores just now. A lot of you think Mrs. Campbell is just a stranger to these parts. None of them are worth risking your neck over, especially against a bunch like Darabont and his men. But if this bunch took Mrs. Campbell, there's no telling how many other women these bastards might've picked up with them along the way here. There's no telling how many more they'll pick up on their way down to Mexico, if that's where they're headed. The kind of men who did this to us will keep on doing it until someone stops them." He realized he wasn't reaching them, so he added, "And they're not above coming back and doing it again if they think they can get away with it. Next time, maybe they'll kill someone you feel is worthy of your vengeance."

Again, he looked as many men in the eye as he could. "Whether or not you decide to ride out with us tomorrow is on your own conscience. I won't ask again, and I'll be goddamned if I beg any of you to go. We'll be riding out after the burial services tomorrow. The rest is on your conscience."

Mackey and the rest of his party walked out onto the boardwalk, leaving his words to sit with the men of the Tin Horn.

Whether or not any of them would take root was beyond Mackey's knowing or caring.

He knew what he had to do. That was enough for him.

When they all got back to the jailhouse, Billy was the first to speak up. "I'm going with you."

"So am I," Pappy added.

"No you're not. Neither of you." Mackey tossed his hat on the desk and sat down. "I need both of you here to keep an eye on the town while I'm gone. Underhill and Sim are all I need, plus whatever volunteers we get between now and tomorrow morning."

Billy clearly didn't like it, but he held his tongue. He'd talk to Mackey about it later.

Pappy, on the other hand, didn't hold his tongue. "Jesus, Aaron. You need us . . ."

Mackey slammed his hand down on the desk. "Goddamn it, for once in your life don't argue with me. Yes, I need you, but I need you here."

"Like hell you do."

"When word gets out about what Darabont did here," the sheriff said, "there's liable to be some bastards who think this town has become an easy mark again. We still need people who are going to keep that from happening, and those people are you and Billy. I let this town down once because of my own foolishness. I won't let it happen again."

"Your own foolishness?" Pappy repeated. "You mean about going to the dance last night? Christ, Aaron, that wasn't your fault."

Mackey pounded his desk again. "Enough!"

The sound was enough to finally quiet his father.

Mackey ignored the growing ache in his hand and looked up at Underhill. "You'll be ready to ride after the service tomorrow?"

"Hell, give me half an hour and I'll be ready to ride today." Underhill looked back at the empty jail cells. "I know you'll want to get some rest now, but we'll need to talk about the Boudreauxs between now and then."

"They'll be coming with us. Not as your prisoners, but as members of the search party."

Underhill stood a little straighter and thumbed his hat a bit farther back on his head. "I don't like that, sheriff."

"I don't give a damn, marshal. Those boys are fine trackers, almost as good as Sim and Billy here. Since Billy isn't coming, I want them with us. Besides, if the shooting starts, you'll be damned glad to have them." He looked at his father and the marshal. "Now, kindly get the hell out of here. I've got plenty to do before tomorrow and I can't do it with a room full of people gawking at me."

Pappy stormed out of the jail, and Underhill went off to see to his horse. Sim went wherever Sim went when he wasn't there. He didn't need to be reminded to be ready to ride. Sim was always ready for anything.

Billy was the only one who hung back, sitting quietly at his own desk near the stove. Mackey hadn't meant for him to clear out, and Billy knew it. After a time, he said: "You need me with you on the trail, Aaron."

"I need you here more. If things get hot while I'm gone, Pappy's liable to start running the town like a fort. He's a good man. Capable, too, but he needs minding and you're the only man I know he'll listen to."

Billy got up and poured himself the remains of the previous night's coffee. "I've never disobeyed you, Aaron, even when I've disagreed with you. I've got no intention of starting now. I just need to know you're going after Darabont for the right reasons."

Mackey looked at him. "Meaning?"

"Meaning I know how your mind works, and I know how things can get fixed in your head, sometimes the wrong way."

Mackey felt himself beginning to get annoyed, even at Billy. "Meaning?"

"Meaning you can't blame yourself for Darabont burning down Hill House last night. I was outside the dance hall and didn't know anything happened until I smelled the smoke and saw the flames."

Mackey felt his own breath catch as he remembered the smell. "And if I'd been there?"

"You'd have been splayed out with a note pinned to your chest instead of Old Wilkes, and Katherine would still be with Darabont. You're not angry because of the dance. You're angry because you know I'm right."

Mackey watched his right hand ball into a fist on his desk. "I'm angry because Darabont looked me in the eye in front of my own house and still thought he could do this to me. To my town. To my people." His hand reddened and began to tremble. He forced it open and laid it flat on the desk. It hurt enough already. "I can't let that stand, Billy. And I can't let them get away with what they did to Katherine."

Billy drank his cold coffee. "If it's really you they're after, ever think they might've done this to draw you out of town so they can nail you on the open road?"

"That's why I'm leaving you here," Mackey admitted. "They get me, they've still got to go through you."

Billy set his coffee cup down on his desk. "I'd prefer to face him together. Like we've been doing all these years."

"I should've killed the son of a bitch the first night I saw him."

"You couldn't do that," Billy said. "You know that. And so did he."

Mackey did, indeed, know that. He looked at the long shadows thrown by the barred windows across his desk by the late morning sun. "Yeah, well, in a few days, it won't matter either way. Because either you or me is going to kill that son of a bitch, Billy. That's all that matters now."

Chapter 17

"My darling!" Mary said as she rushed to him as soon as he walked into their home. She was always fussy about cleanliness, especially about his boots tracking in mud from Front Street. He was surprised she ignored the grime of his clothes and embraced him; holding him as tightly as she had at the dance. He realized that dance had only been a few hours before, but it already felt like a lifetime ago.

"Did anyone tell you how magnificent you were last night?" she asked. "How incredible you were? While everyone else was running around wondering what to do, you set things in order and did the best you could. You were simply magnificent, my love."

He wasn't in the mood for compliments. He placed his hat on the newel post of the stairs. "I'm not feeling particularly magnificent right now."

"I know." She ran her fingertips along the back of his filthy blue tunic. "But you were, Aaron. You were. You took charge and did the best you could. That's all you could do. That's the man I love."

He eased himself away from her. "That's the man

I've always been. Every day since the day we met." He began to unbutton his uniform. "I just wasn't wearing this damned thing at the time."

She turned away from him. "What the hell are you talking about?"

"Nothing." He had neither the strength nor the inclination to argue. Not now. Not with her and certainly not about this. "All it means is that I'm tired, Mary. Tired all of the way down to my bones, and all I want to do is climb into bed and sleep for a while." He reached out to her and put a hand on her back. "I'd love it if you'd lie down with me for a while."

She didn't come back to him as he had hoped, but she didn't pull away like she normally did. She took his hat from the newel post and brushed at it with her hand. "Word is you'll be riding out after those whores tomorrow."

He closed his eyes. Her gossip network astounded him. He had made the announcement in the Tin Horn less than half an hour before. The only women in the bar at the time had been whores, yet Mary already knew what he had said. "I'm not riding out after the whores, Mary. I'm riding out after the men who attacked our town. Our way of life." He was careful not to mention that Katherine had been kidnapped, as he knew that would be the focus of her rage.

"No one attacked us," she said, "nor the town proper, neither. They burned down a whorehouse way out at the edge of town and burned a couple of whores and the men who worked for them. You act like they burned city hall or a church."

"The edge of town is still in town limits," he said. "And those women lived here. One of them gave birth here and that infant will be buried here. Old Wilkes was up there, too. Maybe you don't think the women are worth much, but I know you cared about Wilkes."

"Wilkes was only up there because of her and it's *her* you're really going after, isn't it?" she said. "Your bloody Katherine."

"Mrs. Campbell happened to be up at Hill House helping one of the girls give birth. The baby we're burying tomorrow was most likely hers. It looks like Darabont's bunch took Mrs. Campbell and maybe some of the other women with them."

"Which is why you're going after them, isn't it?" Her eyes reddened but no tears came. Mary always came close to tears, but never actually cried. "To bring her back here."

"I'd ride after Darabont even if they'd left everyone in the house dead because that's what I'm supposed to do. Men like this can't be allowed to run around loose, Mary. They can't keep . . ."

"The people of this town pay you to protect the town," she said. "They don't pay you to go riding off to bring back a bunch of goddamned filth no one cares about anyway."

"Filth or not, they're our people. If I let this go, who'll bring them back? And who's to say the next group like Darabont's crowd won't do something worse the next time? Underhill said he'd heard about Darabont's bunch as far south as Texas. They might've been doing this kind of thing dozens of times in dozens of places throughout the years. They've gotten away with this for too long and now it's time for someone to stop them."

"And if they've done this as long as you and Underhill say, then why do you need to be the one to stop them?"

"Because that's who I am. That's the man you married."

She laid his hat back on the post and wiped her hands on her apron. "Well, it's not who I am. And I'm not sure I'll be here when you get back."

Mackey didn't know what to say to that. He wasn't sure he was supposed to say anything at all. He simply went upstairs and closed his bedroom door behind him. He heard Mary's sobbing from the parlor as he got undressed.

Chapter 18

Beneath a slate gray sky the next morning, Doc Ridley stood beside the six fresh graves, clutching his worn Bible against his chest as his black frock coat billowed in the wind. He finished his final blessing over the remains of the dead before he croaked his way through the hymn "Rock of Ages." The few townspeople who had attended the ceremony did their best to lend their voices to the feeble effort.

Mackey did not. Neither did Billy or Underhill.

Mackey knew more people should have come to pay their respects. He resented the veterans who had insisted on burying Old Wilkes the following day on their own. None of the men who had worked so long to clear the pile had bothered to come to a graveside ceremony for the whores or the infant or the Swede. Even Pappy had decided to sleep in that morning.

Doc Ridley had turned down the honor of presiding over the funerals at first, but the look in Mackey's eyes had changed his mind.

Mr. Rice's attendance was a pleasant surprise. He had manned the pump after the fire and had drunk with the men in the Tin Horn afterward. He'd also vowed to cover the town's costs for outfitting a posse to bring Darabont to justice. Now, he had come to the graveside ceremony of the town's least fortunate. Mackey began to wonder if there was more to this man than just a railroad and expensive clothes.

While Doc Ridley and the others sang their hymn, Mackey glanced over at the portion of the cemetery some called Mackey's Garden. There were no fresh graves in that part of the graveyard. He had ordered the five men Darabont had staged on the hill to stay where they had been placed. He had no intention of burying them in town limits. The birds and worms would get to them soon enough and they were far enough out of town to keep the stench to a minimum.

When the final prayers had been said and the gravediggers began to fill in the graves, Billy and Underhill trailed Mackey as they rode back to town from Boot Hill.

"Any idea on how many men we got?" Mackey asked Underhill.

"Boudreaux brothers make two. You and me make four. Five if you count the quiet fella Sim Halstead."

Mackey hadn't expected dozens, but he'd been hoping for more than that. "That's all we've got?"

"Two old drunks from the Pony House offered to sign up for drinking money," Underhill said, "but I decided to decline their gracious offer. A couple more of your father's friends offered, too, but the trail's no place for a bunch of fat old men with creaky bones."

Mackey held down another coughing fit. Such bouts were slower in coming and happening less frequently. "We might regret that decision before all this is over."

From behind them, Billy said: "Riders coming, Aaron. Looks like Jeb Taylor and three men."

Mackey looked down the road and saw the rancher leading three riders he had never seen before. He watched them ride over to the jailhouse, where they hitched their mounts to the post.

When Mackey and the others reached the jail, Taylor said, "I heard you're looking for men to ride out with you after those bastards who burned down Hill House and took those women."

"Looking for good men," Mackey said, "and willing."

"Well, that's just what I brought you." Taylor thumbed back at the three men with him. Mackey could tell two of them were Mexican and looked to be in their mid-twenties. The other one was a stout, red haired German man with a thick beard. He wasn't as big as Taylor, but plenty big in his own right.

"This here is Javier and Solomon," Taylor explained. "They're brothers, see? A couple of *vaqueros* who've been riding with me for more than a year now. Capable as hell and seem to know about this man you're pursuing."

Mackey had picked up a fair amount of Spanish when he had been stationed in Apache country, so he spoke to them in Spanish now. "What do you know about Darabont and his men?"

The older of the two men spoke first. "We aren't brothers, sir. We're cousins. Taylor thinks all Mexicans are related. He is an ignorant bastard."

Mackey liked him already. "I know he is, but I didn't ask you about him. I asked you about Darabont."

The younger of the two men said, "Darabont raided our family's ranch outside of Juarez while we were bringing our cattle to market. When we got back home, we found our ranch burned and all of our family dead. The women . . ." His voice faltered and he looked away.

Mackey didn't need to hear the rest. In English, he said to Taylor, "And who's the little man you've brought with you?"

"Calls himself Mattias Brahm of Bavaria," Taylor said. "Seems life on a ranch don't suit him much and he's itching to take part in something like this. His English ain't great, but he's strong as hell and can fight as good as he cooks, which is saying something because he sets a damned fine table."

"Beef stew is my specialty," said the German.

"Not likely to have the fixings for beef stew out on the trail, Mr. Brahm," Underhill said.

Brahm patted the large knife sheathed on his ample belly. "All I need is meat. I cut what I need."

Mackey might not have liked Taylor, but he'd never doubted his judgment in the quality of the men he hired to work for him. If he said these men were good, they were. "We're glad to have all of you with us. Marshall Underhill will be my second in command out on the trail. He'll take you over to the general store and see to it that you're outfitted properly. We'll head out in an hour."

And for the first time in the five years since he'd known the rancher, Taylor extended his hand to Mackey. "It's a fine thing you're doing, Aaron. I'm sure you'll catch all sorts of hellfire for doing it, but don't listen to them. Doing right ain't always popular. I'd be going with you if I didn't have the ranch to tend to."

Mackey shook the rancher's hand. "We'll bring your men back to you as soon as we can, Jeb."

"With Darabont's head in a sack, I hope." To Billy, Taylor said, "You need anything while he's gone, you know where to find me."

Billy said that he did.

Taylor unhitched his mount and swung up into the saddle. To his men, he said, "You boys are Taylor men from the JT Ranch. I expect you to act accordingly and make us proud." To the cousins, he said in Spanish, "And I'm not ignorant. Just a bastard."

Taylor spurred his horse and headed back on the road toward his ranch at a gallop.

With Taylor's three men, Mackey knew his force had just doubled in size. He figured Darabont's group still outnumbered him, but he'd rather be riding after them with eight men than with five.

The time had come to get things started. "Underhill, take these men over to my old man's store. See to it that they're outfitted with everything they need."

But Underhill was in no hurry. "Now just wait a goddamned minute, Aaron. I'm not your . . ."

The crack of a single shot echoed from the hillside.

Mackey looked up in time to see Taylor slump over his saddle horn. A second shot rang out and knocked him off his mount. His horse ran on back home as Taylor's body lay flat in the tall grass along the trail.

The three men Taylor had brought with him rode out to where their boss had fallen. Mackey, Billy, and Underhill rode out behind them. They came to a halt when they saw Taylor lying facedown in the tall grass. Two bullets clean through his back about six inches apart.

Mackey climbed down and rolled him over to see if the rancher was still breathing. His vacant eyes looked up at the high blue sky.

Two more shots rang out, the bullets striking the ground about a foot away from where Mackey stood. Billy and Underhill already had their rifles out, using their mounts as cover as they scanned the hillside for something to shoot at.

But Mackey didn't flinch or run for cover. Neither did Adair, who stood in the same spot where he'd left her. If the shooter had meant to hit him, he'd already be lying dead next to Taylor in the grass. He stood up and looked at the hillside instead. All he saw were the jagged rocks and boulders among the tall grass that led up to the top of the hill that surrounded Dover Station.

"That was some mighty fine shooting, wasn't it, sheriff?" a familiar voice echoed from the hillside. "Even by cavalry standards."

"Congratulations, Darabont," Mackey yelled back. "You just killed an innocent man."

"Don't be so naïve, sheriff. Innocence is a relative term. Surely they taught you army boys that back at the Point."

A round of laughter echoed throughout the hillside. Mackey tried to get a fix on where Darabont might be, but the contour of the valley made it impossible. "I figure you've got a point to make, so go ahead and make it while you still have time."

A single loud cackle came from the rocks above. "Christ, how I love your bravado, sheriff. I guess that's why I'm going to do my level best to make sure you die last. But I do have a point to make and, over the coming days, I intend on making it very loud and very clear. Not just to you, but to everybody in your pretty town. You people killed some of ours. You're going to learn there's a price for that. A price that can only be paid in blood."

Mackey walked closer to the hillside. "Billy and me are the only ones who did any killing, Darabont. You got a score to settle, then settle it with us. We'll meet you and your boys anywhere you want. Yours against mine, just like it was at the Tin Horn. It's only fair."

Another chorus of laughter rolled down the hillside, Darabont's grating cackle loudest of all. The sound was not unlike the yips he'd heard from coyotes and wolves at night on the desert plains of Apache country. He figured that was the point.

"Jesus," Underhill said loud enough for Mackey to hear. "There's dozens of them up there."

Billy kept eyeing the hillside. "Don't know that for sure. Echoes don't mean a damned thing."

Mackey didn't respond. He didn't move. He simply stood there alone, waiting for the laughter to die down.

"Fair has nothing to do with what's happening here, sheriff," Darabont went on. "You and I will settle accounts soon enough. Your nigger deputy, too. Got something extra special in store for him."

Billy fired at a rock in the center of the hillside. One of Darabont's men flinched from behind it, but not enough to present much of a target.

Darabont said, "What we've got planned for you folks is what your instructors back at the Point would call a good old-fashioned siege. No one comes into town and no one leaves. All your telegraph wires have been cut and my men have blocked the roads. Yanked out a good section of the train tracks north and south of here, too, so you can forget about anyone coming to rescue you by rail. We'll also kill anyone on the roads and that means stagecoaches, too. That dead man at your feet is only the first victim. There will be many, many more."

"That's a tall order for bunch like you," Mackey yelled back. "Anyone can burn down a whorehouse and steal women. Sieges take discipline. A lot more discipline than you think."

"Then it should prove to be an interesting experiment on both sides, won't it, sheriff?"

Barely moving his lips, Mackey whispered to Billy, "You got a fix on him yet?"

"No. I think he keeps moving around, high up among the rocks up there."

Mackey had figured as much. It's what he would've done if he were in Darabont's position. "How about you sprout a pair of balls and come out and face me. Man to man. Right here in front of all your men. You'll look like a big shot if you gun me down. Think of the songs they'll sing and the books they'll write about The Man Who Killed the Hero of Adobe Flats."

Rifle shots rang out from the hillside as bullets began to pepper the ground at Mackey's feet, but Mackey didn't budge.

After the shooting stopped, Darabont called out, "My men are impressed with death, sheriff. They're impressed by the amount of gold we take and how much blood we spill getting it. Don't worry. Your time will come in the manner of my choosing. Tell Mayor Mason I'll be sending an emissary down in due time with our terms. For now, you and your men can ride back to town without incident."

Mackey saw no point in standing there any longer. He climbed back into the saddle and led Underhill and Billy back into town.

They suddenly had plenty of work to do.

Chapter 19

Back at the jailhouse, Mackey brought Taylor's men inside along with Billy and Underhill. The first thing he did was unlock the Boudreauxs from their cell.

He knew he had to get men with rifles in place at both ends of town, but first he had to figure out what he had. In Spanish, he asked the two Mexicans, "You just saw your boss gunned down on the road. You still up for this?"

Both said they were.

"Either of you boys handy with a rifle?"

Both nodded again, with Solomon adding, "We have brought our own."

"Glad to hear it," Mackey said. "I need one of you take up position near the livery at this end of Front Street. I need the other one to go to the other end of town and takes up position on the top floor of Katie's Place in the room facing west. That'll give us a good vantage point if these bastards decide to ride into town from either end. We'll get more men into position as we get organized, but for now, you boys are it. I'll send one of the Boudreaux boys with each of you, too. I'll send Billy with you to square it away with Old Wilkes."

"Wilkes is dead," Billy reminded him, "but I'll talk to whoever's running the place. Make sure they keep quiet."

With everything that had just happened, Mackey had forgotten about poor Old Wilkes dying last night. His death should have been the worst event of the past year. Unfortunately, it he'd already damned near forgotten it.

To Billy, he said, "After you get Solomon and one of the Boudreauxs in position, get the mayor, Doc Ridley, and Pappy in here, but do it quietly. The town's probably already buzzing from the gunshots they've heard. If word gets out about this too soon, we'll have a goddamned panic on our hands. Darabont would like nothing better than to get people running out of here so he can set to killing. We'll fill them in on everything once they get here."

Billy, the two *vaqueros*, and the Boudreauxs got going, leaving Brahm, the German, and Underhill in the jailhouse with Mackey. The sheriff asked the German, "You any good with a rifle?"

The German teetered a thick hand back and forth. "Better with a pistol and a knife." He balled his hand into a fist the size of a small ham. "Even better with my fists."

"Let's hope you don't have to prove it before all of this is done. For now, I need you to mount up and keep an eye on the street for me. Warn anyone you see on the street to get back inside. Don't let anyone leave town. Drag them off their horse if you have to. Nothing gets out. Wagons, riders, no one." He dug an old badge out of his drawer, blew the dust off it and tossed it to him. "Pin this on. If anyone gives you any trouble, tell them to come talk to me."

The German left, leaving Underhill and Mackey alone in the jail.

Mackey could tell Underhill had something to say. "Spit it out, marshal. Might as well get whatever's on your mind out in the open."

"The current situation aside, the Boudreauxs are still my prisoners, sheriff."

"They're Darabont's prisoners, just like the rest of the town," Mackey said. "But you saw how close those boys came to putting a bullet between our eyes. They're two of the best shots in the territory and I need them out there doing what they do best. If they try to run for it, Darabont's men will shoot them down." Mackey went over to the small oven and began filling it with wood. He stuffed in an old edition of *The Dover Station Record*, struck a match and started a fire.

Underhill watched Mackey dig out some coffee grinds from the burlap sack and begin to brew some coffee. "What the hell are you doing?"

"Making coffee."

"The town's under siege and you're keeping house?"

"I'm keeping a semblance of order, marshal. Something you'd appreciate if you'd been through something like this before."

"You speak to me like I'm a tenderfoot. I've seen my share of blood in my time."

"That so?" Mackey set the coffee pot on the stove and faced him. "You ever been in a siege before?"

"Been in my share of tight spots."

"But not a siege. Because if you had, you'd know

the appearances of normalcy, little things like making coffee, are essential to maintaining order and morale within the besieged area. Whether it's a fort, or a town, or a squad pinned down in an arroyo, panic and disorder get you killed. Sticking to as normal a routine as the predicament allows leads to discipline and discipline increases our chances of living. Things like making coffee leads to people remaining calm and remaining calm quells panic. Panic kills."

Underhill folded his arms and glared out the window at the hillside. "We ought to be riding up there and gunning down those sons of bitches before they get a foothold."

"They've probably been dug in since last night. And we're not going to hit them until we have a better of idea of where they are and how many they are. The best time for that will be when Darabont makes his demands. Until then, you and that federal star on your chest are going to help me keep order."

"How?"

"By sitting right next to me and agreeing with everything I'm about to tell Mayor Mason and Doc Ridley. I want them to see the big, bad United States marshal backing me up and doing what I tell them to do. Agreement from you will make them less likely to argue."

"And keep them fancy investors at ease."

"They're the mayor's problem," Mackey said, though he doubted Mr. Rice would lose his cool so easily.

Billy came through the door with Doc Ridley, Mayor Mason, and Pappy in tow.

Doc Ridley was still wearing his black frock coat from the funeral service. The dusty Bible was still tucked under his left arm. "Thought you would've been on the trail of your whores by now, Aaron."

"Something's come up since then." He motioned to the coffeepot. "Coffee will be ready in a couple of minutes. When it is, I'd suggest you take some. You're going to need it."

Chapter 20

It didn't take long for Mackey to explain the situation. He kept the details sparse because he knew there would be plenty of questions.

He concluded by saying, "I want to move all the women and children into Harrington's press office. It's the sturdiest building in town and the printing equipment will give them plenty of cover if shooting starts."

Everyone agreed, though Mayor Mason looked paler than normal. "I can't believe Jeb Taylor is dead. Christ, he lived through Shiloh. Bull Run."

Pappy puffed on his pipe like he'd been discussing the weather with his cronies back at his store. "Didn't live through this Darabont bastard, though, did he?"

If Mason had heard him, he didn't show it. "How many of them are up there?"

"At least the four men he brought to my house to brace me the other night," Mackey said. "Probably a lot more than that. No way of knowing for sure yet."

Doc Ridley clutched his Bible as he slumped in his chair. "There'll be panic when word of this gets out."

"Not if we do it right," Mackey said. "That's why I need all three of you to quietly spread the word that people are going to have to stay indoors for a while."

"They'll want to know why," the mayor said. "They won't stay put just on our say so. They . . ."

But Mackey already had a plan. "Tell them we've got word of hostiles stalking the town, but keep it vague. Don't tie it to what happened at the Tin Horn or up at Hill House last night. If people think they'll get burned alive, they'll panic and just might get themselves killed."

Pappy took the pipe from his mouth. "I'll take to arming all the old soldiers we've got in town. Between the rifles I've got in my store and Mason's got at his, we should have plenty. Ammunition won't be a problem for a while, either."

"Get a handle on how many men are in town before you run around handing out rifles," Mackey said. "When you hand them out, hand them out quietly in your store and tell the men where we need them. I want them spaced out equally throughout town. That includes the side streets, not just at the ends of Front Street. I want good shots facing the hills, too. Darabont's not stupid, and there's no reason to expect he'll just come charging in at us from the thoroughfare."

"If he comes at all," Doc Ridley said. "Bastard could just sit up there and starve us out if he's of a mind to."

"It won't last that long, doctor," Underhill said. "You've got my word on that."

But Doc Ridley didn't look convinced. "Forgive me for not swooning at the assurance of federal influence, Underhill, but your assurances don't mean much. Not with the telegraph wires cut and the train tracks pulled. Right now, you're in the same mess as the rest of us."

Mackey had no interest in watching Ridley and Underhill spar. "You'll need to arm yourself too, Doc. I know you've become a peaceable man since the war, but these are not peaceable times. It'll mean a lot if the people see you fighting alongside us."

"Being peaceable doesn't imply cowardice, Aaron," Ridley said. "I'll kill whoever needs killing."

Mackey was glad to hear it. "It's important to re-member these men have already killed a lot of people and defiled their own dead. There's no way of know-ing what they intend on doing. They could start taking pot shots at people through their windows. Might conduct night raids to try to break our spirit and whittle us down a bit. Since we don't know what they'll do, we've got to be ready for whatever happens. If we have enough men, I'd like to have them watch the town in shifts."

"This is a fighting town, boy," Pappy boasted. "We built this town, and we'll defend it."

"There's something else." Mackey wasn't sure he should mention it yet, but since they were all in the same mess, he decided to level with them. "We still have one ace up our sleeve. Sim Halstead rode out at first light to scout out Darabont's trail."

"So?" Underhill said. "What kind of chance does one mute have against men like Darabont's bunch."

Mackey glared at him, trying to silently remind him of what they'd agreed to earlier. "Sim might not talk, but he's the best tracker I've ever seen. My guess is that he must have seen signs of a big party in the area and is scouting out Darabont's men. He's probably doubling back here toward us as we speak. I expect he'll make his way back into town come nightfall and let us know what he finds."

"Nightfall," Mason said. "God, the stage from Butte is scheduled to come in at five o'clock tonight. We need to warn them they're riding into a trap."

Mackey knew the stagecoach schedule. "No way we can do that unless Sim leaves some kind of sign for them on the trail. But they won't be his priority. Gauging the size of Darabont's force will be. Until then, we keep our heads down, get our defenses in order and wait for Darabont to make his demands."

"But what if this Sim is already dead?" Underhill asked.

"Then we won't be hearing from him, will we?" Pappy said. "But he's not dead. Sim's too smart to let himself get killed by the likes of Darabont's men."

"And there's Jeb Taylor's boys," Doc Ridley said, his voice thick with old Confederate pride. "Jeb's horse probably rode back to the ranch after he fell. They'll be riding out here to see what happened to him. And when they do, they'll bring thunder with them."

From his spot at the open doorway, Billy said, "I think they've got problems of their own, mayor." He pointed out toward the west. "Come look."

Everyone rushed to the door to see what Billy was pointing at. A thick column of black smoke billowed up from behind the trees in the distance. At about the place where Mackey figured the JT ranch house was located.

"Christ Jesus," Mayor Mason said. "It can't be. Taylor had at least fifty men working his spread."

Mackey wouldn't have believed it either if he

hadn't seen it. "Darabont probably hit them first before coming here. Fifty cow hands aren't a match for Darabont's crew."

"How can you say that?" Doc Ridley said. "Fifty men defending their home . . ."

But his voice trailed off as he looked at the thick, black smoke rising in the distant gray sky. It couldn't be happening, but it was.

Billy brought up his Sharps and moved down the boardwalk toward a man walking toward town. "Looks like we've got company."

Mackey saw one of Darabont's men walking down the trail toward them holding a torn piece of white cloth stuck on a thin tree branch.

The sheriff moved his holster closer to his buckle. "You men have a lot of work to do. Best be on about your business. I'll go see what this bastard has to say."

Chapter 21

Mackey recognized the messenger as one of the men who had been with Darabont the night he had come to his house—a toothless, scrawny man with long stringy hair and nasty eyes beneath a faded hat with a torn brim.

Mackey walked out to meet him where Front Street met the road out of town. He decided to leave his rifle back at the jailhouse in favor of keeping his hands free. The handle of his Colt jutted out over his buckle within easy reach.

The messenger stopped and waived his flimsy white rag at the sheriff. "Flag of truce, lawman. Means you can't hurt me none, least while I'm holdin' it. That's the law."

Mackey stopped at the edge of the boardwalk, which he figured was well out of range of Darabont's rifles in the hills. "State your business."

"You ain't the mayor. Mr. Darabont says I gotta speak to the mayor and only to the mayor."

"I'm as close to the mayor as you're going to get, so state your business or go away."

The messenger shrugged. "Don't make no difference to me. Just repeatin' what the man said to say." He dug out a piece of paper from his vest pocket and held it out to Mackey.

Mackey was too far away to take it. He wouldn't have taken it, even if he'd been closer.

The messenger said, "These here are what Mr. Darabont is callin' his list of demands. Mr. Darabont wants you to know these are his rules and his rules are final. He said that means you don't get to change them."

Mackey stayed on the boardwalk. "What does it say?"

"How the hell should I know? Can't hardly write my name much less read." The man spat a stream of tobacco juice into the thoroughfare. "But he told me he wants all the street lamps to get lit as per usual. That's important. Says if you keep the town dark, he starts torturing one of the women we got. Says you're supposed to give me your answer." He held the paper out to him again. "It's all written down for you right here better than I could ever tell it. Here. Take it, read it and give me your answer."

Mackey pulled his Colt and fired a single shot into the messenger's belly.

The man dropped his makeshift flag as he stumbled back a few steps before dropping to the ground, cradling his bleeding belly. "He shot me, boys!" he yelled out as loud as he could. He kicked at the dirt to try to get back on his feet, but kept falling down. "This son of a bitch shot me under a flag of . . ."

Mackey's next shot hit him in the head. As the man fell quiet, a strong wind picked up and took the letter he'd been clutching. Mackey saw it blowing eastward and away from town. He didn't go after it. He had no intention of reading it anyway.

From the edge of the boardwalk, Mackey opened the cylinder of the Colt, pulled out the two dead bullets and inserted two new rounds from his belt before snapping the cylinder shut.

A scattering of rifle fire broke out along the hillside. The bullets fell well short of the boardwalk, kicking up dirt as they hit. A few managed to plunk the messenger's corpse as the riflemen tried to find their range, but no rounds came close to the sheriff.

Mackey made a point of stepping on the white rag as he walked back to the jail.

When Mackey reached the jail, he found his father restraining a red-faced Brian Mason just inside the doorway. "What the hell is the matter with you? That man came under a flag of truce!"

Mackey walked past him toward the stove. He needed coffee. "Flag of truce only means something in an engagement between two armies. Brian. Darabont's men aren't an army so the tradition doesn't apply."

Pappy surprised him by saying, "You should've at least read Darabont's demands, Aaron."

"What for? He's going to do what he wants anyway. Besides, that bastard said Darabont was specific about keeping all the street lamps lit tonight. I planned on doing that anyway."

"He did?" Pappy relaxed his grip on the mayor's shoulder. "But why? He'd have an advantage in the dark."

"Who knows? Who cares?" He took a sip of coffee. The warmth felt good in his throat. "It won't make any difference. He's dug in up there and we're dug in down here. Just a matter of who makes the first mistake. And I believe he just did."

Underhill didn't look convinced. "How?"

As was his custom, Billy answered for him. "Because now we know where they're positioned. And how far they can shoot from where they are. Mighty useful information."

Underhill clearly still didn't like it. "What about the tradition of not shooting the messenger and all that?"

"Henry the Fourth," Mackey said as he sat behind his desk.

"Henry the who?" Underhill asked.

"More like Henry the What." Mackey poured coffee into his mug. "It's a play by Shakespeare. Don't worry, marshal. Darabont's an educated man. He appreciates the reference." He looked at Underhill and Pappy. "You two best get to work fortifying the town. They're liable to make a run at us just after nightfall. Take the mayor here with you. Help give the people a bit more . . . confidence."

The three men left, while Billy kept watching the street from the jailhouse window. His Sharps rifle was next to him, leaning against the wall. "You know I'd never speak against you in front of anyone, Aaron. Not even Pappy."

"I know. But you will now."

"Shooting that man puts you in a damned awkward place, especially if Darabont takes to torturing one of the women he's got."

Mackey sipped his coffee. "He's going to do what he's going to do, Billy. You know that."

"Sure I do, but one of those women is Katherine."

Mackey set his mug on the desk. "I know, but they're down a man and that might make a difference."

Billy kept looking out the window. "The town might feel different about it if they hear a woman screaming all night. They might start blaming you for bringing this on them in the first place."

Mackey set his mug on the desk. "Just means we'll have to end this damned thing before any panic sets in." He needed to change the subject. The thought of Darabont working over Katherine was too much for him right then. "You get a look at their positions when they started firing at me?"

"Yep."

"Think you'll be able to hit them from here?"

"Not from here. Too far away, even for the Sharps. But the Boudreauxs and me should be able to nail a few if we hit them from either the blacksmith shop or the livery."

Mackey thought of the man he'd just killed, lying dead at the end of Front Street. "Some might call what I did murder."

Billy spat into the spittoon by the door. "I wouldn't."

Chapter 22

Mackey might not have had much success in raising a posse to go after Darabont, but Pappy had managed to scrounge up forty townsmen willing and able to defend the town.

Most of them were former soldiers who had fought on opposite sides of the war, but Mackey knew that war had been a long time ago. They were different men now. Shopkeepers and townsmen; travelers and cow punchers in off the trail; loggers and miners who'd been in town for one reason or another and found themselves stuck there by Darabont's siege. Many of them had been friends of Jeb Taylor and Old Wilkes and customers of the whores who'd been killed. Some were kids who'd grown up listening to the war stories of their fathers and thought this might be their chance for a glory all their own.

It wasn't the army he wanted, but the only army he had.

Mackey and Billy had broken up the men into four shifts of ten men at a time, keeping watch around the clock. Mackey placed the men in a standard defensive formation in buildings around the town. All forty were ordered to come running to their assigned positions if any shooting started.

The rest of the men were either too drunk or too timid to be of much use unless Darabont's men rode down Front Street. Even then, they'd probably do more harm than good.

Mackey decided Dover Station was as ready as it could be. It probably wouldn't be enough against an all-out assault, but it was all he had.

The second shift of ten men had taken over for the two Mexicans, Brahm, and the Boudreauxs, taking up their positions at the head and rear of Front Street and all the buildings in between.

The first shift was drinking coffee in the jailhouse while Billy, Underhill, and Mackey were out on the jailhouse porch. Billy and Underhill were on their feet, rifles in hand, watching for anything to shoot at, but finding nothing. They kept looking anyway.

Mackey was in his rocker; his Winchester leaned against the wall to his right. He felt a tinge of weakness from his pneumonia, but he wasn't as weak as he had been only the day before. Fear and anger could do wonderful things.

He knew they might be out of range of Darabont's rifles, but his men would see them in front of the jailhouse. He wanted them to see how relaxed he was. He wasn't hunkered down somewhere. He appeared to be just a man in a rocking chair, at peace with his surroundings.

It was going on sundown and long, straight shadows were cast across Front Street. It was almost quitting time at the various businesses around town. Usually the street would be busy with people closing up shop and going home. But no one was going home tonight, and the shops were staying open later than they'd intended. Maybe all night because there was nowhere else to go. No one wanted to risk having Darabont's men loot their stores, either.

Mackey knew the stagecoach from Butte was due to arrive any minute. He wished he could've been able to warn them off somehow, maybe send a rider out to keep them away, but he couldn't. Maybe Sim Halstead had managed to tip them off, but he doubted it. Sim would've been busy with other things.

Thinking of the stage reminded him of Katherine and the other women Darabont had taken. He figured she'd be comforting the other captives if she could, keeping their spirits up. It was her way. It was who she was.

Mackey realized he was gripping the armrest of his rocker too hard. He opened his hands and closed his eyes as he willed his anger to subside. There'd be time for anger and rage, but now was the time for order and planning. He'd know more when Sim came back.

Sim *had* to come back.

He tried to distract himself by listening to Underhill talking to Billy. "How many of them you figure there are up there?" Underhill asked the deputy. "Your men were watching them the longest from both ends of Front Street."

"The Boudreaux boys counted about twenty on this side," Billy said. "Solomon counted as many from Katie's place. They couldn't get a clear shot at any of them, so they didn't waste the bullets, but they could see them up in the hills. Saw some cigarette smoke drift up from behind the rocks." He nodded toward the top of the hill. "My guess is they've got the captives up there somewhere. Probably got a wagon or something with the rest of their supplies."

Mackey watched Underhill mindlessly drum his fingers on the stock of his rifle as he watched the dying light on the hillside. The marshal was nervous. Mackey couldn't blame him.

Underhill said, "Bastards gotta move some time, don't they? Get something to eat. Take a dump. Stretch their legs."

"Most likely will do that when it gets dark," Billy said. "That's what I'd do in their place." He looked back at Mackey. "That's what we did, wasn't it?"

Mackey remembered. He kept rocking.

"At that Adobe Flats thing?" Underhill asked.

Mackey kept quiet and kept rocking. That was a different time and different place. Apache were different from Darabont's men. Disciplined and predictable. They hit hard and moved on fast. Darabont was no Apache. There was no sense in trying to relate the two.

Underhill kept talking the way nervous men do. "I stopped by the newspaper office earlier. Is your wife the skinny Irish girl with yellow hair?"

"Yep," Mackey said. "That would be Mary."

"She was whipping everyone into shape pretty good. Taking charge and getting everyone settled."

"Yep," Mackey repeated. "That would be Mary."

He looked like he wanted to say more on the subject, but didn't. That didn't stop him from talking. "Your buddy Sim must've gotten himself caught or shot. Probably would've been back by now if he hadn't."

"He's waiting until after dark to make his way into

town," Billy said. "He'll probably take care of a few of those bastards, too, on his way in."

Mackey saw that Underhill looked like he had more to say but had decided against it.

Mackey kept rocking, looking up Front Street; praying for dark. Praying for something to break.

Don't be dead, Sim.

The sun had just disappeared behind Snake Hill when it happened.

Mackey heard it before he saw it. The sound of a team of panicked horses running toward Front Street at a full gallop.

He'd just gotten to his feet when they came into view. The horses had good reason to panic.

They were hitched to a burning stagecoach.

Smoke and flame billowed out of the coach as the team of horses careened around the corner and onto Front Street. The coach bucked and rocked wildly as the four-horse team ran flat out in a useless attempt to escape the burning cargo they were pulling behind them.

Mackey yelled into the defenders drinking coffee in the jailhouse. "Get back to your positions! They'll be coming now. Shoot anything you see. Move!"

As the men spilled out of the jail and ran in their respective directions, Mackey watched the horses barrel toward the jailhouse, their bodies thick with sweat and their eyes wide with panic. The burning coach's wheels warbled and almost flipped over several times. If one of the wheels came loose on Front Street, the coach could slam into one of the buildings and start one hell of a fire.

That was probably what Darabont was counting on.
And there was only one way to stop it.

Mackey brought his Winchester to his shoulder,
aimed and fired at the two lead horses, then the two
behind them. Underhill and Billy did the same.

The team of horses buckled and crashed to the
ground. The burning stagecoach snapped loose from
the harness and tumbled over them, crashing onto
the hardening mud of Front Street. The burning
coach shattered on impact, sending burning embers
all over the boardwalk near the livery and the blacksmith on either side of the thoroughfare. One wheel
of the coach bounced free, burning as it wobbled up
Front Street until it fell over in front of the Tin Horn.

Rifle fire erupted from both ends of Front Street.
Mackey could understand a few of them getting jumpy
and firing at random, but not all of them at once.

Since the blacksmith shop was closer, he decided to
run there. Billy and Underhill were right behind him.

Mackey ran past the body of the messenger he'd
killed earlier that day. Bullets kicked up dirt at their
feet as they ran within range of Darabont's rifles. Two
of the townsmen were firing up at the hill, their bullets ricocheting off the rocks. The Boudreauxs fired
from the livery stable across Front Street. He remembered he had posted one of them down to Katie's
Place on the other side of town, but this was no time
to argue.

Mackey took cover in the doorway of the blacksmith's shop. He brought his Winchester to his shoulder; covering Billy and Underhill as they ran toward
his position. A bullet struck the front of the building,
inches away from his head. He spotted the shooter

crouching behind a distant boulder to his right, well out of range of the Boudreauxs' rifles.

But not his.

Mackey aimed at the boulder, waiting for the man to reappear for another shot. He figured the man was either reloading or hoping to flank the Boudreauxs' position at the stable. He hoped the dying sunlight held out just a little longer.

When the man moved, he didn't show much of himself, but enough for a man of Mackey's skill. The sheriff fired once and watched the man go down in a puff of red dust.

A series of loud, rebel yells and cheers echoed from behind him down Front Street. He figured Pappy's boys must be in the thick of it on the south end of town.

Mackey ducked into the blacksmith's shop and saw Underhill at the far left of the structure, looking for anyone trying to flank the building. Billy was at the center window, scanning the hillside for more targets with his Sharps.

"See any of them?"

Billy fired, and a man yelped in the distance. "Not anymore."

"What about you, Underhill?"

"I've got two over here, but they're biding their time behind the fence over there."

Mackey joined him at the window and aimed at where Underhill was targeting. It was a broken wooden corral whose bottom rail had dropped long ago, and the grass and weeds had grown thick around it.

Underhill said, "I think they're trying to get around to the cemetery and aim down at us from there."

Hoping to make them break cover, Mackey fired twice into the overgrowth. One of the men jumped as a bullet hit him in the leg. Underhill shot him through the chest.

The weeds moved as the other man crawled farther along the fence line.

Underhill fired again. The man cried out as he scrambled to his feet and made a dash toward the cover of the cemetery. Mackey fired once and brought the man down.

The man had fallen within range of Darabont's guns, but close enough for Mackey to reach before he died. He couldn't count on Sim getting back any time soon. He needed to get the wounded man to tell him how many were with him.

He laid his Winchester against the wall. "I'm going out there. Cover me."

Before either man could stop him, Mackey drew his pistol and darted out from the cover of the black-smith's workshop and ran toward where the last Dara-bont man had fallen.

Bullets flew in both directions as Mackey ran. He didn't think about how many times he'd almost been killed. He didn't dare.

He slid to a halt in the tall grass next to the man he'd just shot. He was bleeding from the leg and a gaping hole in the side of his chest. Mackey kept low as he quickly looked for other gunmen approaching from the rocky hillside, but saw no one.

The man was groaning, but Mackey shook him hard. "How many of you are up there? Tell me and I'll finish you quick."

"Like you finished ol' Phil?" The dying man coughed blood up at him, but missed.

Mackey undid the man's gun belt and hurled it back toward the blacksmith's shop. He did the same with the man's rifle. "Last chance. Chest wounds hurt like hell and can take a long time to kill a man. Tell me how many are up there."

"Too many for you townies to handle." The man tried to spit more blood at him, but dribbled on himself instead. "Darabont's gonna have fun with you, boy."

Mackey moved away from the man. He decided to use the tall grass and the dying light to his advantage. He stayed low as he crawled slow and steady to the other man who had fallen by the fence. The man was already dead, a hole in his throat. As he pulled the dead man's rig from his body, bullets slammed into the fence post next to him and in the rail above him. Mackey pulled the dead man's gun belt free as he scrambled back to the blacksmith shop.

Billy's Sharps barked twice and Underhill's rifle once and Mackey scrambled for cover.

Underhill didn't look happy to see him. "That was a damned fool thing to do, sheriff."

"I got their weapons and rigs. That's means two less guns and ammunition for Darabont and more for us. How many did you boys get?"

"Three that time," Billy told him. "Looks like our marshal friend isn't just pretty. The boy can shoot, too."

Underhill fed more rounds into his rifle. "My pile will be higher than yours before we're done."

Billy smiled as he reloaded as well.

Mackey asked the other townsmen how many they had killed. Between the group of them, they'd hit two. He went to the doorway of the blacksmith's and yelled across to the Boudreauxs in the livery. "How many you boy tally?"

"Two as they were coming down hill," one of the

brothers called back, though Mackey couldn't tell which. "There's one bastard still dug in behind a rock right over there."

Billy moved next to Mackey and said, "I think that bastard behind the rock was the one shooting at you just now. He can pick off anyone on the street from that position."

Mackey knew someone would have to flush the gunman out. And there was only one man who wasn't already in position. "I'll run across to the livery, try to draw his fire."

"From where he is," Underhill said, "it'll be awful hard for him to miss you. And you're liable to draw every rifle on the hill."

Mackey was counting on it. "Lucky for me you boys are such good shots."

Billy brought the rifle up to his shoulder and aimed at the hillside. "I'm ready whenever you are."

Chapter 23

As Mackey bolted from the blacksmith's shop, the hillside erupted with gunfire he hadn't seen since his days in the cavalry. Every shot hit well short of their mark, but he knew it only took one lucky round to make the difference.

At least now he knew why Darabont's men were so desperate to get down that hill.

They were too far out of range to hit the town.

Amid the gunfire, he heard the loud crack of Billy's Sharps as he dove through the doorway of the livery. He crawled back to the doorway and took a look back at the hillside. He saw the man lying dead in the dirt behind the boulder.

He saw Billy crouched low behind the window of the blacksmith's shop, trying to get a higher angle on the men on the hill. It would be a hell of a shot from that distance, but Billy had always been an artist with a Sharps.

Jack Boudreaux had taken up position behind a bale of hay. His brother was on the ground, preferring to fire from a prone position. Two of Pappy's men were up in the hayloft.

"How you boys holding out?" Mackey asked aloud.

They all said they were doing just fine. Henry said, "Good thing for you Billy picked off that bastard at the boulder."

From the hayloft, one of the men said, "You see that burning wagon those bastards sent in? Jesus, I never saw nothing like that in my life."

Mackey couldn't let them dwell on it. "That was just a distraction, boys. We've made them pay for it, and we're not done yet. We showed those bastards the men of Dover Station aren't just dairy farmers."

The men whooped and cheered, which had been Mackey's intention. To Jack, he said, "Think you can still find where Darabont's men fell after nightfall?"

"Sure," said the older Boudreaux. "But why?"

"Because I'll need you to strip their guns and ammunition before Darabont does."

Henry Boudreaux looked up at him from his spot on the ground. "What for? Hell, between what we got in Mason's store and at Pappy's place, we've got more than enough to go around."

"We do, but Darabont doesn't and that's the point," Mackey said. "The more guns and bullets he has, the longer this'll go on. If we cut into his supply of men and lead, we'll foul up his plan. He'll either give up or do something stupid. And if he does, we'll be ready."

Jack Boudreaux craned his neck to look up at the darkening sky. "Looks like it'll be a nice night for a stroll. Might bring Henry with me. Make quicker work of it."

Mackey didn't like that idea. "You two are the best

shots we've got. I'll need one of you boys to stay back
here and cover the other. I can't risk losing both of
you on something like this if something goes wrong."

"I'll go then," Jack said. "I'm the oldest. And better
looking."

"My ass," Henry said from behind his rifle.

Mackey drew more fire from Darabont's men as he
ran from the livery, but he was able to slow his pace as
he got closer to the jail. His lungs were finally beginning to ache again, and he didn't want to risk his
pneumonia coming back.

He passed the remnants of the burning coach,
where some of the men and women of the town had
begun trying to stomp out the flames with heavy
blankets. Mr. Rice was among them, closest to the
wagon. He figured no one had asked Rice to help, especially Mayor Mason. It was something that needed
to be done and Rice and the others took it upon
themselves to do it. Mackey knew that was why they'd
make it through this one way or the other.

He didn't bother to see if there were bodies in the
coach. If there were, they were already dead. Mackey
had to tend to the living.

He walked down Front Street, offering a few words
of encouragement to anyone he saw while reminding
them to stay sharp. He found the two *vaqueros* from
the JT Ranch along with Pappy and some of the other
men in position down at Katie's Place.

Pappy gave a report before Mackey asked for one.
"We nailed three of the sons of bitches as they came
down the hill. I think they were trying to get closer to

get better range on our position. They won't make that mistake again."

Mackey had never doubted his father's resolve, but he didn't share his confidence. "Did you send anyone on foot to check the west side of town?"

"No. Been too busy here to . . ."

"Stay here and keep your men ready," Mackey said as he headed in that direction. He fed new rounds into his Winchester as he walked. Darabont's men had already tried to flank their position from both sides at the other end of town. There was no reason why they wouldn't have tried the same thing at both ends.

Mackey moved slowly along the boardwalk. He realized Pappy was on the boardwalk across the street; his Winchester aimed at the ground as he covered his son.

He couldn't be angry at his father. That old bastard had never been good at following orders.

Mackey noticed a few scared townspeople peeking out from behind lace curtains and window shades. He nodded at each one he saw, hoping it might bolster their confidence, but unsure if it had any effect.

When they reached the corner of Grant and Jackson Streets, Pappy brought his rifle to his shoulder and fired at a man across the street. Mackey tried to get a bead on the man, too, but the man was already on his back. A small red stain began to spread on his dusty shirt.

Being a stopping point for stagecoaches and the train, Dover Station had a lot of people come in and out of town on a regular basis. Still, Mackey had a knack for recognizing anyone who spent any extended period of time in town. That's why he knew this man must've been one of Darabont's men. He had never seen this man before in his life.

Mackey signaled Pappy to check his side of the street for anyone lurking around the corner.

Pappy crept forward, rifle at his shoulder. A few steps later, he stopped and fired up Jackson Street. Mackey brought up his rifle as he turned the corner on Jackson and dropped to one knee. A man was running toward an alley behind Mason's General Store. Mackey fired and clipped the man in the leg just before he darted down the alley. The impact of the bullet caused the man to stumble but keep his footing.

Mackey managed to duck back behind the corner of the building as two more rifles appeared from the mouth of the alley. Bullets slammed into the wood where his head had been only a moment before.

From his side of the street, Pappy crossed Jackson, then Grant Street so he was directly opposite his son. Mackey knew his father might not have been good at taking orders, but he was glad the old man had disobeyed him this time.

He watched Pappy feed more cartridges into his rifle as he thought about the men in the alley. He knew it was more of a narrow courtyard than an alley, with a large wooden wall between them. The owners of the building grew tired of drunks using the alley as a shortcut to the saloons on the west end of town, so they'd agreed to put up a tall wooden fence to discourage trespassers. The fence had been shot at a couple of times, but, when Mackey last checked, still stood.

That meant the three men were still in the alley.

They were most likely desperate and most certainly trapped.

He'd like to grab one of them alive if possible. He'd like to get one of them to tell him what Darabont had in store.

After signaling Pappy to cover him, Mackey jogged down Jackson toward the alley. He kept his Winchester at his side as he paused at the mouth of the alley. He heard two men talking as they rattled doorknobs.

One of them said, "These bastards got everything locked up tight."

Another said, "Try busting a window or something. We're sitting ducks out here."

"We gotta do something quick before . . ."

Mackey rounded the corner and found one of Darabont's men holding up the man he'd wounded. A third man was about to break a window with his pistol butt.

Mackey brought up the Winchester to his shoulder and shot the man in the chest.

The second gunman allowed his wounded friend to drop as he grabbed at the pistol on his hip. Mackey levered another round and shot him in the head.

From his spot on the ground, the wounded gunman threw up his hands. "Don't shoot me again, goddamn it. I got a pistol on my hip, but I ain't going for it."

But that didn't make Mackey feel any better. "Unbuckle your belt with your left hand and leave it where it lies."

As the man followed Mackey's orders, Pappy rounded the corner. "Well, looks like we got ourselves a prisoner. We're gonna have lots of fun with you, boy."

"I'll cover you while you get him to his feet,"

Mackey said. "I'll run him down to the jail," Mackey said. "Get five of your men posted around this side of town. I don't want Darabont flanking us again. Make sure you adjust the relief schedule accordingly and make sure the men know it. I don't want them getting anxious and bleary-eyed."

"Jesus," his father said. "Feels like I'm back in the army. Any other orders?"

"Yeah. Grab these men's guns and ammunition. Add them to our stockpile. We're starting to cut into Darabont's supply of men and ammo. He's liable to hit us hard come nightfall and I don't want him getting back anything he lost."

"Christ, Aaron. I was just joking."

Mackey shoved his prisoner out of the alley. "I wasn't."

Chapter 24

The efficiency of the rumor mill of Dover Station
had always amazed Mackey, and it didn't disappoint.
The boardwalks were filled with townspeople who
had turned out to see Mackey walk the wounded prisoner up Front Street. They heckled and shouted and
called for the man to be strung up. Mackey kept the
prisoner moving.

He knew word of the men they had killed had
probably already spread through town. The number
of dead Darabont men had likely been inflated to
more than a dozen, though Mackey figured they'd
only killed about eight or ten. If it helped bolster town
confidence and stave off panic, he'd allow it to flourish. If it advanced to the point of fostering careless-
ness or a lack of vigilance, he'd clamp down on it.
Night was fast approaching, and Darabont was probably planning something special for the dark.

Mackey steered the prisoner past the still-smoldering
carriage in the middle of Front Street. A few of the older
women were crying on the boardwalk, being consoled
by their husbands at the sight of the carnage inside

the carriage. Now that the smoke had cleared, it was easier to see the charred remains of four people still inside the overturned coach.

Mackey pushed the limping prisoner up to the boardwalk and into the jailhouse where Billy and Underhill had cleared the boardwalk of any spectators.

"Got a surprise for you inside," Billy said as he followed them into the jail. "First bit of good news we've had in a while."

Sim Halstead was standing by the stove drinking coffee. Mackey wasn't surprised to see Halstead had found a way to get back into town before dark, even with all the guards posted around the perimeter. The former scout had a knack for finding a way to get wherever he wanted to go.

"Glad you made it back," Mackey said. "I'll be with you in a second."

Mackey threw the bleeding man into a cell and locked the iron door. "We'll get Doc Ridley to tend to your wounds after you start talking."

The wounded man grabbed the bars. "I ain't talkin' 'til this here wound gets tended to. After that, and a meal, I'll tell you anything you want to hear."

Mackey slammed his elbow into the man's fingers gripping the bars. The prisoner yelped and fell back on the cot. "Speak when spoken to or you'll die in that cell."

The man cradled his sore hands as blood had already begun to pool on the sheet from the leg wound. The prisoner grabbed his leg above the bullet hole to stem the flow of blood. "I seen what you did to Matty and Anson back there. You're one cold son of a bitch, mister."

Mackey went to the stove and took the cup of

coffee Sim handed him. "Tell me your name and where you're from."

"Name's Dan Berrie out of Nebraska."

"You one of Darabont's regulars?"

"Regulars?" Berrie scoffed. "Ain't nothin' regular about Darabont or anyone who rides with him. I fell in with them on the trail back north from Mexico about a month ago. Said they'd just finished cuttin' a swath a week wide and a month long through Texas and Oklahoma and would keep on going clear to Canada. Told me I could ride with them if I was of a mind to, and I was, so I did."

But Mackey didn't care about that. "How many of you are up in the hills now?"

Berrie shook his head. "Not until I see a doctor."

"Tell me or I gag you and shoot you in the belly. Doctor won't be much good to you then."

"About forty," Berrie told him, "give or take."

Mackey hid his disappointment. He had figured the number was closer to twenty, which would have been bad enough. Forty was even worse, even if he was down to around thirty after the earlier shoot-out. "If you want that leg wound looked after, I'll need more than 'give or take.'"

"Give or take is all I got, mister. We ain't never had attendance or nothin' formal." Berrie winced as he gripped his leg tighter. "Had nearer to fifty when we rode into the territory, but given the number you plugged the other day and today, I'd say you're lookin' at forty still up in them hills as of this very moment."

He decided forty was as close to the real number as he would get from Berrie. "What's Darabont's plan?"

Berrie laughed. "Hell, mister. Darabont ain't got a plan. We needed provisions and heard tell of this town of yours having lots of things we needed, what with the railroad being here and all. That's why we sent some boys down here to look the place over. When they didn't come back, Darabont took some men and rode down here to look for them. Guess that's when he ran into you."

"You guessed right."

Berrie winced as he flexed his hand before grabbing his bleeding leg again. "When he came back, he was madder than hell. That's why we hit that whorehouse up yonder. He burned it down and took them whores on a whim. Darabont set up them men you killed like Jesus on account of sending a message to you. Nobody planned it. He just decided to set a flame to it and take those women as we were getting ready to leave."

The image of Katherine bound and gagged against a wagon wheel flashed in his mind. "How many captives do you have?"

"About ten, including them whores we took from that joy house out yonder."

He could feel Underhill, Sim, and Billy watching him, but he asked his next question anyway. "Are any of the women hurt?"

"Not too badly. Darabont wants them healthy and pretty for re-sale down in Mexico," Berrie said, "or as near to Mexico as he can sell 'em off. He's real sure this high-talkin' gal we took is too old to sell, but might be worth keepin' on a while. Says she adds class to the outfit."

"Aaron," Billy said.

Mackey realized Sim had come to his side and put a hand on Mackey's rifle. He'd forgotten he was still holding it. And didn't realize he was beginning to aim it at Berrie.

Mackey pushed away from the cell and put his rifle back in the rack. He'd clean it later. In the meantime, there was plenty to do. To Billy, he said, "Might as well fetch Doc Ridley. Get that man's wound tended to."

"Don't have to fetch him. Been here since after you started your interrogation, but I made him wait outside. Didn't want him lousing up your flow with the prisoner."

Mackey nodded at the door. "Let him in. Better stay with him while he's working. I'd just as soon shoot both of the sons of bitches."

As Billy went back to help, Doc Ridley worked on Berrie's leg, Sim and Underhill sat and sipped coffee while Mackey read through the report Sim had written out. It had always amazed him that an old scout with little education had managed to keep such an elegant hand.

"I doubled back when I followed the trail this morning and saw that Darabont's men headed back towards town. Approximately fifty men are camped along the hillside in a crescent formation. No tents. Supplies and rations appear low, so expect them to try raiding the town for supplies. A couple of men were busy repairing rifles and pistols, so armaments appear to be in poor condition. An old covered wagon in the middle of their camp up in the trees. I heard women's voices in there, but couldn't see them. Too many guards near them to get close. I managed to sneak back into town during the shooting, killing one on my way down to get through."

Mackey set the sheets aside. Between what he'd gotten out of Berrie and Sim's report, he figured he had a close-enough idea of what he was facing and what Darabont might be planning. "We saw a column of smoke earlier. That Jeb Taylor's ranch?"

Sim nodded.

"Any survivors?"

Sim shrugged.

From the doorway, Underhill chimed in. "What about the miners? The loggers? Other people outside of town?"

Sim slowly drew his thumb across his throat.

"All of them?"

Another shrug.

Mackey knew what a shrug from Sim Halstead meant. If any of the loggers or miners survived, it wasn't enough to do the town any good. Not against a bunch like Darabont's men.

He sat back in his chair and hooked his heel under the lip of his desk. "The only way we're going to beat Darabont's men is to kill them ourselves. Can't expect any help from the outside. Not before Darabont makes his move, anyway."

Underhill cleared his throat, as if to remind them he was still there. "Since Darabont hit that mining camp, he might have grabbed any dynamite those rock scrappers might've kept up there."

Mackey knew even one or two sticks could wreak havoc amongst the wooden buildings of Dover Station.

"If they found any, they'll be using it on us come nightfall, especially if they're as desperate for provisions as Berrie said they are." He handed the sheets comprising Sim's report to Underhill. "From what Sim writes there, I've got a feeling this siege is more about them being broke than it is about avenging their fallen friends."

Underhill barely glanced at the pages. "So what?"

"So, desperate men are more predictable than vengeful ones," Mackey explained. "Less committed and more erratic. That charge they just made down the hill in broad daylight proves that out."

Underhill put the sheets back on Mackey's desk without even reading them. "Think they could've gotten anything useful off that stagecoach before they set flame to it?"

"It's possible," Mackey admitted. "This run usually just has passengers, but it could've been carrying money. Maybe a few rifles for some store further along their run. Not much in the way of food, though. Not enough to feed the forty or so men they've got left."

He remembered the image of the burned bodies in the coach right outside on Front Street and quickly put it out of his mind. The dead were better off, and Mackey had troubles of his own.

To Underhill, he said, "I'd appreciate it if you'd get an accurate account of the number of men we've killed on both sides of town. I'm figuring it's close to ten, but I want a hard number within the hour. Make sure all bodies within reach have been stripped of weapons and ammunition. I don't want Darabont getting a single round out of us if we can help it. Then have Pappy double up guards around his store and Mason's store to make sure Darabont can't pilfer anything."

The marshal seemed to appreciate the responsibility. "Think that old man of yours will listen to anything I tell him?"

"If he doesn't, tell him to come see me."

The marshal touched the brim of his hat and went off to carry out his assignment. Mackey figured it'd be good for the town to see more of the federal lawman at a time like this. Might put their mind at ease. He already had enough to worry about with Darabont on the hillside. He didn't need enemies inside his own camp.

He knew Mayor Mason and his wealthy friends wouldn't like hearing the JT Ranch and the mining camp and logging operation were gone. The thoughts of a quick profit had brought Frazer Rice to Dover Station in the first place. Now that they were gone, it'd be a while before those concerns turned a profit.

He knew a conversation with Sim would be a one-way conversation, but sometimes, airing out a thought was the best way to find out if it made sense. "Seeing how desperate they are, I figure Darabont will take another run at us tonight."

Sim blinked and drank his coffee. That was another way he signaled agreement.

"I'd like to hit them now, but not while they're in fixed positions on the hill and certainly not with night coming on. I plan on hitting them hard at first light."

Sim set his cup down and pulled the pages of his report closer to him. He picked up a pencil and wrote: *Just like at Adobe Flats.*

Sim had been with him at the battle. "We'll have to kill them all."

Sim underlined what he'd just written. *Just like at Adobe Flats.*

Chapter 25

Doc Ridley and Billy came out from the cells. Ridley's hands were still damp from working on Berrie. "The son of a bitch will live, I'm sorry to say." He dried his hands with one of the towels he always carried with him. "Did you get anything out of him?"

"I got enough." Mackey saw no reason to tell him more than that. The less the doctor knew, the less he could tell his wife who would spread it around town as quickly as she could. The old battle-axe had a unique talent for changing the information she heard just enough to make a bad situation worse. If he told Ridley how many they were facing, the townspeople would soon believe Darabont had thousands of men with him. Forty was bad enough. "We'll gather the dead at the undertaker's for the time being. Don't know if you'll have enough on them to identify them for death certificates. Not sure it matters, either."

Doc Ridley had always believed in individual human dignity. He believed each life deserved acknowledgment, especially in death. He didn't look like he appreciated Mackey's glib comment about the certificates, but he didn't argue about it, either.

Mackey asked a question Ridley would love to answer. "How's the mood of the town through all this?"

The doctor dried his hands. "You mean are they starting to turn against you. You want to know if word about Darabont's demands have gotten to them?"

Sometimes, Ridley was too smart for his own good. "Who told them about the demands?"

"Word spreads even in the best of times," Ridley said. "Worse when people are scared. In the absence of fact, rumor takes hold. Maybe if you told them what Darabont wants, it might settle them some."

Or scare them worse than they already are, Mackey thought. "I didn't ask for advice, Doc. I asked about the mood of the town."

"They're resolved for the moment, or at least they were until that burning carriage came down Front Street. That flat shook up some folks and for good reason. But they're willing to fight, if that's what you're asking."

Ridley dropped his towel into his medical bag. "I owe you an apology for what I said to you up at Hill House, Aaron. That wasn't your fault and neither is any of this. I was just overwhelmed by the sight of so much carnage, especially the baby."

Mackey hadn't been expecting an apology. He wasn't even sure he wanted one. He certainly wasn't ready for it. Then something Doc Ridley had just said hit him.

Seeing things.

Billy asked, "You getting sick again, Aaron?"

"Far from it. Do you remember how far we can go outside before we're in range of Darabont's rifles?"

"Don't need to remember," Billy said. "There's still a dead guy at the spot where you killed him. Why?"

"Because I need you to round up every torch you can find in town," Mackey said, "then post them around the perimeter out of range of their rifles."

Billy smiled. "I thought Darabont told us not to do that."

"Which is exactly why we're going to do it. Then order all buildings to keep the shades drawn and the lights low. Not seeing what they're walking into will make these bastards think twice about hitting us after dark."

"And what if they come anyway?" Doc Ridley asked.

Mackey drained his cup and set it back on the desk. "We make them pay."

Chapter 26

That night, Mackey had every man who could carry a gun stationed in every building in town. Even those he wouldn't arm with a slingshot, much less a gun, had been stationed as lookouts near alleys and the forgotten edges of town. Every back door that could be locked had been locked. If it didn't have a lock, it had been barricaded or nailed shut. Lookouts were expected to call out if they saw or heard anything strange.

He'd broken responsibility for the town defenses into two sectors. Billy was in charge of the north end of town; Pappy the southern end near Katie's Place. Of the forty armed men and ten lookouts he'd pressed into service, every one of them would work through the night. He'd wanted to work them in shifts, but the possibility of Darabont using dynamite changed his plans.

A ring of torches around Dover Station burned an uneasy light in the gentle evening breeze. Mackey's men lay waiting, out of sight and in the shadows, for Darabont's men to attack the town.

With Billy overseeing the north end, Mackey and Underhill walked the interior perimeter together. It had been dark for more than an hour by then and Mackey was surprised Darabont hadn't made a move yet. Then again, he was surprised Darabont had laid siege when his own supplies were so low. Very little about the man made much sense to Mackey. Maybe that's what made him so dangerous.

The two men stopped at the dead center of town— Mary Mason's Dress Shoppe—while Underhill lit a cigarette. He offered one to Mackey, but he turned it down. He was just starting to feel better and didn't want to push it.

"I've got to hand it to you," Underhill said as he smoked. "You got this town buttoned up pretty good. I'm impressed."

But Mackey wasn't given to accepting flattery. "This is their town. They're defending it."

"As opposed to how they sat on their asses when you asked for volunteers to ride after Darabont and his men."

Mackey wasn't sure that's what he'd been angling at, but he didn't deny it. "Guess they see defending their town as a lot more important than avenging it."

"Most people are like that," Underhill said. "They'll fight danger if it's within easy reach, but aren't apt to do much about it once it's out of sight. Not everyone in town is like that, though. Like that quiet fella. What's his name? Sim?"

"That's his name. Sim Halstead. He's a good man."

Underhill took a drag. "What's his story, anyhow?"

"He served with me in the army," Mackey explained. "He was my sergeant and Billy was my scout. Sim stayed on as a scout after I left, then made his way here a year or so later."

"How come he don't talk?"

Mackey knew what he was getting at, but dodged it. "Sim never does something without a reason and his reasons are his own. If you want to know why he doesn't talk, ask him. Maybe he'll tell you."

"Unlikely."

"Never know until you ask. Maybe you can charm him into breaking the fast."

Underhill laughed. "Even more unlikely, though not as unlikely as a cavalry big shot cooling his heels in a town in the middle of nowhere."

"I was never a big shot, just a captain. They're a dime a dozen as far as the army's concerned."

"I heard different," Underhill said. "I heard some of those old boys at the dance call you 'Captain Mackey.' Also heard them talk about you and what you did at a place called Adobe Flats."

Mackey didn't like talking about Adobe Flats with the other men who'd been there like Billy and Sim. He sure as hell didn't want to talk about it with a total stranger like Underhill. "All I did was put the men in position, Underhill. They did the fighting."

"And just like here, you led. Leadership's a rare quality, captain. Everyone wants to be boss, but few can lead. Still can't figure out why you're here. You ought to be a major by now. Hell, maybe even a colonel."

Mackey realized he was running out of reasons to dislike Underhill. He might be brash and fancy, but he'd held his ground when the lead flew and killed more than his share of Darabont men. Mackey guessed Underhill didn't deserve to be treated like a fool all the time, even if he was from Texas.

He decided to keep the details to a minimum. "A couple of junior officers under my command beat the hell out of an Apache prisoner. While pulling them off him, I hit one of them too hard. Scrambled his brains permanently."

Underhill took another drag on his cigarette. "Got no use for Apaches myself, but beating a prisoner's pretty low in my book. Can't see why the army would throw you out for that, even if one of the men got hurt."

"His father is a senator from a southern state," Mackey said, "and became something of an institution after the war. He wanted me court-martialed and thrown in the stockade for what I'd done to his boy. The army refused." The next part was harder to say. "Asked me to quietly resign my commission instead."

Underhill stopped smoking. "Must've stung, going out like that."

Mackey was about to answer, but down the alley, he saw a lit stick of dynamite tumbling through the night sky, high over the torches.

Mackey brought his Winchester up to his shoulder, but the stick exploded in mid-air; shattering every window on that side of town.

Rifle fire began to erupt all over town, and Mackey knew Darabont must be making some kind of move.

He told Underhill to head south toward Katie's Place while he broke to the north. From the sound of the rifles, it sounded like both ends of town were seeing action. The stick that had just exploded could've caused one man to get jumpy and fire, but not forty guns all at once.

As soon as he reached the north end of Front

Street, another stick exploded well in front of the blacksmith's shop, sending dirt and rock hurtling through the air. Another explosion echoed up Front Street from the south end of town. He saw another stick of dynamite fly toward the stable, only to be shot out of the sky. He figured one of the Boudreaux boys had done that.

Mackey stayed low as he ran to Billy's position at one of the broken windows in the blacksmith shop.

"How many have they lobbed at us so far?" Mackey asked his deputy.

"About seven," Billy said. "I shot two of them out of the air myself. The rest were either duds or blew up well short. I think that dynamite is in bad shape. Surprised they didn't blow up on Darabont when he moved them."

"Must've gotten some old sticks from one of the miners," Mackey said. "Just like Underhill figured."

"Even a busted clock is right twice a day," Billy said. "Where is he, anyway?"

"Sent him to the south end of town with Pappy when things started popping."

Billy grinned as he watched the sky for more dynamite sticks. "Your old man will love that."

Mackey didn't doubt it. "Keep an eye on things here. I'm going to see how we're faring elsewhere in town."

More rifle fire rang out from the hillside as he jogged from the blacksmith shop to the south end of town. Shots rang out at him every time he ran past an alley, so he figured Darabont's men had found a way closer to town by getting farther down the hill. Come first light, Mackey would have to find a way of driving Darabont out.

But first, he'd have to make it to daylight.

As he made his way south, he was glad to hear the rifle fire from his own men was sporadic. That meant the men were picking their targets and not firing wild into the darkness. Better on ammo and even better on morale.

When he reached the offices of *The Dover Station Record*, Charles Everett Harrington came out of his print shop. Mackey had to pull him out of the way as bullets peppered the ground at his feet.

The newspaper man looked like he was about to faint. "Sorry. I'm not used to this."

"Run out like that again, you won't be used to anything. How's everything in there?"

"All those screaming, whiney children only reaffirms my bachelorhood," Harrington said. "But the women are doing all they can to make the best of the situation. Mrs. Mackey is particularly good at enforcing order."

Mackey wasn't surprised. Mary had always been good at telling people what to do. He thought of going in to see her, but not now. He still had to check on the south side of town and had no time to be sentimental.

Thinking of Mary made him think of Katherine; something he'd been trying to avoid all day. Where she was. If she was hurt. What Darabont and his men might be doing to her.

He pushed it as far back in his mind as he could.

Harrington helped by asking, "What's the overall situation, Aaron? The explosions have caused some concern in town, especially with the children."

"Bastards got hold of some dynamite from one of the mines. None of them have landed close enough to do much damage yet, but all it takes is one stick to get through."

"How do you know he didn't bring the TNT with him?"

"I don't. But it's unlikely. And if they got it from the miners, then I'd say that wasn't good news for them. Not the way Darabont's bunch does things."

Harrington flinched as another volley rose up near the center of town. "It's dark now. Why don't we try getting some of the women and children out of town under the cover of darkness? We could get them out on foot toward the JT Ranch. It might be burnt to the ground, but anything's better than leaving them here to die."

But Mackey wouldn't even consider it. "Can't risk them being on the trail alone. If Darabont's men heard them, they'd have even more leverage on us than they do now."

Harrington didn't seem convinced, but another explosion sounded at the south end of town, followed by the crackle of rifles. Mackey forgot about Harrington's questions and started running in that direction.

Chapter 27

The situation at the south end of town was much worse.

He found Underhill and Pappy eyeing the hillside from the alley between Katie's Place and a clothing store next door.

Pappy cut off Underhill as he reported, "All present and accounted for, captain. No casualties and no sign of the heathen bastards since earlier today. But a stick of TNT blew up most of the livery and four horses. It cost us an area of good cover in a forward area and four good mounts, but all of our men got out alive with most of their ammo. Those torches are keeping the enemy up in the rocks."

Mackey looked at the charred remains of the stable. The structure still stood, but the fire had weakened it. One good wind could knock the whole thing over into a smoldering heap.

To Underhill, he asked, "Got any idea on how many sticks they threw at us."

This time, it was the marshal's turn to cut Pappy off. "I counted ten since I got here. The one that hit the livery was a lucky shot." He patted his Winchester. "The man who threw it ran out of luck soon after."

"Let's hope it keeps that way." Mackey peered into the darkness, but all he saw was black beyond the torches. "Come morning, we'll start scouting around and finish this up once and for all. I've got a feeling Darabont's getting reckless and . . ."

A woman's shriek pierced the night air. The effect was more destructive than all of the dynamite Darabont had thrown at them.

None of the men said a word. None of them looked at each other. None of them even moved. They remained frozen in place; looking up into the darkness in the direction of the scream.

The echo of the first shriek had died out, quickly followed by a longer, louder shriek than the one that had come before it.

"Christ," Pappy whispered. "That's not coming from town, is it?"

"No," Underhill said. "Those animals are torturing some poor girl up in the hills. It's an old Indian trick. Let the screams of a captured enemy carry through camp. Break down our morale." The marshal turned his head and spat into the street. "Godless bastards."

Mackey felt himself gripping the Winchester tighter as a third shriek echoed through the valley. This one wasn't as loud or as long as the first two had been, but sounded much worse. Deeper. He wondered if it was Katherine. He wondered if Darabont had found out who she was and how much she meant to him.

As soon as the echo of the woman's pain died, Darabont's drawl rang out. "People of Dover Station. I submitted reasonable terms to your sheriff. He replied by killing one of my men. That is why I am appealing directly to all of you. The troubles that have been visited upon your town can end this instant, provided you grant me one simple wish. Tear the star from Aaron Mackey's shirt, strip him of his weapons and throw him out into the street. Do that, and you people can go back to your lives. If you keep him as your sheriff, I'll keep raining hellfire down upon you until nothing stands of your wretched little burg. One man in exchange for your town and your lives. We'll be watching. You have until sun-up to decide."

Mackey was already in the street before his father could grab him. He walked toward the unseen hillside, tossing his Winchester in the street, then his pistol as he walked. When he reached the last torch at the perimeter, he held up his hands and turned in a complete circle to show he was unarmed.

"Why wait? I'm right here. Want my badge?" He unpinned it and dropped it into the street. "You've got it. Now turn those people loose and come get me if you've got the balls."

The same chorus of laughter on the hillside after Taylor had been killed greeted him now. In the darkness, it sounded even louder.

"I'm afraid that won't do, Sheriff Mackey," Darabont called out. "You can't just turn yourself in. That would be heroic, and you've already had enough laudatory praise heaped upon you. No, your people have to hand you over to me. They have to make the choice. They have to save themselves. It's the principle of the thing."

"To hell with principle," Mackey said. "And to hell with you. I'm here. Alone and unarmed. Right out in the open. Where are you?"

The only sound he heard was the night wind blowing through the hillside.

Mackey kept pushing. "You men who are with Darabont. Here I am, all alone and your leader won't even come face me. You'll torture a woman, but you haven't got the sand to take a shot at one unarmed man all alone? What does that say about you? What does that say about the man you're following?"

He couldn't see the dozens of pairs of eyes on him, but he could feel every one. He hoped one of them took a shot at him. They might miss. They might not. But the muzzle flare would give away their position, and Darabont would lose another gun hand. Maybe more if Darabont's men panicked and made themselves targets.

But no one took a shot. He didn't even hear a sound.

Mackey took that as an answer. "Don't say I never gave you a chance. And don't expect mercy when I start to kill you."

As he began to pick up his gun belt and star off the ground, the screams of the dying woman started up again.

Mackey pinned his star on his shirt, took his Winchester, and walked back toward the barricade.

Pappy grabbed his son by the throat and pinned him against the wall. Underhill began to intervene, but Billy held him back.

Pappy moved his face to within an inch of his son's. "What the hell were you doing just now? Trying to get yourself killed?"

Mackey didn't try to struggle under his father's

grip. He knew he'd never break it. The old man had hands like a vice. "I was trying to get him to do something stupid."

"You're the only one who did anything stupid, boy. You getting shot would've gutted this town. Where would we be then?"

"He's torturing women up there and lobbing dynamite down at us and calling for my head on a plate," Mackey said. "What do you want me to do? Hide behind cover like a goddamned rabbit?"

Pappy pulled his son off the wall and slammed him against it again. "I expect you to be what this town needs right now. And right now, this town needs a leader, not another corpse."

Billy stepped close, but not too close. "What we need is for you two to quit yelling at each other. You're giving Darabont exactly what he wants. The enemy's up in the hills, not down here with us."

Pappy released his son with a shove and moved away.

Mackey tried not to show how much his chest hurt. He remembered warning Underhill about his father's strength. He'd just been reminded of it himself.

Underhill stayed out of Pappy's way as he joined Billy and Mackey. "Wish my old man cared about me that much."

Mackey rubbed his chest and stifled a cough. "Sometimes he cares too much."

"Nice to be thought of, though." Underhill tilted his head back toward Front Street. "How do you think the good citizens of Dover Station will take to Darabont's offer?"

"They'll ignore it," Billy said.

"I wouldn't be so sure, deputy. Scared people can be mighty unpredictable. It's more likely than not that some of them will think he's making a good offer. Best to be prepared for that eventuality."

"This town's different than most towns you've been in, Underhill. Most of these men have been in combat. They know you can't appease a man like Darabont. If anything, they'll want to protect Mackey just because Darabont wants him."

Mackey took his Winchester and began walking back toward the jailhouse. "By God, fellas. I've never felt so wanted in my life."

Chapter 28

Word of Darabont's message was already sweeping through town as Mackey walked back to the jailhouse. He heard them whispering about it, only to hush when they saw him approaching, only to go back to discussing it when they thought him out of earshot. He didn't have to hear what they were saying to know what they were talking about. He knew they weren't ready to throw him out yet, but they were thinking about it.

When they reached the jailhouse, Mackey sat at his desk and began levering cartridges out of his rifle and began cleaning it. He knew it would get plenty of action in the hours ahead. It was only wise to keep it pristine. Billy sat next to the stove and began doing the same thing.

From his cell in the back, Berrie called out, "You kill any more of my friends, sheriff?"

"Keep running your mouth and I'll kill you for certain." Mackey went back to cleaning his rifle.

Underhill took a seat just inside the door. "Don't

you think you ought to be out there speaking to the people instead of in here cleaning your guns?"

Mackey kept doing what he was doing. "This cleaning has a purpose. Keeps the gun clean and in fine working order. Talking to a scared mob has no purpose. They just hear sound and stay scared. The men guarding the town are the only people that matter right now. They'll hold. Billy here will go out in a while and check on the men, make sure they've got plenty of ammunition and food."

Underhill cleared his throat, the way he always seemed to do when he didn't like an idea. "Why Billy? Why don't you do it?"

Billy, as was his custom, answered for Mackey. "Because the sheriff will get mobbed with questions as soon as he hits the boardwalk. But if I do it, they'll ask me how he's doing and I'll tell them he's fine and he's brave and he ain't goin' nowhere. If he says it, it'll sound like a lie. If I say it, well, that means at least one more person believes in him and is sticking by him. It'll help reinforce the notion that maybe they should, too."

"Sounds complicated."

Mackey pulled the cleaning rod out of the rifle barrel. "Dover Station is a complicated town, Underhill. Best you get some sleep. I intend on taking five men with me and hitting that hill at first light. If you want to be one of them, you'll need rest."

The chair creaked as Underhill sat forward. "Five against them?"

Mackey kept cleaning. "That's what I said."

"Seems kind of sparse, don't you think?"

Mackey looked up from his rifle. It may have been

five years since his cavalry days, but he still wasn't used to having his tactics questioned. "We can afford to lose five without losing the town. Any more than five, things might get dicey if we don't come back."

"You planning on bringing my prisoners with you?"

"You, me, Billy, and the Boudreaux boys," Mackey said. "Sim's out there right now scouting Darabont's positions as best he can, but he'll pitch in when the time comes. That'll bring the total number to six if it makes you feel any better."

"The Boudreaux boys." Underhill spat into the spittoon by the door. "You put a lot of stock in those raping murderers, don't you?"

Mackey set the rifle aside. "I thought you'd give that nonsense up by now."

"Enforcing the law ain't nonsense, Mackey."

"You're not enforcing a goddamned thing and you know it."

Underhill lifted his head a couple of inches. "I'm afraid I don't grasp your meaning."

"Sure you do. If those boys were guilty, they would've put one through your head by now and blamed Darabont's men for it. None of the men in town would've called them liars, either. The Boudreaux brothers didn't rape anybody. And I'd wager those ladies' husbands weren't shot in the back like you said. Were they?"

Underhill looked away.

Mackey didn't. "You've probably seen your share of trail jumpings. I'd wager that scene didn't look like an ambush to you."

Underhill looked at his shoes.

"What did that scene look like anyway?"

Underhill looked at his fingernails. "Both men were found on their backs behind boulders on a hillside just outside of El Paso. Both shot clean through the head, most likely by a rifle."

Billy nodded. "Bet those men were still clutching their rifles when you found them. Had all their gear, too."

Underhill snapped. "I do what I'm told, same as you. And when the judge tells me to go after them, I go after them."

"We've been meaning to ask you about that," Mackey said. "Seems awful far to trail two men you figured were just defending themselves. Seems awful personal to me. Like maybe the Boudreauxs weren't the first to take a poke at those ladies."

Underhill and Billy got to their feet at the same time. He froze when the blade of Billy's Bowie knife touched his throat.

Mackey remained seated. "Guess I hit a nerve just then."

The marshal turned scarlet, but remained silent.

"You even a lawman, Underhill?"

The big man slowly stepped back from Billy's knife edge; keeping his hands away from his sides. Billy let him, but kept the knife ready.

Mackey's hand casually moved to his stomach; less than an inch from the pistol butt on his belt. "Tell the truth, now."

Underhill sat back down. "Probably not anymore. The judge and me weren't on the best terms back then. The reasons don't matter much now, I guess. The women were sporting ladies and their husbands were more like regular customers who didn't take kindly to them being with other men. They had to force the ladies to swear out a complaint, but I figured bringing the Boudreauxs back might put me in good with the judge again. He told me to come back with them or not at all. Gave me a month to find them." He looked at the floor. "It's been a lot longer than a month."

Mackey said. "This judge never swore out a warrant for the Boudreauxs, did he?"

"On the word of whores?" Underhill shook his head. "No, but he still wanted to talk to those boys. I stayed on their trail, though, all the way up here."

"On a bogus damned charge," Billy said.

"I had to be somewhere," Underhill admitted. "Figured if I brought them in, the judge might change his opinion of me. Didn't count on it taking so long or leading me so far."

Once again, the screams of the tortured woman began to echo again through the valley around Dover Station.

Underhill added, "Didn't count on this, either."

Mackey stood up and walked past Billy and Underhill out onto the boardwalk.

Katherine?

There was no way to tell if it was her or not. The woman's pain was carried from the darkness on the night wind, past the burning torches that ringed the town until it reached Front Street. He looked up and down the street as if he might be able to see the woman, even though he knew Darabont and his bastards had the poor girl up in the hillside some place.

Darabont's men were making her pay. Not for Mackey's sins or for the town's refusal to give up their sheriff. Darabont was torturing her for a sin committed against him long ago. The sin his mother had committed by giving birth to him in the first place.

It can't be Katherine, can it? God, please no.

Mackey caught himself and stopped that nonsense. Pleading to God had never gotten him anywhere before and he doubted it would start now. He told himself her voice was too delicate to carry that far, no matter what Darabont and his men did to her. He told himself she'd charm Darabont into sparing her life, that he wouldn't waste such a precious captive as her. He told himself these things several times a second as he stood helpless on the porch. He told himself over and over again as the woman's screams grew louder and longer each time.

He told himself these things enough to the point where he almost believed it himself, though deep down, he knew you couldn't tell much from a scream beyond the horrible pain that caused it.

And, as was his custom, Billy once again gave voice to what was on his mind. "You know that's not her, don't you?"

But Mackey wasn't so sure.

Mackey realized Underhill had joined them on the porch. Whatever tension had been between the three of them had passed. The truth had a way of cleansing things once it was in the air.

"I might've come up here for one reason, Aaron," Underhill said, "but I'm here now. And I'm with you and this town until the bitter end. No matter what happens. You've got my promise on that."

His words did little to soothe the ache in his belly as the woman's screams reached him.

"Come sunrise, I'm going to hold you to that."

Chapter 29

About an hour before dawn the next morning, Mackey and the others crouched at the foot of the hill on the north end of town near the blacksmith's shop. The torches had all burned out by then, and all forty riflemen guarding the town waited for something to move in the brightening hillside.

Mackey watched Sim make his way up the hillside in the near dark. The air was completely still, devoid of insect noise or chirping birds. Every living thing seemed to sense something was about to happen and didn't dare make a sound.

Mackey watched Sim quietly scale the hill without so much as knocking a pebble out of place. He always marveled at the way the old scout moved, his movements smooth and flowing; one motion building the next. He watched Sim move around the brush and rocks of the hillside until he disappeared among the overgrowth.

Underhill was crouched next to Mackey behind the rail fence. "Jesus, that fella's quiet."

Neither Mackey nor Billy nor the Boudreauxs said a word. Sim's talent spoke for itself.

A few moments later, Mackey saw Sim's outline at the top of the hill against the brightening sky. He waved his arms, beckoning them to climb up to join him.

Mackey broke cover and charged up the hill, his Winchester in hand. Billy, Underhill, and the Boudreauxs followed.

When he reached Sim's position, he saw why Sim had beckoned them up. Darabont's men were long gone. Their footprints were evident in the dirt and stones along the brightening hillside.

Sim pointed to something in the near distance; a broken wagon propped over on its side. As he began to walk toward it, he saw something else. Something tied to the wagon wheel above the smoldering coals of the dying fire. When he realized it was someone, not something, he wanted to turn away, but couldn't. He didn't have the luxury.

It was the body of a woman. Not Katherine, he knew, but a woman just the same. Probably one of the girls Darabont had taken from Hill House. And given the charred condition of her remains, most definitely the woman whose screams they had heard all night.

The wind shifted just as Billy and the others scrambled up behind him. The Boudreauxs gagged at the scent and backed away.

Underhill stopped walking. "My God."

Billy and Sim said nothing.

During their years in Apache country, Sim, Billy, and Mackey had seen the bodies of settlers and bandits and members of rival tribes who had been lashed to wagon wheels and roasted over low flames. The sight was impossible to forget. The smell even more so.

Both Boudreaux boys wretched and threw up.

A wooden sign had been hung around her blackened neck with twine. It read:

BELLA DETESTA MATRIBUS.

"What the hell does it say?" Billy asked.

"It's Latin," Mackey said. "From the writings of Horace." Mackey realized he was gripping the stock of the Winchester too tightly and stopped. "It says, 'War, the horror of mothers.'"

"Sometimes," Billy said, "I'm glad I'm not an educated man."

Underhill was the only one who hadn't turned away, other than Sim. "That poor woman. She's the one who gave birth to that baby, isn't she? He cooked her. That miserable bastard . . ."

Mackey had already heard enough. "We all see it, Underhill. No need to breathe more life into it than it already has."

The wind shifted again and the stench dampened a little.

Billy looked over the remnants of the campsite. "Looks like they've been gone a while. Since before last night."

Sim nodded.

"Bet they let out after we stopped their men from getting into position," Billy said. "Probably left behind a handful of men to lob dynamite at us to keep us at bay."

Sim nodded again.

Mackey could tell Billy didn't want to say what was on his mind. But they all knew it needed saying. "Took the rest of the women with them." He didn't have to say Katherine was still with Darabont.

None of them had to say what that meant.

To Sim, Mackey said, "Got any idea where they're headed?"

Sim pointed at a trail of hoofprints that lead south through the timberland.

Mackey didn't have to ask the old scout if he was ready to ride. Sim Halstead was always ready. "I'll need you to start tracking those bastards as best you can. We'll be riding out behind you as soon as we can get provisions."

Sim walked down the hillside to get his horse. To Billy, Mackey said, "Head back to town and have the men stand down from their positions. Tell them the town's safe for the moment, but they'll need to stay vigilant. No telling if Darabont and his men might double back and hit the town another way."

He stole another glance at the dead woman. Even in death, she looked anything but peaceful. "Then get the undertaker up here to get her. Tell him to bring a coffin with him and bury her as soon as possible. Tell him to be quiet about it. I don't want any of those busybodies in town seeing her like this. Bastards wouldn't look at her in life. I won't let them see her in death. I'll stay here with her until he shows up. Remind him I'm an impatient man."

"What about the men Darabont propped up? He's been holding on to them for us all this time."

"Have him dump them in the woods. No way those bastards get buried in the same ground as our own."

Mackey motioned for the Boudreauxs to come over. They were still wiping their sickness from their mouths with the backs of their hands. "I know this was tough for you boys to see, but dead people and dead game aren't all that different. I need you boys stocked up and ready to ride within the hour. I need you to fetch those two Mexicans and Brahm from the JT Ranch and tell them we'll meet them at the livery before noon if they still want to go. Any others who want to join are welcome, but don't beg."

As the brothers went off to carry out the various tasks they'd been given, Mackey and Underhill stood alone on the hilltop with the remains of the dead woman. Neither of them mentioned the sight of her sagging belly.

She had been the whore who'd given birth. She'd been the woman Katherine had been helping at Hill House.

Mackey found himself mourning the girl, even though he'd never met her. He mourned her dead child. He mourned Old Wilkes and all the others who'd died in the fire. The people Darabont had killed.

He didn't know if he should thank God that Katherine was still alive.

A buzzard squawked as it began to circle overhead, catching the scent of new death on the hilltop. Mackey raised his Winchester and shot the damned thing out of the sky. It dropped on the far side of the hill opposite Dover Station.

Underhill watched Mackey lever a new cartridge into the rifle. "I know your blood is still up, Aaron, but I don't think it's a good idea for us to leave this town without any law."

"I agree. That's why you're staying behind. I need Billy with me, and the town will need watching while we're gone. If Darabont sends a few stragglers back to cause trouble, you'll be needed here."

"And what if nobody comes back?"

"That federal star might not be legal anymore, but

no one needs to know that. It'll be enough to keep the town in order until we get back."

Underhill was silent for a moment. "And if you don't come back?"

Mackey felt phlegm in his throat and spat it out. "Then you'll have yourself a sheriff's badge if you want it."

Underhill looked back at the town below them. "This ain't my town, Aaron."

Mackey could see the people begin to come out of hiding. Billy must've told some of the townsmen to stand down, because he could hear shouts and cheers beginning to rise up in the streets. The townspeople began to come outside and gather around the riflemen who had left their posts around the perimeter. Many of them fired their rifles into the air in celebration. Many threw their hats aloft like they had the day Lee had surrendered.

Mackey was sure the boasting had already begun and knew, by nightfall, the number of Darabont's dead would reach five hundred men and their defense would include repelling a charge of Darabont's men at full gallop.

They cheered because they thought their war was over now because, for them, it was. The reason for the siege was a distant memory. The dead whores had already been forgotten; Katherine, too. And he knew none of them would ride out with him to chase down Darabont.

Mackey watched their celebration and found himself hating every single one of them. "It's not my town either. Not anymore."

Chapter 30

Mackey and Underhill walked in front while Billy rode shotgun as the undertaker drove the buckboard carrying the dead woman's coffin off the hilltop. They went down a side street and back up Front Street.

The cemetery was closer to the hillside where they had found her body, but this procession was not about brevity or convenience. Mackey wanted the town to see the woman whose suffering they had heard all night.

He wanted them to see the woman who they refused to avenge.

Townspeople craned their necks to look inside the wagon and seemed disappointed to see she had already been placed in the coffin. The only men who removed their hats were the drunks from the Tin Horn who did so more out of habit than respect.

He heard the people murmur questions to each other as the humble procession passed by. *Which one was she? Was she one of theirs? Was it one of those women Darabont took from "that place"?* They kept their questions to themselves. No one asked Mackey anything.

Mackey and Underhill had to keep the horses

steady as they approached the burned-out wreckage of the stagecoach. The horses stiffened at the smell of the dead horses lying bloated in the street, but the wagon kept moving.

Mayor Mason flagged him down from the board-walk in front of the jailhouse. Other than Doc Ridley, Mason was the last person he wanted to speak to, but he was still the mayor and entitled to answers.

Mackey told Billy to continue the circuit through town, then up to the cemetery for burial while he and Underhill went to see Mason at the jailhouse.

"Who was she?" Mason asked as he followed the two lawmen inside.

Underhill went to the coffeepot, shook it, and realized it was empty. "I'll go fill this up and put on a fresh pot. Think we could all use some."

"Pump's out back." Mackey laid his hat on the desk as he dropped into his chair. He hadn't sat down for hours and suddenly felt every second of it. His lungs began to ache for the first time in over a day, reminding him he still had pneumonia.

Mayor Mason stood in the doorway, waiting for an answer. "Aaron, was it one of the Hill House girls or . . . ?"

"A decent woman? That's what you really want to know, isn't it?"

"Aaron, I . . ."

"What difference does it make? She's dead and she died horribly. A lot of people died here over the last couple of days, not that any of you bastards give a damn. Don't worry, Brian. She'll be buried in an hour and then you won't have to worry about it anymore."

Mason took off his bowler and played with the brim. "You mean she'll be buried in the cemetery?"

"Within the hour."

"I hate to ask again, but everyone wants to know. Was she a woman from the JT or the mining camps or . . ."

Mackey pounded the desk. "Instead of firing off a lot of damned fool questions, how about calling for a group of men to ride out with me to chase down Darabont's bunch?"

"You know they won't do that."

Knowing it and finally hearing it were two different things. "Then get some of the men together to pull that stage coach and the dead horses out of Front Street. The men of this town ought to be good for something more than worrying about their own asses."

Mason surprised him by not flinching and remaining calm. "I've already asked your father to handle that. Are Darabont's men really gone?"

"Looks like most of them pulled out sometime last night, probably after we stopped them from getting any closer. The dynamite they threw last night was likely just a diversion, probably meant to keep us at bay during the night while the rest of them cleared out. I plan on closing the gap on them starting at noon today."

Mason looked up from the floor. "Why are you going after them?"

"If you've got to ask the question, you wouldn't understand the answer."

"But you'll be going into the field with a skeleton crew. You're outgunned and out manned."

"This isn't over just because they ran off," Mackey said. "They can't be allowed to get away with what they did here today. There's no telling what a man like Darabont might do. He could come back and finish up what he started or he could just keep riding south.

It doesn't matter what he does. It only matters what we do, and that's why we've got to stop him."

"But he's gone for now," Mason argued. "Best to stay here and harden our defenses. To . . ."

"That woman you heard screaming last night was lashed to a wagon wheel and roasted to death. Looks like she was the mother of that baby we pulled out of the rubble at Hill House."

Mason lowered himself into the chair by the door. "Good heavens."

Mackey rubbed his sore hand. He'd hit the desk too hard. "Heaven's got nothing to do with anything that's happened here the last few days."

"Are you taking Billy with you?"

"I am."

Mason wiped at his mouth with the back of his hand. "We both know I can't fight you and win, Aaron, but I don't like the idea of you leaving the town unguarded right now. Your father's men are riding high with glory now that they've helped run off Darabont. I'm afraid mob rule might take over in your absence."

"That's why I'm leaving Underhill behind."

"I'm sure the marshal is a good man. We owe him thanks for how he helped defend the town. But he's not you, and I don't think anyone else could have held this town together against Darabont's men. You were too busy protecting us to see how terrified they were, especially last night after the explosions started. They all heard about Darabont's demands to give you up, but not one of them entertained the notion. Not even Doc Ridley and certainly not Mr. Rice."

Mackey was in no mood for compliments, even though he could tell Mason was sincere. "Their confidence didn't do the people who burned to death up at Hill House much good. Old Wilkes or that woman in the buckboard or her dead baby, either, not to mention the people Darabont took with him." He felt his throat close in on him. He swallowed hard. *Katherine*.

"I told you no one blames you for that, Aaron."

"I had the chance to shoot that son of a bitch when he was standing in front of my door and I let him go." He glared at Mason. "Because of you and your damned investors."

"No. Not because of me, Aaron, and not because of Mr. Rice and his investors. You didn't kill him because you're not like Darabont. You didn't kill him because you're not a murderer. You're brutal and harsh, but you obey the law even though you bend it when you must. I know you killed that messenger, but as far as I'm concerned, that was war." He looked over at the jail cell. "Just like whatever you do to get him to tell you where Darabont went was war, too."

Mackey closed his eyes. He'd almost forgotten about Berrie. It felt like he'd brought him in a month ago. It had only been yesterday.

"Defending the town was one thing," Mason went on, "but riding out after them is different. That's not about defending the town and it's not about justice. It's about revenge, and even I know there's no future in that."

Mackey looked at him, when a new voice came from the porch. "It's not about vengeance," the voice said. "It's about justice."

Mr. Rice walked into the jail. He held a Winchester in his right hand, and his gray hair stuck up at odd angles. His expensive city clothes were dusty and grimy. There was a slight tear at the left shoulder of his jacket.

He looked ten years younger than the morning Mackey had seen him at the railroad station.

Mason stood. "Mr. Rice. I . . ."

"Sheriff Mackey is right," Rice said as he put the Winchester he'd been holding in the rifle rack. "You let a man like this Darabont scourge go, how long before word of what he did here gets around? How long before some other bastard tries doing the same thing. Six months? A year? I won't invest in a town with a bull's-eye on its back, Mason, and neither will my partners." He nodded at Mackey. "Go get this bastard, son. I'll foot the bill for the whole thing. Whatever it costs, just get him."

After everything he'd been through the past few days, Mackey enjoyed seeing Mason flustered. He ran his tongue inside his mouth and said, "You mean you're still willing to invest here? Even after all that's happened?"

"Hell, yes," Rice said. "The people of Dover Station have grit and determination. They hang together, and that's rare these days. Who's in charge while you're gone?"

"U.S. Marshal Underhill."

Rice seemed pleased. "I've heard the men talk after your deputy called for volunteers. I wouldn't expect many to ride out with you, except for the Mexicans and the German who volunteered. I can send out a call to hire more, but they wouldn't get here for at least a week."

"More likely a month at the earliest," Mackey said. "I'll ride out with who I have. Anyone forced to ride will just be a drag on the rest of us."

"But you can't just ride off without surveying the

damage to our interests," Mason said. "The loggers. The miners. Taylor's ranch. Others who . . ."

"Best to consider all of them dead or missing," Mackey said. "Darabont was plenty busy before he hit us. Anyone still alive probably got scooped up by Darabont's men. I'm not going to waste another day looking for what I know I'll find. I'll put that time to better use riding him down."

Mason clearly wanted to continue the discussion, but Rice beckoned him toward the door. "Let's you and me get a riding party together and scout out these places tomorrow after the burials. See what's been done and what we need to rebuild. We're more apt to get volunteers if they know I'm interested in helping. The sheriff's got enough to worry about."

Mackey watched the politician and the financier walk out of his jailhouse. He realized that for the first time in a few days, he was completely alone. It was likely to be the last time he'd be alone for some time.

He hoped Underhill took his time filling that coffeepot.

Chapter 31

Pappy was waiting for him as soon as he stepped out of the jail. "Word is you're going out after Darabont."

"For once, the word is correct." Mackey kept walking toward his house. "Billy and me and some of the others will be hitting the trail by noon."

"I'm coming, too."

"Nope. Only room for one boss on the trail, and I don't need you second-guessing my orders. Besides, I need you here to help Underhill keep watch over the town in case Darabont sends some men back here."

"Underhill? You're leaving that goddamned Texan in charge? What about Billy?"

"Billy's the second best tracker I know next to Sim. I'll need him out there with me, which leaves Underhill the odd man out. He's better suited to town work now."

Pappy had no trouble keeping pace with his son. "This is about her, isn't it? Not Darabont or Old Wilkes or any of the others. This is about rescuing Katherine."

Mackey had rarely won an argument with his father

before and knew he wouldn't win this one, either. "It's about more than her," he lied. "It's about the loggers and the miners and the ranchers he killed. It's about not allowing him to get away with what he did to this town. And it's about making sure he doesn't do it to anyone else again."

"And what if she's already dead?"

"Then I'll bury her."

"And what if he kills you? You're worth a hundred Darabonts, and you know it."

But that was just it. He didn't know it. He just knew Katherine was worth the risk. "If I die, Billy will see to it I get a Christian burial."

"Stubborn son of a bitch," Pappy said. "Stubborn and stupid for throwing your life away on a woman who ain't even yours."

Pappy stopped walking.

Mackey didn't.

Mackey found Mary on the bench outside their home. Her eyes were red and hollow, the way they always were when she'd been crying and now was beyond tears. If she saw him, she didn't show it, not even when he sat next to her.

Mackey took off his hat and toyed with it in his hands. He waited for her to say something, but she didn't, so he said, "Long day."

A single tear ran down her face, but her voice was surprisingly strong. "I suppose you'll be leaving after them, won't you?"

"Who told you?"

"No one. I just know you."

"I've got no choice, Mary. I can't . . ."

"You can't?" The lines around her mouth deepened. "You're the sheriff who just saved this miserable town. You can do any goddamned thing you want, including letting that rabble keep going on their way."

"And if they come back?"

"We fought them off before. We can do it again."

"Next time they'd be ready."

"If there even is a next time. Christ, Aaron. They're gone. You won. Can't you just let them go? It's not as though they killed anyone important."

"They killed Old Wilkes. And burned out the JT, and probably killed most of the miners and loggers, not to mention those women up at . . ."

"Whores," Mary spat. "And whores don't count as women. I know the woman you're after, and she's a whore, too. No better than the rest of them."

Mackey closed his eyes. He'd been fighting and arguing and staying strong for days. He just wanted to go upstairs and gather his things, but he didn't want to leave it like this. "I'm not going after anyone but Darabont."

"You're going after her the same way she came out here after you," Mary said. "You've got the courage to defend a town, to walk out in the darkness and let them kill you. But you don't have the courage you need most; to let those animals go and take her with them."

He'd been having the same argument all morning. He didn't want to argue any more. "Underhill will be minding things while I'm gone. He's a good man."

"With far more sense than you have. You can't beat these men, Aaron. They're not Apaches. They're wild, rotten dogs who do whatever they want whenever they please. Well, I've been married to you long enough to know there's no amount of pleading I can do to make you stay, so I won't even try. But the second you're out of sight with whatever idiots are dumb enough to follow you, I'm going right over to Mason's Store and buying a black dress out of the Sears and Roebuck catalogue. For it's a widow I'll be by the time it gets here."

Mackey slowly stood up and walked inside. He waited for her to join him. He prayed that she would. But she didn't. She didn't move at all.

He allowed himself one final glance at her before he headed upstairs. He tried to remember her as that bright young girl with the windblown hair who'd beamed up at him that miserable day when he'd gotten off the train all those years ago.

But that young girl was gone, just like the man in that uniform had gone. All that was left was the bitter, angry woman sitting on the bench outside the house they'd built together.

Mackey went up the stairs two steps at a time.

Mary was gone by the time Mackey came back downstairs with his field pack. He loaded what he could on Adair without weighing her down too much. The rest would go on the pack animals Billy had already secured.

He untied Adair from the post and swung up into the saddle. He didn't know if this would be the last time he'd see Mary or his house or his town. He didn't allow himself to think of such things. Such thoughts were cheap in town, but expensive on the trail. Questions like that could cost him his life.

He rode past the jailhouse and to the cemetery that lay just beyond the blacksmith. He saw the diggers were already filling in the dead whore's grave while the undertaker murmured readings from the Bible. He figured the bastard would charge the town extra for the prayers.

Only Underhill stood off to the side, hat in hand, while the men went about their grim work.

Mackey thought about joining the tail end of the service, but decided not to. He hadn't even known the girl. He couldn't even recall ever seeing her before that morning. In that way, praying over her now would make him no better than the rest of the people in town.

He watched Billy ride out from the livery, trail ready and eager to ride. Next to the stable, both Boudreaux boys, the two Mexicans from the JT Ranch, and the big German named Brahm. Three pack mules for the seven of them, thanks to Billy's preparation. Mackey figured most of it was ammunition.

Mackey rode over to the men and asked the question even though he already knew the answer. "You boys ready?"

Billy nodded. So did the others.

Mackey swung Adair south and headed toward the trail. Billy and the others followed, leaving Dover Station behind.

And no one had come out to say good-bye. Not even Pappy.

Chapter 32

Billy spent the rest of the afternoon riding ahead of the others, scouting out the trail. Mackey knew Sim was tracking far out ahead of them by now, but it helped to have him at the head of the group. He'd assigned the *vaqueros* to serve as outriders, loping along either side to broaden their range of view. They were used to ranging cattle, so it seemed a natural fit for their talents. Mackey, Brahm, and the Boudreauxs rode clustered in the center.

He didn't have a pocket watch, but judging by the sun, he could tell they had maybe an hour or so of sunlight left. There'd been no sign of Sim in all that time, which meant Darabont's men must've gotten a bigger head start than he had thought. Mackey knew the old scout's methods and knew he'd be back after nightfall. He always had been before.

Mackey looked up when he heard Billy's familiar whistle that told him he'd spotted something. Billy was pointing out at a lone rider off to the right in the near distance, slumped forward in the saddle atop a horse that ambled along as it nosed the tall grass.

Mackey ordered the rest of the group to stop. "Stay here and rifles at the ready. This might be a straggler or it might be a trap. Get ready to shoot at anything that's not Billy or me."

Mackey and Billy converged on the stranger from different angles.

As he rode closer, Mackey could see the horse was a brown bay speckled with white. The rider was just a kid, probably no older than twenty. His skin and clothes were blackened by soot and his body moved with every movement of the horse. Mackey had no idea what was keeping him from falling out of the saddle.

Billy and Mackey reached him at the same time. Billy took hold of the horse's reins while Mackey shook the boy awake. "What's your name?"

The kid looked at him with dull, bloodshot eyes. "I know you," the young man slurred through parched lips. "You're the sheriff."

"That's right. What's your name? Where'd you come from?"

"I'm from the JT Ranch. We . . ." The kid's eyes rolled up into the back of his head and he went limp. Mackey grabbed him under the arm before he fell out of the saddle.

Billy helped Mackey lay the kid across his saddle and lead the horse back to the others. Mackey knew it was uncomfortable, but without a wagon, it was the only way either of them knew to get the boy moving.

"This boy looks familiar to me," Billy said. "Those *vaqueros* and Brahm will be happy one of their old friends is alive."

Mackey pulled the horse's reins as he led it back to the others. He had one more mouth to feed and no time for sentiment.

* * *

Billy had been right. The arrival of the kid into the group had improved the mood of the *vaqueros* and Brahm. They took turns tending to the young man they'd known as Sandborne. Brahm filled him up with as much coffee and biscuits and bacon as the young man's belly could hold.

After dinner, some color seemed to return to the boy's face. Mackey thought he looked like he might be strong enough to answer some questions.

The low fire crackled and spat out cinders as Mackey asked, "You feeling up to telling us what happened to you?"

"I'll tell you what I know," Sandborne said, "but I'm afraid it ain't much. Whole thing's kinda murky."

"It's not a race," Billy told him. "Take your time and tell it your way."

That's what Sandborne began to do. "Me and some of the boys were out tending the herd in the north field when some riders came over the hill and hit us before we knew what was happening. I can't tell you how many on account of everything happening so fast, but it was more people than I'd ever seen in one place before. The bastards started shooting at us as soon as they were in range. Hit some of us, I guess, because I remember seeing some JT men fall off their horses."

"You get hit?" asked Solomon, one of the *vaqueros*.

The kid shook his head, then winced from the effort. "No, but the noise scared my horse something awful and he threw me. I landed near a tree and must've hit my head or something because I got knocked out."

Mackey looked at the purple bruise on his left temple. He'd seen men die from blows like that. The kid was lucky.

Sandborne went on. "When I woke up, the hay barn in the north field had already burned all the way through and was smoldering something awful. The bunkhouse and all the barns and Mr. Tyler's ranch house, too, were still burning. The rail fences had all been busted in several places and the cattle had scattered. Guess all that commotion must've stampeded the herd, or else those raiders scattered them. My head hurt something fierce and I couldn't get my bearings long enough to stand on my own two feet."

To Mackey, Billy said, "Bet they butchered themselves some cattle while they were at it. Could give them enough provisions for the trail."

But Mackey didn't care about their provisions. "You know if anybody else made it out of there?"

"Didn't see anyone else around when I woke up. No one was looking for me either. I was so bleary-eyed, I couldn't see more than a couple of feet in front of me." He thumbed back over to where they'd picketed the horses. "That's when my own horse wandered by and I managed to climb up. I meant to ride into town, but, well, the rest is a blur until you woke me up. What the hell happened, anyway?"

Mackey quickly told him about Darabont, and how he'd hit the miners and the loggers and the town, too.

The kid's eyes went wide. "He did all that? What happened?"

Billy grinned. "We're still here, ain't we, boy?"

"We're riding out after him now," Mackey added. "I hate to tell you this, but Mr. Taylor got killed first. He'd ridden into town with Manuel and Solomon and

Brahm here to offer them as part of our posse. He got shot on his way back to the ranch, just before they raided it. He died as best as he could."

The kid swallowed hard. "Mr. Taylor wasn't an easy man, Mr. Mackey, but he was a good man. I'd be proud to ride along with you if you'll have me. Ain't like I got much to go back to anyway."

Mackey figured he would. "You might think about that differently after your head clears. In the meantime, you'll ride with us until you're feeling better. After that, we'll see."

The two *vaqueros* and Brahm began peppering young Sandborne with questions of who else had been in the north field with him. The Boudreauxs listened, but kept to themselves.

Billy set his dish aside and began building a cigarette. He looked around at the darkness surrounding them and spoke quietly to Mackey. "You see who's out there?"

"Yeah." Mackey sipped his coffee. Brahm's coffee wasn't as good as Billy's, but it was close. "Figured I'd give them a minute to get reacquainted before I ruin their evening. The more relaxed they are, the better this will go."

Billy licked the cigarette paper and rolled it tight. "Damned shame, too. Nice fire. Sorry it's gonna have to get ruined on account of this."

"Yeah. Wasn't our doing, though." Mackey drank his coffee and decided it was time to break the news to the men. He didn't bother asking them to quiet down. The less formal, the better. Instead, he simply spoke over them. "Any of you men take the train up to Dover Station?"

All of the men stopped talking. They looked at

each other and shook their heads. Manuel said, "We never had enough money for a train ticket."

"That means you all spent time on the trail getting here. You've seen what can happen across open land and you know about the dangers and people you can meet along the way."

He looked at each man, waiting for them to nod. Some of them did.

Mackey continued. "And since you followed Billy and me out here after Darabont, I suppose you boys trust us."

Jack Boudreaux spoke first. "Sure we do, Aaron. We wouldn't be here if we didn't."

Mackey finished his coffee and set it aside. "That's good, because I'm going to need you boys to stay as still as you are right now. When I leave, do exactly as Billy tells you."

The men traded glances as they watched Mackey slowly get to his feet. From his spot at the fire, Brahm asked, "Where are you going, boss?"

Mackey slowly unbuckled his gun belt and let it drop to the ground. "For the past fifteen minutes or so, we've been surrounded by a band of Blackfoot Indians." He held his arms away from his sides and slowly turned in a full circle to show he wasn't armed. "Don't move and don't say a word and we'll all make it out of here just fine."

Brahm reached for his rifle.

"Don't do that." Mackey kept his voice calm. "I've dealt with these folks for years and I know how to handle them. Just stay in the light where they can see you and keep your hands in the open. They mean us no harm."

"How the hell you know that, sheriff?" Solomon asked.

Billy answered for him. "Because we'd already be dead if that's what they wanted."

Mackey spoke to the darkness in *Siksika*, the language of the Blackfoot tribe. "I have no weapons. I mean you no harm. These men mean you no harm. Tell me what you want of me."

A lone Blackfoot warrior stepped from the edge of the darkness. As was the way of his people, he had used the weakness of his enemy to his advantage. In this case, Mackey knew it was the white man's need for firelight at night. In his own tongue, the warrior replied, "If you are their leader, come with us."

Mackey looked down at Billy. "Keep them close. Keep them alive. I'll be back as soon as I can."

"We'll be here." He looked around the edges of the campfire. "I got a feeling we'll have plenty of company, too."

Mackey followed the Blackfoot warrior into the darkness.

Chapter 33

Mackey followed the warrior back to a small settlement he judged to be about a mile from where he and his men had made camp. Even in the dim light of the settlement's main fire, he could see what had happened there and knew why he had been brought to that place.

The camp had been attacked. Wigwams had been burned out; the scent of burnt canvas and charred lodge poles still hung in the air. He smelled the unmistakable scent of burnt flesh, too—just like in the wreckage of Hill House and on the hillside earlier that morning and from when he had still been in the cavalry.

Darabont had done this.

A group of seven members of the Blackfoot tribe sat around the great fire. Sim Halstead sat next to a very old man; speaking with his hands in the sign language of the Blackfoot people. His hands moved just as fluidly as those of his host.

Sim stopped signing when Mackey approached the

fire. The chief looked up also, his high cheekbones and strong jaw line looking fierce in the firelight. His nose cast a long shadow across the lines on the long planes of his face.

The chief did not extend his hand, nor did he attempt to rise. Mackey had not expected him to, for this man was Wolf Child, the chief who had led his people through many seasons. He bade no greeting to any man, white or otherwise.

Mackey had seen the man several times since his father had brought him to what would eventually become the town of Dover Station. The chief had been much younger then, but every bit as imposing as he was now. Pappy and the chief could never be considered friends, but had managed to forge something of a truce that had held many decades. Their people lived apart from each other without incident.

Even now, as a much older man, Wolf Child's presence made Mackey as uneasy as it had when he was a boy.

As the warrior who had brought Mackey to the village spoke to the chief, Mackey made sure he stood in the firelight, wanting all of the men of the tribe to see him clearly. He held out his arms as he slowly turned as he had turned back at camp, so all could see he was unarmed.

When the warrior gestured for him to speak, Mackey spoke in the chief's own language. "I come to you in peace and without weapons." He was careful not to look at Wolf Child directly, for to do so could be considered a great insult. "My people and I mean you no harm. We come in peace as we always have."

"You may come in peace, Young One, but your people have not."

"You call me Young One. Then you must remember me and my father."

Wolf Child grunted. "Loud One is difficult to forget. Have you followed in his ways?"

Mackey knew the Blackfoot tribe called Pappy "The Loud One," but Pappy didn't speak their language and had been told the term meant "Great Friend." Mackey had never seen any reason to tell his father otherwise. "I am like him in all honorable ways, great chief, but quieter."

Wolf Child himself grew quiet for a time. Mackey kept his eyes on Sim, who looked as calm as he always did. If they were in danger, Sim would have signaled him somehow.

When the chief did speak, he said, "You call me Great Chief, yet you see my people are dead. Our people were murdered by the same white men who attacked your village." He motioned toward Sim. "The Quiet One has told us this. Our women and children and old men were butchered like buffalo while I led my men in a great hunt to feed them. You call me Great Chief. A great chief protects his people. An old man allows his people to be slaughtered. I am an old man."

All of the remaining men of the village told him he was wrong, muttering praises and accolades in his name. He silenced them with the slightest turn of his great head.

Mackey said, "I grieve, too. My village has also lost men and women and children. This is why I have hunted these men until now. These men are not of my village and not of my people. From now on, I will also hunt them for you and for the people they have taken from you."

Wolf Child grew very still. Mackey felt a coldness pass through his body as the chief glared at him. He could have blamed it on the remnants of his pneumonia, but knew better. "You believe that I am so weak that I need a white man to kill for me? The same white men who hack holes into our mountains and cut down our trees while the cattle you have brought eat of our grass and defile it with their dung."

"The buffalo does the same as a cow," Mackey said.

"The buffalo have always been here," Wolf Child answered. "This has always been their land and ours."

Mackey found a way to keep his voice from quivering as he answered. "Wolf Child needs no man—white or otherwise—to do anything for him. I meant no offense, only brotherhood as our two peoples have lived together in peace for many seasons. We have shown thanks for your kindness by sharing our bounty with you. Any deeds committed against your people have been punished. Just as the shadow of a weak man cannot dim the fire of a great one, this man Darabont cannot harm your name."

The men of the village voiced their agreement with Mackey and, this time, the chief did not silence them.

Mackey nodded at Sim. "You have allowed my friend to share the comfort of your fire. I know he has told you what has happened in my village."

For the first time, Wolf Child looked at him. Mackey damned near flinched. "You would not still be alive if he had not. My young men thirst for vengeance. Old men should not know such thirst, but yet I do. Your lives would have been taken for those we lost had the Quiet One not told us of what had happened. Our friend tells us you seek justice for what has happened to you. Our people suffered first. Their justice should be first."

"These men will suffer for what they did to my people and yours, great chief. This I swear to you."

The old man grunted and looked into the fire. When he spoke, it seemed to be to everyone within earshot and not just to Mackey. "Long ago, when the white man first came to our lands, our people rode out to meet them. The Loud One spoke of peace and life. We had heard the lies of the white man before, but we allowed him to bring his people to our land. We were happy to see his words of peace and life were real. When the Young One wore a Blue Coat, we knew he hunted the Apache and the Comanche. These men are animals meant to be hunted. When the Young One returned, we feared he would hunt us as well, but he has kept the peace The Loud One had promised. I saw truth in the words of the father then. There is truth in the words of his son now. This is why I will send two of my warriors with you to help hunt the man who hurt my people. They will help you find the justice we both seek. This is my word."

Mackey was in no position to argue. He only had seven men against at least forty of Darabont's crew.

Besides, Wolf Child didn't seem to be in a negotiating mood. "I will be proud to have them with me. They can share our fire and . . ."

"They will need nothing from you or any white man." He looked at the scorched remains of his village, then back at the fire. "The white man has given them vengeance. That will be enough."

The chief signed to Sim, who signed back. Then the scout stood up and motioned Mackey to follow him.

Sim led him back toward camp through the darkness, without a moon or a torch. Mackey didn't know how he did it, especially since he'd never been there before, but he did.

Sim was like that.

The Blackfoot did not follow.

Chapter 34

There were times when Mackey believed that Sim's silence posed a problem. This was one of those times.

As they trailed Sim's horse behind them on the walk back to his posse's camp, Mackey had been full of questions for Sim about what he had found on the trail. How far ahead was Darabont? How many were with him? Does he have provisions? Did Katherine leave any clues farther up the trail?

But since Sim didn't speak, every question had to wait until they men reached the light of Brahm's campfire. Sim had his coffee and handed Mackey the notebook that had a full accounting of all he'd seen and done that day.

Mackey tilted the notebook to get a better angle on the light. Billy looked over his shoulder as he read it.

Sim's elegant handwriting read: *"We killed far more men than we thought. Darabont's men are about twenty-five in number. I found one man buried just off the trail. Whoever buried him made a half-hearted attempt to hide the grave. Tracks show they have a wagon with them. The ruts left by the wheels tell me the wagon is still loaded heavy. Could be*

*provisions. Could be captives. I don't know which. Judging
by the scat of their horses, I'd say the bulk of the force is about
a day ahead of us. If we push hard through tomorrow, we
can catch up to at least his rear guard by dawn the next day."*

Mackey closed the notebook and handed it back to
the scout. "How was the dead man you found killed?"

Sim pointed to a rifle, then to the right side of his
chest.

"Probably got winged chucking dynamite sticks,"
Billy said.

Mackey thought so, too. "You wrote that he has
twenty-five men. You used to think it was forty. Did we
kill that many or did they separate from him?"

Sim shrugged and drank his coffee.

"Does it look like he's got anyone watching their
back trail?"

Sim nodded and held up two fingers. Two men.

Billy looked encouraged. "Guess he can't spare the
men for a proper rear guard."

But Mackey wasn't so sure. "The half-breed Darabont called Concho looked like a tracker to me. He's
probably out front scouting for them now. If Darabont's men think we're getting close, he'll put Concho
on their back trail to make it tougher for us to follow."
To Sim, he said, "You keep an eye out for him. He's
dangerous."

Sim drank his coffee. He didn't look worried. He
never did.

Mackey realized the rest of his men of the posse
were looking at him, their faces blank. He couldn't
blame them. They'd just watched him having a one-
way conversation with a mute.

He decided to give them a quick rundown of Sim's
notes. "Looks like we're up against twenty-five men or

so, which is fewer than we thought, but still outnumber us more than three to one. They're pulling a heavy wagon and about a day ahead of us. The Indian who pulled me out of here is with a Blackfoot tribe that Darabont hit while he was coming to Dover Station. They're giving us two of their warriors to help us track down Darabont's men. They'll come in handy if lead starts to fly, too. If we're lucky, they'll help keep the lead from flying at all."

Brahm grumbled as he began to gather the used dishes for washing. "I ain't cooking for no heathen savages."

"You won't have to," Mackey said. "They're on their own and won't be bedding with us either. They've got their own score to settle. Now I want everyone to get plenty of rest. You'll need it. Billy and I will take watch tonight. You boys'll pick up the slack starting tomorrow." He felt compelled to add, "I know we didn't see any action today, but we made up a lot of ground and found young Sandborne here in the process. You handled yourselves well when the Blackfoot surrounded us. We're off to a good start." He even smiled, which made the others smile, too. Yes, they were beginning to become a group. "Now get some sleep you sons of bitches."

Chapter 35

Mackey had taken first watch. Billy, a light sleeper whether on the trail or in town, took the second. Sim headed out to scout the trail well before dawn and was long gone before any of the men woke up. After a quick breakfast they doused the fire, packed up camp and hit the trail themselves.

To prevent monotony from setting in, Mackey had the Boudreauxs serve as outriders and the *vaqueros* guarded the flank. Sandborne and Brahm stayed with the pack mules. He figured the easier pace would be a good way for the kid to get his bearings while his head wound healed.

Billy was about to ride ahead to take point when Sim came riding back toward them at a good gallop. There was no sign of the two Blackfoot scouts anywhere in sight.

"Halt!" Mackey called out to his men. "Get your rifles out and ready and wait for my command."

Sim brought his mount up short in front of Mackey and Billy. He whipped out his notebook and handed it to Mackey.

"*Wolf Child's scouts spotted Darabont's rear guard by the stream about a mile ahead. Four men hanging back in an ambush. Two on the ground. Two up in trees on the far side of the river. Looks like they plan to hit us as we cross.*"

Mackey handed the notebook back to Sim. "Any sign that they spotted you?"

Sim shook his head.

Billy asked, "Is there good enough cover before the crossing where we could get within rifle range?"

Sim pointed at Billy, then the Boudreauxs, and nodded. Mackey understood. Enough cover for them to take out targets.

Mackey asked, "They close enough for us to go in on foot or ride?"

Sim walked two fingers along the back of his hand. *On foot.*

Mackey beckoned the Boudreauxs to ride back in toward the group. "Brahm, Javier, and Solomon: you stay here with Sandborne and the horses." When the Boudreauxs got there, he said, "I'm going to need you boys to come with us on foot. Bring your rifles."

Henry Boudreaux climbed down from the saddle. "Where we going, sheriff?"

Mackey pulled his rifle free from his saddle's scabbard. "Whittle some bastards down to size."

Mackey knew moving on foot was a hell of a lot slower than riding in, but necessary. They would be harder to hear if they crept in on foot. They left the mounts farther back with Brahm, Sandborne, and the *vaqueros*.

Sim led the way through the forest as Mackey, Billy,

and the Boudreauxs followed. When they got closer, Sim signaled them to walk single file, literally walking in Sim's footsteps. A snapped branch or a broken twig could be enough to give away their position. Darabont's men could open fire on them before they were ready. Or worse, they might escape and lie in wait for them somewhere farther down the trail. One of them might ride back and tell Darabont they'd been spotted. Mackey could not allow that to happen.

Sim crouched just short of the edge of a small wooded clearing near a creek. Sunlight filtered down through the leaves and shimmered on the surface of the rolling water. He pointed to a large felled tree on the other side of the creek. It was long and gnarled, with peeling bark and a thick carpet of moss growing along the side. The bare heads of two men were barely visible over the log, their rifles at rest, pointing toward the sky. They were careless about maintaining cover because they were bored. Bad news for them. Good fortune for Mackey.

Sim pointed up at the tree line above the fallen log. It took Mackey a moment to see what he was pointing at: two men perched in the notches of trees about ten feet off the ground. They weren't up very high, but high enough to rain fire down into Mackey's men as they would have been crossing the creek. The shots would've most likely spooked the horses and sent animals and riders in all directions. Mackey's men would have been on foot in the creek bed, easy pickings for gunmen lying in wait.

To Sim, Mackey whispered, "Where are Wolf Child's men?"

Sim used the old Apache hand signals he'd learned

in the cavalry to tell him: *They rode around and are still tracking our prey.*

Mackey had always been better with a pistol than a rifle, so he started assigning his men their targets. He pointed at Henry Boudreaux and motioned for him to get the man on the left side of the log. He gestured for his brother Jack to take the one on the right. He had Billy aim at the man in the tree on the left. And Sim would take the one in the tree on the right.

To all of them, he whispered, "Wait for my signal."

Back at West Point, Mackey had heard some of his instructors talk about their experiences in battle. Some of them said everything seemed to speed up when lead started to fly and cannon roared.

But the time before a battle had always been just the opposite for Mackey. Things always slowed down to a point where he saw everything clearly and knew exactly what to do. This was one of those times.

He waited until all four of his men had crept into position within the overgrowth. He waited until they'd had time to sight on their targets. He waited for each man to grow absolutely still. When they were, he sensed they were ready. He said, "Fire!"

The Boudreauxs fired a split second before Sim and Billy. Mackey watched the brothers' bullets strike both men behind the mossy log, red mist appearing behind their heads as they fell backward.

Mackey looked up in time to see Sim and Billy's targets drop from their perches like squirrels hit with a slingshot. One landed on top of the mossy log with a wet smack. If the bullet hadn't killed him, the landing had.

The last man fell from the tree and landed in the

creek bed feet first. He crumpled into the water, and the screams that followed proved he was still alive.

Mackey was already running toward the screaming man as Billy and the others got to their feet.

The crippled, bleeding gunman was struggling to keep his face above the water. The creek was only calf-high, but deep enough to drown a man if he couldn't keep his balance.

Mackey grabbed the gunman by the collar and dragged him onto dry land. The man screamed himself hoarse from the pain and, once they got to dry land, he understood why.

The bullet had gone clean through the right shoulder, but the shinbone of his left leg poked through his pants leg. The right leg was at an unnatural angle as well. He must've broken both legs as he hit the creek bed.

The man looked up at Mackey and rasped, "If you're a Christian man at all, you'll kill me quick."

Mackey nudged the man's broken leg with his boot. The man screamed out.

"You one of Darabont's men?"

"We all are," the man groaned. "Before he left us on that hillside, he told us to camp here and wait for you to come across. Said you'd probably have only three men with you, so the pickings would be easy."

Mackey looked at the three dead men. "Looks like he was wrong. How many of you are there?"

"Me and three other guys. We . . ."

Mackey moved his boot closer to the man's broken leg. "Not here. How many with Darabont. And don't lie because I already have a good idea of the number."

He looked at Mackey's Winchester. "You gonna do the Christian thing and kill me if I tell you?"

"I'll do the Irish thing and stomp on your legs if you don't."

The gunman swallowed hard. "Probably had thirty or so when he pulled out of that hillside a couple of days ago. Lost a lot of men taking that ranch. Miners and loggers cost us a few more, but we got the dynamite, for all the good it did us."

"How many captives does he have with him?"

"Ten. A couple of girls we picked up along the way and a full grown woman from that town you're from."

"She alive?" Mackey said quicker than he'd intended.

"He's treating her real special. Keeps her away from the other women on account of him fearing he doesn't want her putting ideas into their heads. Some of the boys want to shoot her, but Darabont said he's saving her."

Mackey thought that had to be Katherine, but he wouldn't ask him. Not in front of the others.

"Darabont taking them to Mexico?"

"You said you was going to kill me, damn it. Now I answered all your questions and . . ."

Mackey brought up his boot to stomp the man's leg, but the man quickly cried out, " He's heading west, that's all I know."

Mackey lowered his boot. "West? Where west?"

"He didn't tell us. He was thinking California or maybe Utah or Canada. Maybe hopping a boat somewhere, but you never know with him. He ain't much for telling us what he's thinking. He just does it. All I know is he plans to avoid Fort Custer at all costs. Says he doesn't want to run into any of them soldier boys on patrol."

"Darabont's smarter than he looks," Billy said. "You sure he didn't tell you any more than that?"

"All I know is he told us he was heading south for a while and we could catch up to him after we finished you off. He could be anywhere by now. All he told us was to follow his trail. That's it, mister, I swear!"

Mackey had heard enough lies to know the truth when he heard it. To Billy, he said, "Find out where these bastards picketed their horses and ride back to the others. Sim, I want you to take one of their horses and keep heading out on the trail; see if you can't meet up with Wolf Child's men. We'll be along as soon as we can with your mount. We'll camp along the trail just after sunset. You shouldn't have any trouble finding us."

As Billy and Sim went to search for the gunmen's horses, the dying man yelled to Mackey, "Where you going? Ain't you gonna kill me? You promised! You said you'd kill me if I told you everything and that's what I done."

The man was still yelling when they found the mounts and saddled up. The Boudreauxs shared a horse while Billy, Sim and Mackey got their own. Sim rode off down the trail at a good clip while Mackey led the men back to the others.

As they crossed the creek bed, the man kept yelling, "Concho is going to kill you, you son of a bitch. He's going to gut you and everyone you're with. He ain't like nothing you ever came up against, you bastard. He's the end. The worst. He's gonna skin you bastards alive, you hear me? Bastards!"

They did hear him and kept on hearing most of the way back down the trail to where they had left the others. There, they switched for their usual mounts, trailed Sim and the dead men's horses behind their own and headed back across the creek bed.

By the time they crossed the creek bed again, the man was no longer screaming. His shoulder wound had bled out.

Mackey was glad he hadn't wasted the bullet. He had a feeling he'd need every round in the days ahead.

Chapter 36

Mackey had Henry Boudreaux ride point and kept Billy and the others close to him. More of Darabont's men could be nearby. The brush was thicker here, and he didn't want to lose outriders to another ambush in the greenery. He wanted to have his men close in case anything popped. They were still only eight against twenty or more. Sandborne was still recovering from his head wound, so he couldn't be counted on for much. That made it over two-to-one against. Better odds than before, but not good enough where he could afford to be reckless.

Mackey knew his group had fared well in their first couple of engagements, but they hadn't seen much action. Until now, everyone had kept their head and followed orders. Even during the run-in with the Blackfeet, they all kept their powder dry. He took some comfort in that. Not much, but some.

Mackey turned when he heard Billy ride up beside him. "You believe what that bastard said about them avoiding Fort Custer?"

"I believe that's what he told them."

"But you don't believe it's true."

"I think Darabont saw what he was up against when he saw how we defended the town. He probably figured we'd spot those four bastards back there and would most likely kill them before they talked. He was hoping we'd lose a few on our side in the bargain and maybe turn back, but I'll bet he didn't think we'd get any of them alive. If I was him, I'd have told them the opposite of where I was heading just to be sure."

Billy rode a little taller in the saddle. "You're a smart man, Sheriff Mackey, because that's exactly what I was thinking, too."

"Where do you think they're riding next?"

"The trail will tell the tale, but I'd imagine it'll be straight for Fort Custer. He's most likely low on supplies and men and ammunition. Probably ride into town looking for any of the above or all three, just like he did in Dover Station. He'll be more careful this time, though. Tougher to track, too. Fort Custer's a busy place and it'll be easier for his tracks to blend in with the others."

Billy seemed to think about that for a moment. "Wish we knew what the rest of his men looked like."

"No need. They know what we look like. And I've got a feeling that'll be enough when the time comes."

Billy had ridden with Mackey long enough to know when to ask questions and when not to. This was one of the times he knew enough to keep his mouth shut. "A while back, I heard Captain Peters got himself named as commander of Fort Custer."

"I heard the same thing, though he's Major Peters now."

"Some history between you two."

Mackey hated it when Billy played coy. Peters had been one of the men who testified against him at his dismissal hearing from the cavalry. "You know there is."

"You planning on talking to him about helping us find Darabont?"

"I'm planning on reporting a massacre on a Blackfoot reservation, which is Peters' duty to investigate. I'm hoping I can wrangle some help with Darabont out of him in the bargain."

Billy rode quietly for a while. "You think he's still sore over what happened?"

"You mean about me beating his cousin half to death?"

Billy's horse threw a stone but he brought her under control. "I was trying to be delicate about it."

"Nothing delicate about caving in a man's skull," Mackey said, "even if he deserved it. I did it, and I paid the consequences for it. And yes, I'd imagine Major Peters is still angry about it."

"Well, seeing as how we're headed to the town right outside his fort, maybe you're not the best one to talk to him. Maybe I should do it."

"Maybe you're forgetting Major Peters is from Virginia and wasn't entirely accepting of people of your persuasion?"

"I didn't forget," Billy admitted. "I'm just trying to make sure you don't cave in his skull, too. As I remember, Peters was as much of a son of a bitch as his cousin."

"Your recollection fails you, deputy. Peters was the grandest son of a bitch I've ever known. Worse than Mayor Mason, if that's possible." Mackey tried a smile. "Don't worry. I'll hold my temper."

"We'd have better luck sending Sim to talk with him before you'd hold on to your temper."

Mackey couldn't argue with that.

It was going on full dark by the time they reached Fort Custer. Mackey knew the way and didn't need a lot of sunlight. Besides, the place looked better at night.

The town that had sprung up around the fort was every bit as squat and ugly as any other town he'd seen around any other fort in the West. The town of Fort Custer featured a general store, four hotels of various quality, a livery, a blacksmith, a couple of trading posts and, of course, plenty of whorehouses and saloons to meet the needs of soldiers and travelers alike.

All the stores were already long closed by the time Mackey led his men into town, but the windows of the saloons and whorehouses glowed with activity and possibility.

Mackey knew from experience that there were only two types of people in a town like Fort Custer: the men who'd been ordered to be there and the people who lived off them. That meant shopkeepers, bartenders, and whores. Mackey knew everyone had to be somewhere. And whores had to make a living, too.

He dug a bag of dollar coins out of his saddlebags and tossed it to Billy. "Get the mounts situated over at the livery. Have the stable boys give the horses plenty of feed and rest. We'll need them as fresh as possible before we head out after Darabont tomorrow."

"What about the men?"

"Get them set up in rooms wherever you can in

town. I want everyone in the same hotel if possible. Get one for me if you can manage it, but not until each of them has a place to lay their head. I'll sleep in the barn if I need to. Then get them something to eat. They can have beer but no whiskey. I need everyone to have clear heads for the trail tomorrow."

Billy tucked the bag of coins in his pocket. "What about female companionship?"

Mackey thought about that. "If they want that, they'll have to pay for it on their own. Just let them know I only want their trigger fingers to be itchy, nothing else."

Billy was still shaking his head as he led the men toward the livery.

Mackey didn't turn toward the fort right away. He wasn't a hesitant man by nature, but he hesitated now. This would be the first time he had set foot on federal property since his dismissal five years before.

He could remember a time when all he had ever wanted out of life was to be a soldier. He had intended on dying in uniform or being drummed out as an old man against his will. But now, he'd give anything to have all memory of his service scrubbed from his memory and he cursed the day he'd ever heard of Adobe Flats.

He looked through the gates at the squat, crooked buildings just inside the walls of the fort. There was still a light on in the building he knew housed the commander's office. He could always put off meeting Peters until tomorrow, but decided to get it over with.

He brought Adair around and rode through the gates.

* * *

The fort's headquarters building was a ramshackle affair warped by the intense heat of the frontier sun. The building was comprised of blistered wood and uneven beams and a sagging porch. The windows all had cracks from the building's uneven settling in the Montana mud. The building should have been repaired a long time ago. It should've been built right in the first place. But he wasn't in the army anymore. He had no right to complain.

He hitched Adair to the post outside the main building and walked inside.

An aging sergeant with a day's worth of stubble on his fleshy face sat at a table just inside the door. He stifled a yawn as though he'd just woken up from a long nap.

"What do you want?" the sergeant asked.

"I'm here to see Major Peters. Tell him . . ."

"Don't you see what time it is? Major don't take meetings at this time of night and he don't take meetings with drovers who just come in off the trail." The sergeant opened a notebook on his desk. "Make an appointment and maybe he'll see you tomorrow."

Mackey might be a civilian for over five years, but his days in uniform came to the fore. "Sergeant, my name is Captain Aaron Mackey of the United States Cavalry and I want to see Major Peters immediately. Now get your dead ass out of that chair and tell him I'm here before I beat you to death."

"Uh oh." The sergeant flushed and obviously recognized the name. He might not have moved as quickly as Mackey would've liked, but he moved as fast as he could into Peters's office. When he came back outside, he snapped to attention and was a lot paler than when he'd gone in.

"Sorry, sir. The major will see you now."

Mackey strode into the office and slammed the door behind him, ignoring the sergeant's salute.

Chapter 37

Mackey hadn't expected Major Samuel "Pete" Peters to be happy to see him. He wasn't disappointed.

Upon seeing the commanding officer of Fort Custer, Mackey was reminded of something Pappy used to say: *A fish rots from the head down.* Major Peters's condition reflected the rest of his command. His desk was cluttered with papers and opened ledgers. Mackey could see the barrel of a Colt pistol sticking out beneath piles of unread reports.

Peters's uniform was frayed around the collar and cuffs, the buttons dull. His sleeves bore tobacco and wine stains. He was clean-shaven, but his skin was pale and he looked like he hadn't slept in days. His once sandy hair was grayer than Mackey remembered and prematurely thinning.

Just about the only orderly thing about Major Peters was his thin, blond moustache. He'd had it since the day Mackey had first met him, back when Mackey was a young lieutenant and Peters was younger still. The major was Mackey's junior by four years, but that night, he looked at least a decade older.

"Fancy meeting you here," Peters said from behind his desk with all the Virginian aristocratic arrogance he could muster. Mackey could remember a time when the affectation had been amusing. But it didn't seem like an act now. It seemed like a drunk trying to come off better than he was. "I'd offer you a chair, but knowing you as well as I do, you'd probably just take it anyway."

Mackey remembered Peters always loved a great debate and was in no mood to oblige him. He simply sat down in one of the chairs facing the desk. "Been a while, Pete. How've you been faring?"

"Ah, so we've advanced to the pleasantries already. You know, I could have you arrested for impersonating an officer just now. You're not a cavalryman anymore."

Mackey made a point of looking over Peters. "Neither are you."

If Peters took offense, he hid it well. He nodded at the star pinned to Mackey's shirt. "Ah, look at that. I had heard you had become a lawman. I guess that bit of tin takes the sting out of being banished."

"Only thing I regret is not giving you the same beating I threw your cousin." Mackey smiled. "Would have, too, if you hadn't run and gotten the sergeant to pull me off him."

Peters looked away. Mackey used to see a fire in the brash younger man's eyes. Now, he didn't see much of anything at all. "Shall we sit here and discuss the missed opportunities of our youth or do you plan on telling me why you're here. It certainly isn't for your wish for my company."

"I'm here to report an attack on an Indian reservation under your jurisdiction."

Peters's bloodshot eyes narrowed. "Attack? What

attack? Where? On whom? I haven't been informed of any attack?"

Mackey knew Peters and knew his concern was more about his career than about the dead or the damage. "I'm informing you now. It happened a few days ago up at the Blackfoot reservation just outside Dover Station. I know you haven't been up there, even though you've been in command of the fort for over a year, but some of your men might know where it is."

"To hell with you, Aaron. I know exactly where it is."

Mackey grinned. "Good for you. A bastard by the name of Darabont raided a small village up there. Killed a good number of women and children while the men were out hunting. His group then raided my town. I'd like to report that, too."

"Darabont," Peters repeated. "I've heard of him. Thought he was further south than here."

"Yeah, well he's here now and he's raising hell wherever he goes. Got a group of women he's holding captive, too. Plans on selling them once he reaches Mexico, if they live that long."

"And I take it you're going after him."

"That's another reason why I'm here. I'd like you to lend me some men to help bring him in."

"I'm sure you would. How many men do you have with you?"

Mackey hedged. "Enough."

Peters might've been on the downswing of a mediocre career, but he was no fool. "How many, *Sheriff* Mackey?"

"Ten. Got Billy Sunday and Sim Halstead with me, plus two Blackfoot scouts."

"Sergeants Sunday and Halstead. Your old cohorts." Peters smiled. "You always were more at ease with the enlisted men, weren't you? What sort are the others with you?"

If spilling his guts was what it took to get Peters to help, he'd do it. "Four cow punchers and some hunters."

"Sounds like quite an impressive ensemble. Couldn't get anyone worth a damn to go with you, could you?"

"They defended Dover Station well enough. Sent ten of Darabont's men to Hell when the time came."

"I know you've been a civilian for quite some time," Peters said, "but I hope you haven't forgotten that defending a fixed position like a fort or a town is completely different than fighting an engagement on open land? I'd have thought the hero of Adobe Flats would realize that."

"And since you were with me at Adobe Flats, you saw how I can get the most out of men." He had a grin of his own. "Even you."

"You were a fine commander in your day, Aaron. No one can ever take that from you. Not even me, as much as I would like." Peters looked at his filthy tunic and made a show of wiping off an ash that wasn't there. "Alas, raiding a town isn't a federal offense unless it's by hostile natives. I'm afraid I can't help you with Darabont."

"Maybe not, but attacking Indians on a reservation is, which is why I need your help to track down the bastards who did this."

"Of course, after I conduct a full official investigation into the matter."

"We don't have that kind of time and you know it." He could feel his temper beginning to slip away from him. He forced himself to lower his voice. "I've got two scouts from Wolf Child's tribe riding with me right now who can testify to the whole thing. Right here. Tonight, if that'll help ease your conscience."

"Ah, so you're reporting that you've encouraged two scouts to jump the reservation." Peters sucked his teeth as he began taking notes. "First you impersonate an army official, now you've confessed to harboring two renegade Blackfoot dog soldiers. Your federal infractions are piling up more by the second, Aaron."

Mackey gripped the arms of his chair. "Don't do this, Pete."

"I'm doing the only thing I can under the circumstances. My duty. You should appreciate that. Besides, I doubt the sworn testimony of two heathens would hold up under scrutiny from my superiors, especially two that have willfully jumped the reservation under the wing of a disgraced former cavalry officer."

Mackey knew saying anything else would just make it worse. He clamped his mouth shut instead. He hadn't formally turned him down yet and might still come around. He also might want to have some more fun with him before he turned him down. Either way, Mackey had no choice but to sit and see what happens.

Peters sat back in his chair and was in no apparent hurry. He even sighed as he looked around his barren office. He pointed at an old barrel in the middle of the floor. "It's a horrible place, isn't it? Hasn't rained in days, but the roof still leaks. I have to dump that bucket out twice a day even during the mildest spring shower. But I get to hear it all day long, drip, drip, drip like a ticking clock reminding me of the passage of time."

Mackey didn't like the turn this conversation was taking. "Pete, for Christ's sake . . ."

"I shouldn't complain, though, should I? I'm doing

far better than poor William Pike is. You remember Willie? My cousin? The man you beat into a vegetative state?"

"He was beating a prisoner."

"An Apache dog soldier who'd butchered some of our men."

"A shackled prisoner nonetheless. I ordered him to stop and he attacked me. He got what was coming to him."

"You always contended that I was there that night, but that was never proved. Not by you and not by that goddamned redskin either. That didn't prevent you from naming me in your court-martial testimony, did it?"

"They called it a formal hearing of inquiry. I never got court-martialed and neither did you. Unfortunately."

"Yes, unfortunately. And now, fate has brought us both to this same place and this same time." He threw open his hands and laughed. "The ass-end of the army. A place so cold in winter and hot in summer, not even the Indians want to be here. Yet here they stay, so here I stay, babysitting a bunch of heathen savages whose time has already come and gone. I wish they had the good sense to simply die and save everyone the bother."

Mackey felt the bones of his fingers pop as he grabbed the armrest tighter. He made himself stop. "None of this has anything to do with why I'm here right now."

But Peters kept talking. "Do you know why they promoted me to captain, then to major so quickly? Because they had to stick me somewhere after the scandal and no one else wanted me. They loved you, but couldn't keep you after what you had done. They despised me based on your testimony but couldn't do much to me. They were going to shelve me in an office back in Washington, but Willie's father didn't want an office boy in uniform in the family. Might disgrace the family name even further. The good senator pulled strings to keep me in the field, so the army, in their own inimitable way, sent me here."

Peters looked closely at Mackey and, for the first time, the sheriff saw true madness in the major's eyes. "I have no choice but to be here. I'm under orders. But you're here of your own accord, aren't you? You're from this wretched part of the world. You had a family and a town that embraced you after your disgrace brought about by my cousin's actions. And I'm stuck here because of the disgrace to my family's name brought about to my cousin. You've played more of a role in my life than I think you've known, Aaron. And now, you need my help. Life's twists and turns are so funny sometimes, but there's a certain poetic justice to all of this, I think."

Mackey stood up. "You're an officer in the United States Cavalry. Start acting like one and quit your bellyaching. A command is whatever you make of it. You've made a pigsty of yours. You can change that any time you want. Tonight. This instant. And giving me the help I need to run Darabont down is a good place to start."

But Peters wasn't looking at Mackey anymore. He was looking in his general direction, but almost though him, as if he saw something in the near distance of his mind. Something that wasn't actually there but real enough to him. "I'll start my investigation in the morning. Yes, I think I'll do that first thing.

With luck, I'll have a troop in the field within a week. If you want to wait that long, fine. If not?" Peters's eyes refocused on Mackey. "Well, if not, I'm afraid you're on your own. In the wilderness. Just as I have been these many years."

Mackey had never thought much of Peters, but he'd thought him better than this. He might've been disgusted if he didn't have so much on his mind. "What the hell happened to you, Peters?"

The major appeared to give it serious thought before saying, "You. You happened to me." He straightened his filthy tunic. "Now get off my property."

Mackey made sure he left the door open when he left. He unhitched Adair from the post and rode away as quickly as possible. The more distance he put between him and the raving lunatic Peters had become, the better he'd feel.

Chapter 38

After stowing Adair in the livery with the rest of their mounts, he found Billy waiting for him in front of a saloon called The Belle Union. He could hear the sounds of laughter mixed with a tinny piano from across the street.

As was his custom, Billy was building a cigarette. "You talk to Pete?"

"I did. No luck."

"He still mad about what you did to his cousin?"

"He's just mad, as in out of his mind." He leaned against the porch post as he felt a sudden wave of weakness come over him. But this time, it wasn't from the pneumonia, but from the weight of the enormity of the task ahead. He had known all along that getting help from Peters was a long shot, but he hadn't expected to walk off the fort completely empty handed. He thought he'd have at least a squad to help him track down Darabont. It wasn't finding the bastard that mattered. It was about being able to kill him and free the hostages when they found him. About freeing Katherine.

But the army wouldn't help, so they were going to have to end this the way they'd begun it. On their own.

Billy licked his cigarette paper and wrapped his smoke tight. "What are we going to do now, Aaron?"

He wasn't sure. "Sim back yet?"

"No sign of him or the Indians with him."

Mackey hadn't expected Wolf Child's scouts to come into town, but he'd hoped Sim would have come back with a report. There were dozens of reasons why he hadn't come to Fort Custer, and not many of them were good. But he had enough trouble on his hands now without adding wild speculation to it. Sim had been in scrapes all of his life, both in uniform and out. If he hadn't come back to report, there was a reason. Mackey figured he'd find out why in due time, one way or the other.

He decided to think about something he could control. "How are the men holding up?"

"While you were busy dancing with the major," Billy said, "I had Brahm and the Boudreaux boys split up and do some polite asking about Darabont in the saloons around town. No one's admitted to seeing hide nor hair of Darabont's people yet."

"What about the . . ."

Billy held up a hand to stop him. "I talked to a clerk over at the general store just as they were closing. I got him to tell me that no one has placed any big orders, at least not enough to feed twenty men and ten or so hostages in the field."

He wasn't surprised at Billy's resourcefulness. He'd always known what Mackey needed, sometimes before Mackey knew it himself. Mackey also didn't doubt Brahm and the Boudreauxs had done a good job of asking about Darabont.

But sometimes, it wasn't about the question, but how you asked it. And who did the asking.

The germ of an idea began to form in Mackey's mind. "Have any luck getting us rooms anywhere?"

"Some hell hole named the Grand Hotel." Billy spat, then lit his cigarette. "I picked it because it had a lobby and had smaller mice than the ones I saw at the Hotel D 'Luxe on the south end of town." Billy looked at him closely. "Uh oh. I know that look."

The sheriff rapped his deputy on the shoulder and beckoned him to follow him inside the Belle Union Saloon. "Come on. I've got an idea."

The crowd was loud mix of civilians and soldiers in various stages of drunkenness. A scrawny drunk in a bowler was banging out a warbled rendition of "Old Dog Tray" on a tinny piano while whores in bright colored dresses and dark stockings tantalized the men to dream of other things, things that could be had in one of the rooms upstairs. Most of the men just leered at them over their beer or whiskey, but enough would plunk their money down for half an hour of paradise.

The Belle Union was cheap and tawdry and loud as any saloon found in any army town. And Mackey missed it. All of it.

He spotted his men at a table near the door against the wall. He was glad to see all of them had obeyed his orders about avoiding whiskey and had chosen beer instead. None of them had female companionship. The Boudreauxs looked longingly at the working girls, who looked just as longingly at them while they tolerated the curious hands of the drovers and the soldiers at the tables. The kid—Sandborne—glanced furtively at the girls, too shy to look at them directly. The *vaqueros* and Billy drew glares of another kind from the customers, but Brahm's presence ensured they'd do little more than look. The hulking German appeared to be more trouble than he was worth and he looked troublesome enough.

With Billy close behind, Mackey made his way over to his men and spoke to them over the noise of the crowd. "You boys get ready to drink up and pay up. I'm going to make a scene in a minute and we'll need to get to our rooms after that."

"Scene?" Henry Boudreaux asked. "You mean a fight?"

His brother cracked his knuckles. "I don't mind. I could do with a good brawl right about now."

"Nothing like that. The kind of scene that'll make us popular with some folks and unpopular with some others. Either way, we'll need to clear out right after. We're going to have a long day tomorrow."

Mackey ignored Billy's look of concern as he took one of the few empty chairs and stood on it. He shouted, "Can I have your attention, please?" several times before the room quieted down enough for him to speak in a normal voice.

"Some of you may know me, but a good number of you don't. I'm Captain Aaron Mackey, the man who killed all those savages at Adobe Flats."

The soldiers cheered and toasted him with their glasses.

Mackey yelled over them. "Now, I might not be in the army anymore, but I'm here tonight as the sheriff of Dover Station, a town that's a couple of days ride up the trail from here. We got hit by a group of cowardly sons of bitches who ride with a spineless murderer who goes by the name Darabont. This bastard took a lash to my town and killed a lot of women and children in the process. Those he didn't kill, he took with him and intends on selling down in Mexico."

Cries of "kill 'em" and "string 'em up" rose from the crowd. All of it was just hot air and boozy resolve, but he wasn't looking for zealots just then. As soon as they quieted down a bit, he continued. "My men and I intend on hunting these cowards to the ends of the earth if we have to. We're going to find them and string them up by their balls from the nearest tree limb when we do."

The drunkards banged tables and shouted support. Mackey talked over them. "We've got some damned fine men riding with us already, but we could always use more. I just came out of a meeting with Major Peters and he's vowed to lend us some soldiers to hunt these murderous bastards to the ends of the earth if necessary. They'll help, but we could always use more. That's why I'm asking for volunteers who might want to ride out with us to do what's right."

The men cheered again and thumped their fists against the tables and the bar. He felt Billy looking at him, wondering what the hell he was doing, but Mackey stayed in character. "Now, any of you brave men who want to sign up with me can come over to where I'm staying at the Grand Hotel tonight. I'll be in the lobby for a while, then upstairs in my room later. This is a paying job, boys. No volunteers, here. Just make sure you're ready to ride come first light tomorrow morning. We'll take any man who can shoot, who can ride, and wants to help us send these murderous cowards back to Hell where they belong."

More cheers rose up, boozy oaths to be ready filled the air. "Spread the word all over town, boys, and tell them I'll be at the Grand Hotel to sign you up. Now, since I've taken up your good time, next round's on me!"

Even Mackey flinched as a thunderous cheer rose up from most of the patrons of the Belle Union. From his place atop the chair, he noticed not all the men cheered. He saw two men standing at the bar, whose clothes were tattered and trail-dirty, whose long rangy hair hadn't seen a comb or a bar of soap in some time. In many ways, they looked no different than dozens of the rest of the men in the Belle Union that evening save for one important way.

The way they glared at him.

He knew they were his true audience. They were Darabont men.

Mackey stepped down from the chair and motioned for Billy to give him the moneybag. He did, and Mackey gave enough to the bartender to cover a round, with a good tip in the bargain. He reminded him that, if anyone asked, he was in the lobby over at the Grand Hotel.

He politely ignored requests from the soldiers to buy him a drink. Everyone wanted to be with the hero of Adobe Flats.

That's what he was counting on.

As he led his men out of the saloon, Billy said, "I hope you know what you're doing, because I sure as hell don't."

Mackey was surprised at how good he felt. "I just rang the dinner bell. Now let's see if anyone's hungry."

Chapter 39

Like everything else in Fort Custer, the lobby of the Grand Hotel was as misnamed. Mackey took a seat on the threadbare couch against the wall, next to the window facing the street. This wouldn't work unless he could be seen.

Billy had stationed Brahm at the front door of the hotel. He was a menacing presence and would keep the drunks and lightweights away. After all, this wasn't really a recruitment drive. He was setting himself up as bait.

Billy had sent the two *vaqueros* to bed, with the Boudreauxs on the hotel's second floor balcony, rifles ready. The Mexicans would relieve the brothers if the night lasted that long. Sandborne was supposed to be asleep, but Mackey figured the kid would be too excited to get a wink. He couldn't blame him.

Billy positioned himself out of sight at the top of the stairs, his Sharps ready to cover the lobby. Mackey might not have pulled a stunt like this if Billy hadn't been along to back his play.

The innkeeper was glad for the attention Mackey's announcement had given his establishment. He offered him a bottle of whiskey and a free steak dinner with all the trimmings, at a discounted price, of course. Mackey spotted the dead mouse beneath the far end of the couch. He opted for a pot of black coffee instead and hoped it would be strong enough to kill whatever germs were in the pot and cup.

He was about fifteen minutes into his recruitment drive when he saw the first men began to appear. Drunks, mostly, who'd toddled across the thoroughfare from the Belle Union to enlist in Mackey's noble cause. Brahm shooed them away.

The more serious types came later. They were gun hands and drifters, men of few prospects drawn by the promise of easy money and blood. Mackey half listened to them tell him how impressive they were, who they'd ridden with and how many men they'd killed. All the while, he kept an eye on the front door of the Belle Union and for any sign of Darabont's men.

Mackey soothed the ego of each man who'd offered to sign up. He stalled for time, telling them they'd be riding out at first light if they were serious. They all shook his hand and told him they'd be ready. And he watched each one of them trail back into the saloon to celebrate their new assignment at the side of the hero of Adobe Flats. He doubted any of them would be ready to ride in time. He doubted he'd still be in town at first light anyway. For if he was, it would mean his plan had failed.

That's when he spotted one of the men he'd seen at the bar come out of the saloon. Darabont's man. Now that he was on eye level, he could see the man better, even from across the street. He was tall and thinner than his clothes. His duster was splattered with layers of mud, and his face had a lean, sunken look. His duster was pulled back over the handle of the pistol on his right hip, but that didn't mean anything. Lots of men walked around like that, especially in a town like Fort Custer.

But he was eyeing the hotel the same way Mackey was eyeing the Belle Union. He seemed to notice Mackey was watching him, for he spat in the street and wiped his mouth with the back of his hand as he moved up the street and out of Mackey's line of sight.

I see you, Mackey thought. *But where's your buddy?*

Mackey turned when he heard the back door of the hotel open. His hand moved closer to the handle of the Colt jutting up from beneath the table, but he didn't pull. No reason to force something before it happened.

After all, trouble had never had a problem finding Aaron Mackey.

The other Darabont man he'd seen in the bar ambled into the lobby at his own pace. He was as scraggly as his friend on the street, his eyes just as hard.

The man pawed at his mouth with the back of his hand. His duster wasn't pulled back over his pistol butt, but Mackey could see he was wearing a gun belt.

The man stayed by the front desk, where the innkeeper was fussing with the mail in the slots behind the desk.

"You really Aaron Mackey?" the gunman asked. "That feller who done all them things at Adobe Flats?"

The innkeeper answered for him. "Of course it is, mister. That's him right there, in the flesh. Sheriff of Dover Station and the hero of Adobe Flats. As righteous and courageous a man as we've ever had in Fort Custer, and we're damned honored to have him in our hotel."

The man pawed at his beard. "That's what I thought. Well I'll be damned."

"Glad to meet you, friend." Mackey smiled as he sat back on the couch, but kept his hand on the table only an inch from the handle of his Colt. "You here to sign up for our worthy cause?"

"Came to ask you about that. You said this here Darabont feller burned injuns and whores like that was a bad thing to do. In my book, that's what some might call a work of mercy. Whores and injuns ain't worth nothin'."

"Lots of people would agree with you, friend, except for one thing."

The man spat a stream of tobacco into the silver spittoon by the front desk. "What's that?"

"Back in the saloon, I didn't say anything about burning Indians. Or whores, neither."

Mackey saw Billy's rifle flash from atop the landing just as the window facing the street shattered. He heard Brahm yell as Billy fired again. He heard a man cry out and a body hit the boardwalk outside.

But Mackey hadn't moved.

And neither had the gunman in the lobby. Not even when the innkeeper came from behind the desk and ran outside.

"You get him?" Mackey asked Billy without taking his eyes off the stranger.

"I got him." He heard Billy lever a fresh round into the Sharps. "Got this one, too, if you need it."

Mackey and the man kept looking at each other. "That's up to him."

The man smiled a jagged yellow smile, just like

Darabont's. "Sounds like your negra friend's backing your play. Awfully smart."

"I haven't lived this long by being dumb. But no one is backing me now, friend. This is just you and me."

"I'd a thought you'd had your fill of Darabont by now, friend. Crossing him ain't smart. In fact, it's just about the dumbest thing a man could do."

Mackey smiled, too. "How about you show me? Right now."

The man brought up his left hand and the pistol in it.

Mackey pulled the Colt and shot him through the belly before the man could aim.

The man doubled over and tried to keep his balance. He tumbled over, firing once into the floor as he fell onto his back. Mackey quickly got up as the man tried to bring up his gun again. Mackey pinned his arm to the floor beneath his boot, putting all his weight on his wrist. The Darabont man screamed.

Billy and the others came running downstairs as Brahm barreled into the lobby.

"You get him?" Billy asked.

"Of course I did." He opened the Colt's chamber and removed the spent shell; dropping it on the gunman's face. "You boys help the Boudreauxs keep an eye on the street. This bastard might have more friends in town. Have Javier, Solomon, and Sandborne get our horses ready. We'll be riding out as soon as this bastard tells us where we can find Darabont. And Brahm, don't let anyone in here until I saw so. My new friend here and I have some things to discuss."

After the others cleared out, Mackey snapped the Colt's cylinder shut and spoke to the dying man. "It's just you and me now."

The man laughed a wet laugh. "You ride out tonight, you'll be riding straight to hell if Darabont has anything to say about it. You've seen what that man can do at night."

Mackey slid his pistol back into the holster. "Did you know this place has a full kitchen? Food's not so good, so the cook covers it with lots of salt."

"Salt?" Another wet cough. "Who cares about salt?"

"You do, because I'm going to start pouring a whole lot of it into that belly wound unless you tell me where Darabont made camp. You tell me that, I'll let the town doctor look at you. You don't, you'll die in as slow and as painful a way as I can think."

"Bastard. You'll probably do that anyway."

"Only if you lie to me." He put more weight on the gunman's wrist until he screamed out again. "So, where is he camped?"

Chapter 40

Sim Halstead stayed low as he crept through the darkness. He had lost track of the Blackfoot warriors some time ago—maybe an hour or more—but he kept on going. He didn't need them for what he was doing now. He had been hunting white men and red men for half his life. The other half, he'd spent being hunted by them.

He had picketed his horse a quarter of a mile back when he saw the tracks split off. He'd seen similar tracks from the hillside to the creek bed back in Dover Station. That had led to an ambush—albeit a half-assed one—but an ambush just the same. He didn't want Mackey and the others to ride into another one in open ground.

Sim followed the tracks in the pale moonlight. The rider had split off from the rest of Darabont's group and moved off the trail into the timber. It was harder to track the rider through the forest floor, especially at night, but Sim had tracked men through much worse and with less light.

The tracks might've looked like any other horse tracks to another tracker, but Sim knew what to look for. He'd been following this trail for a hundred miles since Dover Station. He'd come to be able to read it like Mr. Rice might read a stock report, and he could glean as much information from it, too. The tracks told him the condition of the mounts, the scat told them how many there were, the gait of the tracks told him which horse might be lame and which mounts were tiring.

He had seen this particular track many times in the many miles since Dover Station. This one had an uneasy gait. Long, then clipped, giving it a certain skitter as it moved. It could've been the nature of the horse or the fault of the rider pulling up on the bit without even realizing it. Either way, it was there and it was definable.

And it led Sim into a stand of tall trees off the main trail.

There were plenty of reasons why a rider might split off from the rest of the group. Given the number of women in Darabont's group, none of those reasons were probably good for the captives riding with them.

As he followed the trail into the stand of trees, he kept his Colt holstered. His Bowie knife was his weapon of choice now. He'd left his Winchester back in the scabbard on his saddle. It was too dark to do much good with a rifle. Any work that needed to be done would be done best up close with a knife or a pistol.

Sim was just inside the cluster of trees when he realized the tracks changed. The horse was no longer being ridden, but led. The footprints of moccasins were barely visible in the soft earth, which was the whole point of wearing them. He had seen these moccasins before, but not on the feet of the Blackfoot warriors tracking with them.

The trail led off too far to the right, too close to the tree and kept going in that direction, into the darkness of the trees beyond. It was too neat; too easy to follow, given Darabont's men knew they were being followed.

Instinct brought Sim away from the tree, stepping backward, Bowie knife ready.

Instinct made him look up. Just as Concho dropped from the tree limb above him.

Instinct made him raise the blade of his Bowie knife as Concho fell on him.

Sim's grip held through the impact, even as the blade slid into Concho's heart, even as the handle of his own knife was crushed into his chest, pinning his hands beneath the gasping renegade.

Concho's knife dropped from his hands, his breath escaping him as the blade punctured his lung until the knife tip poked through his back. He had misjudged the reflexes of the older man and landed too high atop his target.

Sim tried to move, but could not. He tried to flip the Indian off him, but his legs couldn't move. He tried to work his hand free, but found it trapped beneath Concho's weight. He didn't know if he was paralyzed or simply pinned to the ground as Concho was impaled by his Bowie knife.

All he knew was that he couldn't let Concho pull that blade free.

Sim heard Concho's wet coughs and gasps as he fumbled to get to his feet. He saw the Indian roll off him instead and flop over onto his back. He coughed again when he collapsed, sending a spray of blood onto Sim's face. The scout tried to wipe it away, but could not move his hands.

He was paralyzed after all.

He was able to lift his head just enough to see the Bowie knife was no longer in his hands. He looked over and saw it still sticking out of Concho's heaving chest.

Good, Sim thought. *He'll never pull it out on his own. Not with it so deep.*

But he saw that Concho wasn't quite done yet. The renegade was reaching for something with his left hand. It was too far out of Sim's limited vision to see what it was? Was it the knife he had lost when he fell from the tree? Was it a rock?

He never found out what he was reaching for, because Concho stopped moving, coughed a few more times before he grew very still. When he heard the Indian's bladder release, he knew Concho was dead.

Sim was already very still, too, and very much alive. He tried moving his feet again, but could not. He tried simply wiggling his toes, but no luck there, either. His hands were still on his stomach where the handle of his Bowie knife had been. They would not respond to his will, either.

He raised his head and looked himself over as well as he could. He didn't see any blood and decided he was probably just stunned from the impact of Concho falling on him from such a height. He set his head back on the cold ground and closed his eyes, listening to the night sounds of the forest slowly come back to life. The humans had struggled, but now it was over and they had their business to attend to.

The old scout closed his eyes and tried not to think of what might come for him in the night. He tried to think of Aaron and Billy and how they would find him the next morning at the latest.

He only hoped it would not be too late.

Chapter 41

Given the fullness of the moon that evening, Mackey and the others set out well before sunrise to hunt Darabont. The wounded gunman had told him Darabont's men were supposed to follow the trail south and camp past a stand of trees where they would be sheltered from the prying eyes of passersby on the trail. He said the group was low on ammunition and food; the last meat from the cattle they'd slaughtered was beginning to go bad. Darabont had sent the two men to scout the town and purchase provisions the next morning if the town was clear.

The information made sense, so he believed it. It's what Mackey would've done.

He'd fought the urge to kill the man after he'd told the truth. He let the doctor work on him instead. Besides, it would take the man a while to die, even if the doctor did manage to save him. He could always go back and kill the man later if he was lying.

The sky was beginning to brighten with the coming dawn when they saw Sim Halstead's dappled gray hitched to a distant tree just off the main trail. Billy and Mackey spurred their horses into a gallop, stopping next to the mount.

Billy looked at the horse's saddle. "It's Sim's horse, all right." He pointed over at the stand of trees in the near distance. "Looks like he went on foot for some reason. Probably over there."

Mackey didn't like it. Sim was an old cavalryman. He would never have gotten off his horse unless he thought it was necessary. To the others, he said, "You men stay here and stay on your guard. I want rifles out and eyes on all positions. Call out if you see anything move. We'll be right back."

Mackey steered Adair through the overgrowth and into the clearing that led to the stand. Billy followed.

When he got closer, he saw the two men lying on the ground in a clearing within the trees. One was lying on his back, with something sticking out of his chest. The other's body was laying at an unnatural, broken angle.

Mackey was off Adair and running full speed toward them before he realized he was doing it.

The one Darabont had called Concho was the one with the knife sticking out of his chest.

The broken man was Sim; his arms barely clawing the ground as his legs were twisted crooked. He didn't have to examine him to know his back had been broken.

No, no, no, no.

He slid to a halt next to Sim and saw the old scout was still alive, though barely. His eyes were wide as he tried, breathlessly, to get to his feet. His mouth was stained with dry blood and his breath was shallow.

Mackey cradled his old friend's head in his hands.

"You'll be okay. Just sit still a while until we get this sorted out."

But if his old friend heard him, he didn't show it. His eyes were fixed on a point, deep in the gloomy stand of trees. His arms flailed back and he grabbed Mackey's shoulders with both hands. Even as death approached, his old friend had a hell of a grip.

For the first time in as many years as he could remember, Sim's mouth moved and he began to try to speak.

Mackey tried to quiet him. "It'll be okay, Sim. Billy's going to look you over. He's better than any doctor going. You know that."

Sim's mouth quivered as a tear streaked down his cheek. And the man who hadn't spoken in more than a decade struggled to speak now. "Aaron, look." His eyes locked onto the gloom. "It's them. They're still . . . alive. Amy and the boys. They're here. They came!"

Mackey couldn't have seen anything, even if his own eyes weren't filled with tears. It wasn't just because he knew his oldest friend was dying. It was because, for the first time in longer than he could remember, he saw Sim Halstead smiling. "Of course they did. Where else would they be?"

Sim struggled to raise his head from Mackey's hands, to go to the family he'd lost so long ago. The family whose death had caused him to curse God and hold his silence ever since. Sim gasped as his eyes went soft and he was gone.

Billy Sunday took a step back and wept.

Mackey buried his face in the old scout's chest and screamed longer and louder than he had ever screamed before.

Chapter 42

Sim's burial was a blur.

Mackey and Billy dug as deep a grave as they could in the hard ground of the forest and covered it with as many rocks as they could find. It wasn't permanent anyway. Mackey would see to it he was buried in Dover Station where he belonged.

They left Concho where he had fallen, but pulled Sim's knife from his chest.

Mackey wiped the blood on the renegade's clothes and gave it to Billy.

But Billy wouldn't take it. "He'd want you to have it."

Mackey didn't take the knife away. "I was an officer. He'd want an enlisted man to have it."

Billy took the knife and kissed the handle before he tucked it into his belt and climbed into the saddle. "Never thought he'd go out like that."

"He went out fighting. We should all be so lucky."

The two of them rode back along the clearing to the others. They let their horses move at their own pace. Darabont was close by and waiting on supplies. He wasn't going anywhere.

* * *

An hour later, Billy spotted one of Darabont's look-outs on an outcropping just off the trail. The man was leaning against a tree, dozing on his feet instead of keeping an eye on the trail as he'd been assigned to do.

Billy slid out of the saddle and drew Sim's knife. "I'll take care of it."

Mackey and the others watched Billy move slow and steady toward the sleeping man. Billy stepped quickly but quietly around the tree, slipped his hand over the man's mouth and drew the blade across his throat in one fluid motion. No scream, no sound except for the dead man's body hitting the ground. Billy signaled Mackey to come forward.

Mackey motioned for his men to stay where they were before he dismounted and joined Billy at the edge of the outcropping. The two of them belly crawled up the slight rise and peered over the edge down at the camp below.

Darabont's camp was about a quarter of a mile below the outcropping, nestled against the rock wall. The sun had just begun to rise, giving them a good look at the layout.

Mackey counted twenty bedrolls on the ground around a central cook fire. A covered wagon sat un-hitched and farther away from the camp. He figured that's where the captives might be. Where Katherine might be.

This was the closest he had been to her since this whole nightmare had begun.

He pushed every thought of her out of his mind, for this was no time for distractions. Mackey and his men were outgunned and outnumbered, and taking the camp wasn't going to be any easier without Sim. He had wasted enough emotion over Sim's grave.

Now was a time to think.

In the growing light of coming day, Mackey noticed how the trail became a gradual incline that snaked around down to a small box canyon where Darabont and his people had camped. Seeing as how the trail was the only way down and the only way out, Darabont probably had it guarded.

The entire situation reminded Mackey of Darabont's failed siege at Dover Station, only this time he would be in Darabont's position. He hoped the invaders would fare better this time.

Darabont had probably made camp in the box canyon because he didn't think anyone would dare attack a party that size.

Mackey was about to prove him wrong.

Mackey looked back and motioned for the men to hitch their horses and come toward him quietly. To their credit, each man did as he'd told them. For a group of amateurs, they were shaping up into a decent outfit, even young Sandborne.

Billy and Mackey met them halfway between the horses and the outcropping. They gathered in front of him in a tight semi-circle and he spoke in a low voice. "Our targets are at hand, boys. Darabont's men are camped right below us. We're still outmanned and outgunned, but Billy and I have been up against worse odds with the Apache and we're still here to talk about it. If you do what we tell you, chances are you'll be telling your grandkids about this someday."

The men laughed, not out of humor, but because it masked their fear.

To Sandborne and Brahm, Mackey said, "I want

you two up here with the Boudreaux boys peppering those bastards with rifle fire. Call out your targets ahead of time and put them down. Looks like there are about twenty of them, mostly still in their bedrolls, so picking them off as they wake up should be easy. Make sure you tell each other who you're shooting at before you shoot. I don't want you wasting four bullets on one man when you could be taking down four different men at once."

"What will you be doing?" Jack Boudreaux asked.

"Billy, Solomon, Javier, and me will ride into them hard and take down the bastards you miss."

Both Boudreauxs began to protest, but Mackey cut that off quick. "I know you boys want to be in the thick of it, but the *vaqueros* are better riders and better with their pistols than you are. You boys are the best rifle-men we have. I need you up here where you can do some damage. But there's too many of them to pick off from up here. A few of them are bound to get to cover or try to hurt the women we think are in the wagons. If we ride in hard and cut them off, we'll have a better chance of winning this thing."

Billy pointed to the south, and Mackey continued. "This trail forks off to the south and leads down to their camp. Darabont most likely has more guards along the way. I already killed one of them, but we can't sneak up on them on foot without at least one of them getting off a shot and waking the whole camp. That means we'll have to shoot them on our way down. The first shot will be your signal to start picking off your targets in their bedrolls. Hit your man in the chest and put him down."

He paused to allow the men to ask questions. When he didn't hear any, he continued to the tricky part.

"You all know there's a group of captive women down there, but we can't see them. I think they're either near the wagon or inside it. The wagons are all out of range for you boys anyway, so you let Billy and me worry about them. Solomon and Javier here will ride through the camp and put down anyone you boys miss." He looked at the *vaqueros*. "That sit well with you boys?"

Both men nodded. "For Sim," Solomon said.

"And for Mr. Taylor," Javier added.

"Dead men don't need intentions," Billy said. "We're doing this for the living."

Mackey nodded. "And let's hope we're among the living as well when this is all over."

Chapter 43

Mackey led the men, single file, down the trail at a fair clip, holding Adair's reins a bit tighter than normal. The horse could always sense when trouble was coming and liked to charge right at it. But if they rode down the trail at full gallop, they might miss some guards and risk getting shot in the back.

And if they went in too slow or on foot, the camp might wake up before the first shot was fired. Being outmanned, Mackey wanted to avoid that if possible.

Mackey let Adair trot down the sloping trail as he looked for signs of movement among the brightening shadows along the trailside. He heard the unmistakable sound of a hammer being pulled back just ahead of him. "Pete," a voice called out. "Tom? That you, boys?"

Billy's rifle responded, knocking the man from the shadows into the trail. The man had caught a round in the shoulder. Mackey drew his Colt and finished him off with a shot to the head.

The outcropping surrounding the camp flared with rifle fire as the Boudreauxs launched a volley into the sleeping men in the camp below.

Mackey had already given Adair her head, allowing her to gallop flat out down the trail. One Darabont man fired from the shadows but the shot went wide. From behind him, he heard the pistols of the *vaqueros* fire, taking the man down.

Mackey and Billy hit the camp first. Mackey had raided more camps than he cared to count in his life, and each time had been like the first time. The world slowed. Sounds became muffled and blurred as his vision became sharper than he ever thought it could be.

He watched half-dressed men begin to scramble out of their bedrolls, sleep still heavy in their eyes as they reached for their gun belts. As had been their custom since their cavalry days, Mackey took the men on their right and Billy shot the men on the left.

With five shots left in his pistol, Mackey drew careful aim on each target as he raced for the wagon. His skill and training helped him aim, compensating for the movement of Adair, the movement of a Darabont man, the speed of his horse and the recoil of his Colt. A fraction of a second felt like a full minute as he took aim and fired one shot per target. He aimed at each man's chest, firing as he passed. Five shots. Five Darabont men down.

No sign of Darabont himself.

He holstered his empty pistol and drew Adair to a halt as he pulled his Winchester from the saddle scabbard and dismounted. He slapped his horse's hindquarters, sending her on her way. She continued to tear through the camp at top speed, drawing fire from Darabont's men as Billy and the *vaqueros* shot whoever the Boudreauxs and the others had missed.

Mackey dropped to a crouch and brought the rifle

up to his shoulder as a shot rang out from the wagon. *Is that Darabont? Is he killing the women? Katherine?*

But the shot had come from outside the wagon. Two of Darabont's men had taken cover behind the wagon. The burly man and the skinny one who had been with Darabont the night he had visited Mackey's home. Skinny was crouched at the back of the wagon, taking aim with a pistol while Burly was behind him, reloading a shotgun. Skinny fired again at Mackey and missed again.

Mackey took aim and fired, striking Skinny just below the left shoulder, the impact sending him backward into his friend. Burly fell back dropping the shotgun in mid-reload. Mackey dashed a wide arc around the wagon until he had a clear shot at the prone man. Burly saw him and threw up his hands, his eyes wide with fright. "Don't shoot, mister! I give up. I . . ."

Mackey shot him between the eyes.

He shifted his aim when he heard a man from inside the covered wagon cry out, "AARON MACKEY!"

Sporadic gunfire spread throughout the camp, but from the sounds of it, he knew they were his men firing, not Darabont men.

Female screams from inside the wagon. Any one of them could've been Katherine's or none of them. Mackey couldn't care about that now.

Mackey yelled into the darkness of the wagon. "It's over, Darabont. Your men are dead. Let the women go and I promise you justice."

A woman leapt from the back of the wagon and hit the ground hard. She was a blond woman in a filthy nightgown that had once been white. *Not Katherine.*

She shook as she quickly pushed herself beneath the wagon on bloody elbows.

"He's got a gun on the others."

Mackey flinched when two shots erupted from the wagon, not at him but through the floorboard of the wagon. Darabont was shooting at the woman who'd escaped. The women screamed, maybe because they had been hit by the gunfire.

The woman beneath the wagon looked up at Mackey and shook her head. She hadn't been hit.

He heard Darabont shout a whisper inside the wagon. His aim shifted as he saw five of the women stand and crowd toward the back of the wagon bed. The axel groaned beneath the added weight on one end.

His belly grew cold. None of them was Katherine.

They were all skinny and red-faced from crying, shivering from fear and the chilly morning air. Their clothes were tattered. Some of them were bare-breasted and made no attempt to cover themselves. They were beyond modesty. Some looked like they were even beyond surviving. They looked more relieved than frightened. They knew their ordeal was finally over, one way or the other.

Out of the corner of his eye, Mackey saw Billy approaching as he reloaded his rifle. He darted over to the woman beneath the wagon, grabbed her by the leg and pulled her away behind the rear wagon wheel.

Darabont called out from inside the wagon. "Looks like we're back where we started, sheriff. Me with a shitload of hostages and you with just a rifle in your hand."

Mackey listened, gauging exactly where he was in the wagon.

Darabont went on. "I've got women lined up around the interior of the wagon, so any of you bastards shoot in here, you'll hit one of them. But I've kept one back, though. I've grown rather fond of her in our time on the trail. A fancy, highborn lady I think you know. Mrs. Katherine Campbell of Boston. She's quite a woman. She . . ."

Darabont's words dulled as the blood began to roar in Mackey's ears. He gripped the Winchester tighter. The bastard had found out who Katherine was. Somehow he'd always known it would come down to this.

Billy snapped him out of it by whispering to him "The girl said he's lying. The only women in there are bunched up there. He's in the back of the wagon with a gun to Katie's head."

Darabont was still talking as Mackey whispered, "Get the women to drop and I'll take him."

Billy didn't seem to like the idea, but he was in no position to argue. He backed away and got the girls' attention.

When he heard Darabont stop talking, Mackey said, "Your men are dead, Darabont. You've got nowhere to go and no one left to help you. Let the women go, climb down from there and I promise you'll get justice."

"Justice?" Darabont laughed, a high, desperate cackle. "Do I strike you as a man interested in justice?"

"You avenged your dead," Mackey said. "And I've avenged mine. The scales are even now. Let the women go and you and I can end this like we should have at the beginning. One on one, just you and me."

Billy continued gesturing to the women at the edge of the tailgate, and a few of them nodded.

Darabont said, "How about this? I made you a fair offer during the siege. The offer still stands. Drop your rifle, call off your men, and surrender to me."

Mackey glanced over at Billy, who mouthed the word, "Ready."

Mackey nodded and Billy showed the women one finger.

Then two. Some of the women trembled.

"What's it going to be, sheriff?" Darabont called out. "You . . ."

Billy's third finger went up and time slowed once more.

He heard the wagon creak as all five women fell forward out of the wagon. They didn't jump, they just fell flat like sacks of flour.

The mouth of the covered wagon was an empty maw, save for a tiny slit of light just behind the buckboard.

A light that shined between Darabont and Katherine.

Mackey's aim was already true. He squeezed the trigger and fired.

Mackey dropped the Winchester and leapt over the women, hurtling himself into the wagon.

He found Darabont had fallen backward toward the buckboard, pulling the canvas open. His right shoulder gone from the shot, but still conscious. The pistol nowhere in sight.

He found Katherine was in the other corner, screaming through her gag. Her hands and feet bound by rope. Mackey pulled the gag down as Katherine shrieked and cried. He undid the rope that bound her hands and she blindly pummeled his chest, his back, anything she could reach. He held her close to him as she flailed blindly at him.

"It's Aaron, my love. It's me. You're safe, honey. You're safe. It's me."

Billy bolted into the wagon, but Mackey didn't care. He kept absorbing the blows until her strength failed her. She was panting now as Mackey held her tighter than he ever had before.

"It's me, Katherine. Aaron. Your Aaron. You're safe. It's me."

She raised a trembling hand to feel his face. She wasn't clawing at him now, but patting at him blindly. He slowly eased his grip so she could finally see him.

She grabbed his face with both hands and looked up into his eyes. She had only been Darabont's prisoner for a few days, but looked like she had been with him for years. New streaks of silver were in her hair. Lines on her face that hadn't been there before. Her cheeks fallow and her eyes wild. Seeing this strong, graceful woman laid low broke his heart.

"Aaron," she said feebly. "It can't be. You . . . you're a ghost. He said you were dead. He said he killed you. He said he drowned you himself."

Mackey smiled as he felt a tear run down his own cheek. "He lied, honey. I'm right here. It's all over and you're safe."

She thumbed away his tear. "It really is you, isn't it? I knew you'd come. I told him you would. I told him no matter what happened, you'd come, even if you came by yourself."

"And you were right, but I'm not alone. Brought Billy with me. He's right here, see?"

He moved to his left, blocking her view of Darabont so she could see his deputy.

She looked at him as though she were seeing him for the first time. "Billy?"

Mackey couldn't tell for certain, but he thought Billy was crying, too. "Good to see you, Miss Kate. You always were a vision in the morning."

Mackey undid the rope binding her feet. "Go to Billy. He'll take care of you for a minute."

She threw her arms around his neck and held on tight. "I won't let you go. Not ever."

He helped her to her feet and swept him up into her arms. He hadn't held her like that since Boston. She barely weighed anything. "Just got to finish something here, first, my love. I'll be with you in a minute."

Billy jumped down from the wagon and Mackey handed her to him. She tried to walk but was unsteady on her feet. Billy practically had to carry her, but she tried to walk.

That was his Katherine. No matter the circumstances, always proud.

He gripped the canvas to keep himself from falling over. She was safe. Katherine was alive.

A wet cough from the back of the wagon brought him back to reality. "How touching," Darabont said. "True love never fails, eh? I should've . . ."

Darabont screamed as Mackey fell on him.

Chapter 44

Billy used a strip of cloth from the burly man's shirt to bandage Mackey's bloody hands.

Mackey was still waiting for the effects of his rage to ebb away. "How long was I in there?"

"Long enough," Billy said. "Ain't seen you like that since that business that got you drummed out of the cavalry. You're still hell and Jesus with your fists, Aaron."

Mackey didn't remember any of it. "How many did it take to pull me away?"

"Solomon, Javier, and both Boudreauxs tried. Brahm was the only one who was able to get a firm grip on you and hold you down until you got right again."

Mackey pawed at something wet and sticky on his neck with the back of his left hand. Blood he knew wasn't his own. It was Darabont's.

"Did I kill him?"

Billy tilted his head to the left. "See for yourself. He's alive, but near enough to death that he'll wish you killed him."

Mackey looked over and saw Darabont tied to the wagon wheel. The image of the charred girl back on the hillside flashed in his mind. Darabont's head was covered in blood, half of his hair ripped away. His nose was shattered, and both eyes were already swollen shut. His jaw hung at an unnatural angle.

"I think you fractured every bone in his head," Billy said. "Broke his jaw, too. Least we won't have to listen to the bastard anymore."

Mackey felt himself laugh for the first time since he could remember. Billy laughed, too, as he bandaged his old friend's bloody hands. "We'll soak these in cold water once the ladies get through bathing. Glad this happened now instead of before the fight. I don't think you broke anything, but you won't be able to hold a gun for a week or so."

He stood up as if waking from a dream. "Katherine? Where's Katherine?"

"She's fine," Billy assured him. "She's helping the ladies clean themselves up. Darabont had plenty of water for the men, but never let the ladies bathe. She said women feel more like women when they're cleaned and proper. That girl I pulled out from under the wagon tells me Katherine kept them together on the trail. Said she kept Darabont off his feed with all that fancy talk of hers."

Mackey's breathe skipped. "Did he . . ."

As was his custom, Deputy Billy Sunday knew what the sheriff meant. "Don't know if he did and I wouldn't go asking her, either. If she's of a mind to tell you that, she will. If not, best leave it alone. What's past is past. You've both still got a lot of living ahead of you. She's quite a woman, Aaron. You're lucky."

He decided Billy was right. On all counts. His rage almost gone, he decided to focus on what he did best. "We take any casualties?"

"Solomon took one in the calf, but it went clear through. Killed his horse, though, but he's fine. Someone slammed Javier in the back with a rifle, but he's fine. Sandborne got blinded by some rock dust from a ricochet, but I think he'll be okay. The sporting ladies have promised to take care of him. The Boudreauxs are charming them, too. They killed most of the Darabont men from the outcropping. Damn those boys can shoot."

"Any Darabont men still alive?"

"Some," Billy said. "But not anymore."

Mackey felt a certain amount of pride course through him.

Billy seemed to feel it too as he began bandaging his other hand. "A damned fine engagement, captain. Looks like you haven't lost your touch for that, either."

He looked over at Darabont. His bloody head had sagged to his chest, but he was still breathing.

"Wouldn't mind touching him some more," Mackey said.

Billy grinned. "You touched him enough for one day. Besides, I don't think our guests would be too happy with you if you did."

Mackey spotted the two lone Blackfoot members on horseback, about a hundred yards away from the camp. They were standing stock still, looking at the carnage.

"Better late than never," Mackey said. "Hurry up so I can see what they want."

Billy finished the bandage. "Just don't lose your temper with them scouts. We got to ride back through the nation to get back home. They'll be more apt to let us pass without incident if you don't kill two of their men."

Mackey stood up and beckoned Wolf Child's men to come into camp. He then went over to the wagon wheel where Darabont was tied and waited for the Blackfoot to approach.

Darabont stirred and struggled to clear his throat. His speech marred by his broken jaw. "I suppose you think you won something here today, sheriff."

Mackey stood silently above Darabont, a man beaten in every way, watching the warriors trot into camp.

Darabont gagged on a laugh. "Why don't you finish what you started and just kill me?"

"Didn't ride after you to kill you, Darabont. I rode after you for justice."

"How noble."

He watched the Blackfoot scouts trot closer. "Not really."

When the scouts stopped in front of them, Mackey asked in English, "Where the hell were you two?"

The older Blackfoot warrior answered in his own language. "Why should we fight the White Man's battles when he does not fight our battles? Wolf Child told us to help you track. We did."

Mackey tried to keep the anger out of his voice. "And you let The Quiet One die."

"The Quiet One told us to continue on the trail to find the one you call Darabont. We did. We were about to tell you where to find him, you were already here."

Mackey knew they were lying. Not about Sim telling them to go ahead. That was something he would have done. But they were lying about not being able to reach them in time. They had found Darabont's camp and figured Mackey and the others would be there eventually. They sat back, waited for the shooting to be over and came in after.

He didn't like it, but couldn't blame them for it. They had never agreed to fight Darabont. They had only agreed to help find him.

The younger warrior said, "We have been true to our word. Now we expect you to be true to your word."

Mackey hadn't planned on handing Darabont over to the Blackfeet so soon. He planned on handing Darabont over to Wolf Child personally. He wanted the credit and the acclaim from the great chief. No telling when it might come in handy later on down the road.

But the going would be slow with five sick women in a wagon, plus his own wounded men. He'd have plenty to worry about in keeping them safe and moving. Having Darabont around wouldn't help them heal any faster. His people had already been through enough already.

And so had Mackey.

The sheriff stepped aside. "Take him. He's yours."

Darabont looked him up and down with his good eye. "So this is how it ends, is it? The great Sheriff Mackey succumbing to revenge after all? Even after all your high talk about justice, you're just going to let these heathens cut my throat after all, aren't you?"

"These men are from that same Blackfoot tribe you raided on your way to Dover Station. Since you attacked them before you attacked us, they have the right to put you on trial first." He took a knee and glared into Darabont's ruined face. "I promised you justice. Never said anything about it being white man's justice."

Darabont began to squirm against his bindings as the oldest warrior stepped forward and slammed Darabont's head back against the wagon wheel, rendering him unconscious.

The warrior drew a blade and cut the ropes tying Darabont to the spoke of the wheel. He grabbed the unconscious man by the collar and began to drag him back toward his horse.

From the front of the wagon, Mackey heard the women, just back from their washing, began to shriek at the sight of Darabont being free from the wagon wheel. Even though he was unconscious, he still terrified them. The five women clustered behind Katherine like frightened girls as she, herself, backed away. Billy and the others tried to calm them, but they recoiled just the same.

Mackey grabbed the warrior's arm.

The warrior brought up his knife to Mackey's throat.

Mackey didn't flinch. In English, he said, "Hurt him."

The warrior's face did not change. In his own language, he said, "Your tongue does not have a word for what he will feel."

Mackey let go of his arm and the warrior withdrew his blade. The women's screams began to subside as they watched the Blackfoot warriors throw Darabont over the back of their spare horse and bind his hands and feet beneath the horse's belly. The men climbed back on their horses and rode away, trailing Darabont's horse behind them.

Mackey watched them until he couldn't see them anymore.

He waited to feel something for Darabont's fate, knowing he was going to experience more pain in the next few days than most people experienced in a lifetime. The Blackfoot tribe would take their time. They wouldn't finish him quickly.

Mackey waited for some semblance of sympathy to reach him. All he felt was that justice would be done, even if it was red man's justice.

He realized Billy was standing beside him. "What do you want us to do now?"

"Strip the dead of everything valuable. Guns, knives, ammunition, then stow it all in the wagon. Round up their horses, too. Should fetch a good price when we get back to town. Leave the dead where they are. No sense in wasting time burying them."

"Consider it done."

"Then get the women together and tell them we're riding out as soon as they're able. We'll camp somewhere else. Tell them the wagon's the only way we can move them for now, but let them ride on horseback if they want. We can take down the canvas if it makes them feel any better. We'll get them clothes and a new wagon at Fort Custer."

"And then we go home?"

"We're going to Dover Station," Mackey said, though he wasn't sure it was home anymore.

Chapter 45

Darabont drifted in and out of consciousness. He had no idea how long he'd been strapped to the horse, only that the warriors hadn't stopped for days. Or was it hours? The pain in his shoulder and from his wounds made it difficult to gauge just how long he'd been traveling. All he knew was that he had fouled himself numerous times and the scouts didn't seem to care.

The dirt road grew greener and the horse's footfalls became lighter as they seemed to reach some sort of camp. His head ached too much to look around, but he heard more voices before the horse finally stopped. He tried to decipher the language, but for all his education, could not. It was heathen talk, based on a language all their own, and he decided they had finally reached whatever destination the warriors had in mind.

He was quite prepared for whatever they had planned for him. He assumed he'd be scalped and most likely castrated. He'd long since prepared himself for that eventuality. One didn't spend as much time on the plains as he had without accepting such outrage was possible at the hands of the heathen horde. He'd made his peace with whatever god had damned him long ago. He had reaped his own vengeance upon His people. He expected no quarter from any god now—heathen or otherwise.

He fought to control his relief when he felt his bindings cut and he was pulled off the horse. He hit the grassy meadow hard and shrieked as every one of his numerous wounds roared to life.

Someone grabbed a handful of his remaining hair and pulled him to his feet. He looked up through swollen eyes, but saw nothing. The world was a vague, swimming expanse. He thought there were other people around him, though he couldn't be sure. His legs were wobbly, but no one came to his aid. He walked only because he was led and knew they'd drag him if they had to. He decided he would not give them that last bit of his dignity.

He did not see the hole until they dropped him into it, feet first. He was still unsteady on his feet, but realized the hole was too narrow for him to fall over. His knees buckled, but he did not sink. Whoever had dug the hole had done an excellent job. It was just enough room for him to breathe.

And then someone began to fill it in.

He tried as best he could to climb out, but with one ruined shoulder, it was impossible. He couldn't move his good arm enough to get purchase anyway.

As much as it hurt his jaw, he dipped his head as the hole was filled in, trying to keep the dirt from getting in his eyes and mouth. He screamed and moaned as best he could through a closed mouth, but the dirt kept coming, covering him completely from his knees, then his hips, then his elbows and his neck until . . . it stopped.

Through swollen eyes, He looked around and realized he could not move his head. He had been completely buried except for his head.

What little he could see was grassy and shaded by large, leafy trees. He had heard of the desert Indians, especially the Apache, who buried their victims in the desert and allowed the sun to kill them slowly. But if he had to choose a place to be buried from the neck up, he could not have picked a nicer spot.

He listened to hear voices, movement, something to show he was not alone, but he heard nothing.

Instead, he felt something pour over his head and down his face. Something thick and warm. He imagined the heathens were probably relieving themselves on him as part of some kind of pagan victory ritual.

But as best as he tried to keep his ruined mouth closed, some of it dripped into his mouth and he realized what it was. It was not urine.

It was honey.

And it didn't take long for the first fly to find him. Then, a second.

And then the ants came.

And for the first time in all the years since he was a boy, Alexander Darabont knew true terror.

Chapter 46

It was just past noon some days later when Sheriff Aaron Mackey led his motley army down Front Street in the same direction from which Darabont had come. The new wagon they had purchased in Fort Custer bore no canvas and the women inside it were smiling and laughing with the Boudreauxs and young Sandborne, who drove the wagon. Brahm and the *vaqueros* brought up the rear with the horses of the men they'd killed in tow.

Katherine was the only woman not in the wagon. She was where she had been since the day she had been rescued, seated right behind him and clutching him tightly. Adair didn't seem to mind the extra weight. Billy trailed close behind.

He had thought about seeing if the telegraph wire had been repaired when they'd stopped near Fort Custer, but decided against it. He doubted it had been repaired yet and even if it had, he knew the town would not welcome news of five female refugees coming to town.

None of the prostitutes of Hill House had survived

Darabont's cruelty, but that would not matter to the townspeople. The women Mackey had rescued were widows from Idaho and schoolteachers from Oklahoma and Texas and a parson's daughter from Nebraska, but that would matter little to the women of Dover Station. They would be seen as damaged women, especially having been in Darabont's clutches for so long. The wives of the town elders would be as curious about their experiences as they would be repelled by them, but they would treat them like second-class citizens just the same.

Mackey's sprawling group slowly drew the attention from townspeople and drunkards and shopkeepers as they rode down the main thoroughfare. None of them cheered or offered him greeting. No one threw hats in the air or celebrated as they had when they'd learned Darabont's siege had ended. He hadn't expected them to. He wasn't sure he wanted them to, either.

From what Mackey could see, Dover Station had sprung back to life from Darabont's attack. His rocking chair sat unattended in front of the jailhouse, and the door was closed. Flatbed wagons were parked in front of his father's store and Mason's store farther down the street. He couldn't tell if they were delivering supplies or picking up supplies, but either way, it was a good sign.

The noise coming from the Tin Horn was loud, but far more subdued than it had been in recent months and far quieter than it had been the afternoon when he and Billy had first tangled with Darabont's men. He, Billy, *and Sim.* God, how Mackey wished the three of them were riding back in together now.

He made sure not to look at his house as he rode by

for fear of what he might find there. If Mary was there, she'd see Katherine clinging to him and become enraged. If she wasn't there, then she had most likely lived up to her promise of leaving him. Either way, he wasn't ready to face the outcome just yet.

He brought his party to a halt at Katie's Place. He waited for Katherine to dismount first before he did. He hitched Adair to the hitching rail in front and started giving orders. To the Boudreauxs and the two *vaqueros*, he said, "Jack and Henry, you help these ladies dismount. Brahm and Sandborne, too. Javier and Solomon, take the horses over to the livery. Have them kept separate from the rest of the horses so Pappy and Mason can look them over later. Then drop the goods we took off the men over at the jail. Mason and my old man can haggle over who gets what later on. Hang around until I come back, and I'll see to it that you're all paid."

The men did as they were told. He thought Katherine would go back inside and help the girls get settled. She'd been so attentive to them during their ordeal and since, he thought she'd continue to be that way, especially now that they were home.

Instead, she stood stock-still on the porch while the Boudreauxs led the girls inside. Billy drifted inside with the others, leaving Mackey alone with her.

He knew everyone in town was looking at them. He put his hands on her shoulders anyway and whispered, "What's wrong?"

She shook her head. "I can't go in there."

"Sure you can. It's your place, remember? Big sign up there has your name on it. You're home."

"No, I'm not. Not anymore. Not after . . . everything.

Not just to me, Aaron, but to this town." She put her hand over his. "To us."

"All the more reason why you need to go inside, honey."

She turned and looked up at him. "You haven't called me that in years. Not since Boston, and now you call me that every day."

"And I'll keep on calling you that for as long as you want me to." He heard himself say it, though he couldn't believe it. And he had never meant anything more in his life.

"Old Wilkes is gone." The tears began to come again. He'd never seen her cry before. Now she cried all the time. He supposed she had a right. "All the girls in Hill House are gone. That poor baby . . ."

"The JT Ranch is gone, too, so that means poor Brahm is out of a job. He's a good cook and could help with the rowdies like Old Wilkes used to do. Sandborne's a friendly sort. Could fill in nicely helping you run the place."

She blinked a tear away. "It's not the same."

"It's not supposed to be. But it can be better."

She looked away from him again. "How long were we gone, Aaron? The whole ride back here, you never told me."

"Does it matter?"

"Very much."

"It took me three days to find you. We took a little longer coming back because I didn't want to rush you girls."

He wasn't sure if he should say what he was thinking and decided to do it anyway. "I've never gone through what you have or what those ladies went through with Darabont. But I've seen plenty of people who've suffered at the hands of Apaches and men like Darabont. Some of them crumbled and were never the same again. Some pushed their way through it and found a way to live. But if you don't walk through that door now, you'll regret it for the rest of your life. If you have the courage to push through it and try to live, I promise you that it'll get better a lot quicker than if you run from it."

"It's not the same." She looked down at the porch step where she stood. "You beat Darabont. I only survived."

He tucked his finger under her chin and raised her face until she looked at him. The silver streaks in her hair were still there, but the lines were less visible and the redness had gone from her eyes. But they were harder than they had been the last time they'd spoken on her porch. He wondered if they always would be. "You kept as many of the women alive as you could without any help from me or anyone. I beat Darabont the only way I know how. Now it's up to you to beat him your own way. And the best way you can do that is to walk inside your hotel and tend to the women who still need you."

She buried her face in his chest. And despite all the people looking at them, he didn't push her away. When she looked up at him again, there weren't any tears. "I guess we both have work to do."

He felt himself smiling. "Best get to it. Both of us. I'll be by later."

He watched her gather herself as she walked through the door of her own hotel.

He'd just unhitched Adair from the railing and climbed up into the saddle when he saw her standing just inside the doorway of the hotel. She looked at the townspeople before she yelled, "I'm proud to love you, Aaron Mackey. And I don't give a damn who knows it."

Smiling, she brushed past Billy as he was coming out of the hotel. The deputy watched her go inside, then looked up at his friend. "Quite a woman, ain't she?"

Mackey managed to say, "Let's get back to the jail."

Chapter 47

Billy had just finished brewing a pot of fresh coffee when Pappy ran across the street. His face flushed more from excitement than the effort. "You came back."

Mackey had already had his fill of sentiment for one day. "Told you I would. Brought back plenty for you and Mason to pick over. Guns, bullets, saddles. Horses, too, over at the livery. You boys can pick over them tomorrow."

"I don't care about that," Pappy said. "I care about you and what happened. Darabont dead?"

"Not yet. Handed him over to Wolf Child's men. He raided their settlement on his way here. Killed a lot of women and children. They'll hurt him worse than a hangman's noose will."

Mackey didn't want to think about it anymore. "Where's Underhill?"

"Out at the JT Ranch. He's been surveying the damage with Mr. Rice for the past couple of days. They ride out at first light and come back each evening. Took a look at the mining camp already. Seems the miners had the good sense to get the hell out of there before Darabont's men could reach them. Wasn't much there, so he left it alone, except for the dynamite he stole. Loggers, too. Some of them have already started filtering back into town, even the hands at the JT who survived. Looks like Rice might want to get into the ranching business. Says they're going to rebuild. Run more horses and cattle. There's talk Underhill might run it for him."

Mackey drank his coffee. "Glad to hear it. You'll need it to help keep the town on its feet."

"Word is they'll have the telegraph up and running in a day or so," Pappy said. "Railroad stopped here yesterday, so it looks like Darabont didn't damage the tracks like he said he had."

Mackey wasn't surprised. "Probably didn't want to waste the dynamite on steel rails when he could use them on us instead."

Pappy looked at his shoes and toed the ground the way he always did when he was about to deliver bad news. "Mary's gone. Left on the first stage that came into town."

Mackey sipped his coffee. "That was to be expected."

"No loss. Bitch even bought her ticket from Mason instead of from me. Spiteful even to the end."

Mackey sipped more coffee. "That was to be expected, too."

Pappy rubbed his nose and changed the subject. "I heard Katherine made it back okay. Some of those captives you brought in, too."

"I know what the next question will be," Mackey said. "They're not whores, just Darabont's captives. None of the women from Hill House survived Darabont's men. You don't want to know the details. Just make sure that damned rumor mill of yours doesn't destroy those women's reputations before they've had a chance to put down roots. They've been through enough already."

His father took a step back. "Jesus, Aaron. I don't deserve that. Here I am, delighted you're back and . . ."

Mackey looked at Billy, and Billy spoke for him. "Sim's dead."

"Sim?" Pappy whispered as he lowered himself into a chair by the door. "After all he's been through. Shiloh. Georgia, even, only to be laid low by the hand of rabble. How?"

"What difference does it make?" Billy touched the handle of the Bowie knife. "Died well, though. Fought until the end."

Pappy rubbed his hands on his pants legs. "One of the best men I knew. We'll give him a fine military burial. As fine as we gave Old Wilkes."

Mackey set his mug on the desk. "That'll make everything better."

Pappy looked at his son. "It's not about making anything better, boy. It's about paying respect."

"Sim had more respect for this town than any of the other men in it."

Pappy was on his feet. "And just what the hell is that supposed to mean?"

"It means he did something when this town was attacked. He could've stayed behind and licked his wounds like the rest of you. He rode out after the whores and the vagabonds you and the rest of them deemed unworthy. He paid for it with his life. And you thank him with a military funeral, like that makes it all better. Well, it doesn't, Pop. Not by a long shot."

"What the hell do you expect me to do?" Pappy said. "What else can anyone do?"

"There was a time when you would've ridden out there with us," Mackey said. "Hell, there was a time when I would've had to fight men from saddling up after a bunch like Darabont. But I guess things change, don't they? Towns change, just like Mayor Mason said they do. People change, too."

The sheriff unpinned his star and dropped it on the desk. "Well I've changed, too. This isn't the same town I grew up in. And it's not my home anymore. You've got Rice and Underhill now to run things. You don't need me and my difficult ways."

Billy's star landed on the desk right next to Aaron's. "Goes for me, too."

"Aaron, you don't mean that. I . . ."

But for the first time since he could remember, Mackey talked over his father. "Billy and I buried Sim on the trail. We'll fetch him home where he belongs. How you honor him after that is up to you. After that, I'm leaving."

Pappy tried to steady him down. "Son, you're upset. After what you've been through, I can't blame you. But . . ."

"I made my decision the day I rode out of here. Sim's death just made it easier to say. Now, get back to your store and back to your gossips. You've got plenty to tell them."

His father had plenty to say, but at that moment, words seemed to escape him. He simply stood and quietly walked out of the jailhouse, back to his store.

Pappy had no sooner disappeared from the doorway when Mackey heard heavy footfalls followed by a clomp on the boardwalk outside the jailhouse. He wasn't surprised when Mr. Rice removed his hat and stepped inside.

Mackey let out a long breath. "I'm sorry, Mr. Rice, but I'm not in the most hospitable mood right now."

"Can't say I blame you," he said, "especially by the way you were greeted on your way into town. That's no way to welcome heroes home from the battlefield, so I hope you'll accept my apologies on their behalf." He stuck out a hand to Billy. "And my welcome and admiration."

Billy shook his hand. So did Mackey. "Thanks, but it's not my home anymore."

"I overheard you say that," Rice admitted. "Didn't mean to eavesdrop, but it was kind of hard not to hear. I didn't want to interfere."

"You're not interfering. It's your town now, not mine."

"Might be my town, but it's your home," Rice said. "And before you jump on me for saying it, you need to hear me out. I'm a little bit older than you and I've done my fair share of wandering. Was a time when I didn't want any of my family's money. I wanted to be a soldier."

"So you've said. But your knee . . ."

"The knee kept me from being a soldier, not acting like one. I realized I had responsibilities I couldn't shirk and duties I needed to perform. Mine was handling my family's affairs. Yours are handling this town's affairs. I can't tell you how many times I've argued with my father and my brothers and uncles over the business decisions I've made. Sometimes I was wrong and sometimes I wasn't, but I made them because they needed to be made. I made them because I couldn't escape who and what I was no matter how much I wanted to. Same thing applies to you." He looked at Billy. "Both of you."

He nodded down at the two stars on the desk. "You can unpin a star, but it doesn't make you any less a lawman, just like being thrown out of the army made you any less of a soldier. You were right about towns changing, and I intend on changing Dover Station for the better. And it'll be a hell of a lot easier if you're around to help me do it. Easier for you, too, because like it or not, this is your home. It's where you're from." He pointed at the stars with his cane. "And that is what you are."

Rice set his cane back on the floor. "You're hurt and angry now, but all I ask is that you give yourself some time before you walk away and do something you'll regret. Underhill isn't a lawman anymore. He wants to be a rancher and I intend on making him one. And I intend on making this town the kind of place men like you will be proud to call home again." He placed his hat back on his head. "You'll have my respect and admiration no matter what you decide."

And with that, Fraser Rice strode out of the jailhouse. Mackey noticed he leaned less on the cane now than when he'd walked in.

Billy cleared his throat as he drank some coffee. "Quite a speech."

Mackey was still looking at the spot where the wealthy man had stood. "Yeah."

Later that afternoon, Mackey and Billy were out on the boardwalk in front of the jail. Mackey rocked back and forth in his rocking chair; his pace steady. Billy sat on the bench building a cigarette in his nimble fingers.

The sun had settled farther in the west and cast long crooked shadows across the thoroughfare. A cool breeze had picked up, and it promised to be a chilly evening. More flatbed wagons had come and gone on Front Street. The boardwalks were a hive of activity, strangers mostly, in city clothes. There was an excitement in the air that Mackey could feel, but barely describe.

Mr. Rice was right. Dover Station was a different town than the one he had left.

Neither man had spoken since Pappy and Mr. Rice had left. It wasn't an uneasy silence. Their silences had never been uneasy. There was simply nothing to say.

Billy lit his cigarette and said, "You going to apologize to your old man?"

"No reason to apologize. I didn't do anything wrong."

"For your tone, not what you said."

Mackey thought he had a point, but he wasn't in an apologizing mood. "I don't know. Maybe later. Figured you'd be sore at me for not telling you I was planning on quitting."

"You didn't have to tell me. I felt it in you the moment you turned toward the trail and rode out of town after Darabont."

Mackey wasn't surprised. Billy had always known his mind even when he didn't know it himself. "You can stay on if you want. I'm sure Underhill would be glad to have you."

"Underhill's a rancher now, remember? Besides, I wouldn't stay on even they did ask me to stay. I rode in here with you, Aaron. I'll ride out the same way."

Mackey thought that would be the case. "I didn't ask you to do that. Didn't ask you to give up your job."

"You didn't have to ask. And you never will."

The two men sat quietly for a while longer. They watched more city people walk past the Tin Horn and head toward the train station. They walked with purpose and promise."

"Still thinking over what Mr. Rice said?"

"A bit." In fact, he hadn't been able to think of anything else since the man left. How he pointed to the stars on the desk. *That's what you are.*

"Mighty persuasive fellow. Guess that's why he's got all that money."

"Family already had money when he was born."

"But he got more of it for them. Something to be said for that."

Mackey watched the city people clap each other on the back as they rounded the corner toward the train station. Their excitement and happiness was almost palpable. "I suppose so."

Billy took a drag on his cigarette. "Think you'll change your mind about quitting?"

"No," he said too quickly. Then, he thought of what he'd said to Katherine and of what Mr. Rice had said to him. About people needing rebuilding, too. "Maybe. I pinned the star back on, didn't I?"

"Yes you did." Billy rubbed a sleeve across the star on his own chest. "And so did I."

They watched a woman in a fashionable dress and parasol stop outside the Tin Horn, straighten her hat, then walk inside.

Mackey said, "Looks like the Tin Horn might be taking on some new talent."

"Looks like."

"She'll probably lend the place a little class. Change it from a hellhole to a respectable place."

Billy smoked his cigarette. "Nothing lasts forever."

Mackey rocked in his rocker. "Thank God for that."

12 -- 22

Look for the next Sheriff Aaron Mackey Western,

DARK TERRITORY

coming in Spring 2019 from Pinnacle Books.